ZAGRIBUD

Presenting *Zagribud*, the sequel to John Russell Fearn's *Liners of Time*—the first-ever unabridged book edition of a classic pre-war serial from the pages of *Amazing Stories*.

Once again Time Liner Pilot Sandford Lee resumes his battle against Elnek Jelfel, the Jovian wizard of science who seems to constantly be winning a victory over Lee and his comrades, but in some mysterious way, they always succeed in saving themselves. *Zagribud* carries out their contests against an interstellar canvas with Jelfel using his scientific powers to ultimately take possession of the Earth and carry out mass vivisection on humanity.

A cosmic saga of super-science from a bygone era of science fiction in the tradition of E. E. 'Doc' Smith!

THE GOLDEN AMAZON SAGA

ZAGRIBUD

JOHN RUSSELL FEARN

WILDSIDE PRESS

This novel was previously published as a serial in *Amazing Stories* magazine, in the December 1937, February 1938, and April 1938 issues.

Published by Wildside Press LLC
www.wildsidepress.com

INTRODUCING "ZAGRIBUD"

BY PHILIP HARBOTTLE

This edition of *Zagribud*, the sequel to John Russell Fearn's *Liners of Time*, is the first-ever unabridged book edition of a classic pre-war serial from the pages of *Amazing Stories*. It sports an illustrative cover by the late Ron Turner, which I had the foresight to commission for possible future use—way back in 1985!

Once again Time Liner Pilot Sandford Lee resumes his battle against Elnek Jelfel, the Jovian wizard of science. *Zagribud* carries out their contests against an interstellar canvas with Jelfel using his occult scientific powers to ultimately take possession of the Earth and carry out mass vivisection on humanity.

It is a cosmic saga of super-science from a bygone era of science fiction in the tradition of E. E. 'Doc' Smith.

As I explained in my introduction to Wildside's new edition of *Liners of Time*, Fearn had written both novels in the white-heat of enthusiasm following *Amazing Stories'* editorial acceptance of his previous submissions whilst he was under the influence of E.E.Smith's "Skylark" serials in the same magazine.

In his novels Fearn had deliberately chosen to invent his own science to explain his cosmic imaginings—substituting sheer imagination for accurate science. The fantastic events are explained away in a welter of pseudo-science that today reads as sheer gobbledegook.

Although this pre-war style of 'super-science' science fiction was soon abandoned by Fearn, and occupied only a small part of his prolific output, latter day literary critics have used it to tar his entire output with the same brush, and furthermore to claim that Fearn's scientific derelictions were due to his own scientific ignorance. In this latter regard they are shamefully ignoring any number of essays by Fearn at the time of these stories (and widely reprinted since), in which he made it clear that his pseudo-science was simply a *deliberate* device to help carry the story to ordinary readers ("I freely admit I do not strive for scientific accuracy by any means; indeed I ignore possibility altogether if I can get a thrill by being particularly fantastic.")

However, despite the critics, in the past twenty years all of Fearn's more than one hundred science fiction novels have been returned to print and modern readers can now appreciate the full range of his work in its historical context.

Zagribud is, as it happens, the very last remaining Fearn science fiction novel to be restored to print. There *was* a much earlier heavily abridged and rewritten version, retitled as *Science Metropolis* and published in 1952 in the UK by Scion Ltd, as by 'Vargo Statten'.

But whereas *Zagribud* ran to some 65,000 words, *Science Metropolis* was cut to only 35,000 words!

To cut the novel by some 30,000 words, Fearn did not indulge in any significant rewriting; instead, he simply *omitted entirely the middle portion of the novel* (chapters 7 through 12) and abridged the final third where it contained characters or plot strands that had been introduced in the excised portion. A curious feature was that Fearn elected to change the names of some of his main characters, including, inter alia, Sandford Lee became Avian Lee, Elnek Jelfel—Finjios Nairn, and Anton Frot—Fran Atos. But many names were retained, such as the heroine Elna Folson, and the great inventor, Lan Ronnit! Why some names and not others? Alas, we shall never know…

When I first read *Science Metropolis* myself in the mid-1950s, I was unaware of its origins, and I will admit that I found it almost unreadable, presented as it was as a 'stand-alone' 1952 novel. The welter of pseudo-science from an obsolete era of SF (written in 1932) did not read well twenty years on.

Later, as Fearn's literary executor, when I finally had the opportunity to have all of his 52 Vargo Statten novels reprinted, I determined that this abridged version would *not* be included. The 1952 *Science Metropolis* thus remains a collectors' curiosity, known and sought after only by a handful of completist collectors. It is an extremely scarce book, allowing dealers to justifiably charge extremely high prices for rarely-offered copies.

But now that Wildside Press have produced a new edition of *Liners of Time*, it seemed to me entirely appropriate that this long-lost unabridged sequel should finally be restored to print. To be best appreciated and understood, it needs to be read after *Liners of Time*.

Some critics will undoubtedly claim that *both* novels should have remained un-reprinted. But, if the reader is able to regard the pseudo-science as historical window dressing and to focus instead on the epic storyline, and sheer sense of wonder, there is much to enjoy. Buried in the hodge-podge of pseudo-science are several fascinating ideas and the seeds of intriguing plot-lines that Fearn would later revisit in his

"Golden Amazon" series and the "Clay Drew" Martian novels. The character of Elnek Jelfel himself was used as the template for the Amazon's nemesis, Sefner Quorne, who featured in seven novels, of which *Quorne Returns* was the most indebted to *Zagribud*. Interested fans of the author are hereby invited to contrast and compare!

Philip Harbottle.
Wallsend,
April, 2015.

INTRODUCTION

Again I send to you, via the Time Line from 2004 A.D., a history of my second and, I hope, my final adventure with Elnek Jelfel, the Jovian wizard of science. In my previous narrative concerning him—"Liners of Time"—I hinted, I think, at the more than obvious possibility of him returning to continue his nefarious work of capturing Earth and Earthlings in the interests of Jovian civilization... He has indeed returned, or, should I say, he did return? I believe now, with my companions, that he has at last ended his life, and in "Zagribud" I have related, for your especial benefit, the details of this second and, if anything, more deadly and scientific battle.

As a result of these struggles I now possess a face totally different from the one with which I was born; at least it will be an everlasting souvenir of a great adventure. The why and wherefore of this condition you will, of course, discover for yourselves.

As before, the critical amongst yon will attempt to question Time. You will ask how I encountered these experiences when they happen in a Time I have already crossed—a fact which is obviously at variance with the law of time. But, when you take this into account, please remember that all my experiences in this second battle took place in a false period of Time—one deliberately created by Jelfel himself, and such a state was therefore not in alignment with natural Time. It therefore became a new and unexplored field, never before crossed. Otherwise the experiences could never have taken place. As I have said before, a man can only do in his life, at a given second, one chosen action—and every time he crosses that time he will repeat that action.... That is why I explain to you now, how my experiences were possible.

Beyond a brief elucidation of that matter I have nothing to add to my story, and leave you now to the narrative itself. Again my thanks, my friends of the past.

SANDFORD LEE,
of the Time Line, 2004, A.D.

CHAPTER I

ELNEK JELFEL RETURNS

The Fourteenth of June 2004 A.D. As far as my eye could see, from my standpoint on the summit of the mighty Time Liner Corporation Building, extended the incredible panorama of unexpected skyline, known to the world as New York. The rearing immensities of buildings, the hurtling air-machines, the silent, personal gliders coming and going in the danger-free Tonium gas—and above it all, the perfect blue of the summer sky, a climate of warm, equable softness controlled by squat cylinders of energy that lay in the heart of the Time Liner Corporation Building itself...

And everywhere, order—precision—duty.

I smiled to myself as my mind went back to that brief period four years before, when I had pitted my relatively puny brains against the scientific genius of Elnek Jelfel, the Jovian—native of a planet which had been eradicated from the heavens of future time. True, the planet Jupiter still shone in the sky of 2004, but only because it was existing in a time prior to its destruction. Again, as I write, I find myself on the verge of one of those incomputable paradoxes that even I, Sandford Lee, Commandant of the Time Way, find difficult to understand.

I was awakened suddenly from my preoccupation at a light touch on my arm. A T.L.C. page stood beside me.

"Doctor Anson would like to see you, sir," he said respectfully, then stood back with a sharp salute.

I frowned and shot him a glance of inquiry. "Is it urgent, Billy? I came up here for a brief relaxation. Tomorrow, you know, I leave for 20,000, and—"

"Doctor Anson asked me to stress the urgency, Commandant."

At that I shrugged. "All right Thanks..."

I descended by the percussion staircase to the apartment of the great Doctor Anson, Specialist in Terrestrial Relativity. His particular occupation was the charting of Time Lines and new cosmic paths. As I entered he greeted me with a welcoming smile.

"Hello, Lee, glad you've come along. Something peculiar has cropped up; I'd be very glad if you will give me your advice."

"Willingly," I assented. "But I confess I fail to see how my knowledge can be of any service to the great Anson."

"Needless flattery, Lee. As a matter of fact, you're the only man who knows enough about Time to conceivably help me... What would you say if I told you that the earth, this age, keeps undergoing strange changes? What would you say if I told you that, for some remarkable reason, we are hovering even now between the Age 2000 and 25000?"

I sat down on the stool by his bench with a thud. "We're *what*?" I asked dazedly.

He nodded slowly, his clever face earnest. "It's true, Lee. Something is happening to time—it's shifting—altering—behaving as though it's crazy. I can't understand it. May of course be some cosmic disturbance affecting the time-band, but as the time-band is of another dimension, the theory doesn't seem tenable. What do you think about it?"

"Possibly something amiss with your instruments," I said presently.

"Not a bit of it, Lee. It's—it's just as though something was trying to superimpose another Time on top of ours. It hasn't been visible yet to the eye, but my Relative Condition machine has responded to the influence."

"Does Templeton, the President, know of this?" I asked sharply.

"Surely—I told him last evening. It was he who thought you might be the man to assist me to explain things. He said something about a man named Elnek Jelfel—"

At that I shot to my feet. "Elnek Jelfel!" I shouted hoarsely. "Good God, did he say that?"

"Something like it," Anson assented. "But Lee, what— Heh! Where are you going?"

I had reached the door in two strides. "To see Templeton—right away," I replied, and, as fast as I could go, made my way through the devious routes of the great, confusing edifice until I reached the Debating Room. The guards moved to one side as I entered. Templeton was alone, not accompanied, as was usual, by his fellow directors of the Corporation.

I marched across the shining floor and saluted smartly.

"President Templeton, may I speak?" I asked with tense quietness. His impartial blue eyes looked up at me. Silently he laid aside his electric pen.

"Why, surely, Commandant Lee. What is the trouble?"

"I have just come from Doctor Anson, President, concerning the strange phenomenon taking place with Time. He said you mentioned Elnek Jelfel. Is that true, sir?"

Templeton hesitated and compressed his lips. He nodded slowly.

"Yes, Lee, I did mention his name." He looked at me keenly. "Lee, you accomplished a wonderful feat by destroying the planet Jupiter, and, as you hoped, Elnek Jelfel and his entire dastardly race—but I am commencing to have grave fears that your efforts were quite useless... You just averted the catastrophe for the time being. Frankly, doesn't this curious effect with Time savour of that Jovian genius of science?"

"I confess it's about what Jelfel would do—but I see nothing to be gained by such a stunt," I answered. "His idea was, as you know, the importation of human beings to Jupiter to be vivisected, and to use Earthly bodies for Jovian brains, so that they could come to Earth and continue their intellectual pursuits on a more congenial planet, and—"

"Quite—quite!" Templeton interjected. "I know all that, Lee. You, however, in the year 22,000, The Age of Problems, flung Jupiter into the sun and you were firmly of the opinion that all the Jovians went with it. But, didn't Jelfel swear he would return? Didn't he die an unnatural death—seemed to just leave his body before you strangled him?"

"Truly," I answered, troubled.

"Well, Lee, doesn't it occur to you that the only way he can return is to come in either a different time, a future time? He can't come back and live over again the same time as before—that would only mean repetition of all his actions. The only way he can attack is to use a time *after* that in which his world was destroyed! To make, as it were, an entirely new field of endeavor. And, the only way to do that is to make earthly civilization—the civilization he desires most strongly at least—change to a point where he can get at it! Just as a target might be moved in order to be properly fired at! Now do you see why I suspect Jelfel?"

"Good heavens!" I muttered. "I never looked at it that way before. These past four years have moved so peacefully that I'd almost forgotten Jelfel ever existed."

Templeton's craggy mouth creased in a smile. "He hasn't even come yet for his first battle, according to normal time!" he commented. "Ah, Lee, Time is indeed a paradox."

"Well, sir, if this time trouble is Jelfel's doing, what are my orders?"

He shrugged dubiously. "At the moment, Commandant, there is nothing you can do. We will discuss it again, before you leave for 20,000 tomorrow. If indeed it *is* Jelfel behind it all, we are going to be up against it!"

I stood back and saluted. "I will report this time tomorrow for further orders," I said obediently. "That in order, President?"

"Perfectly, Lee."

In a troubled frame of mind I departed. The thought of again encountering that scientific and ruthless Jovian was no little worry to carry on my mind. I realized that I had only vanquished him in the first place by reason of an operation on my brain, performed by an amazing brain-planet an incomputable distance in the future. How I should fare now, with my brain long since returned to normal, I did not dare to imagine... Perhaps, after all, I decided, Templeton's conclusions were erroneous.

I returned through the pedestrian ways to the glider grounds sought out my own personal machine, and presently was floating through the Tonium gas toward my abode, two miles to the north. I had only just pushed my glider into its roof-hangar when a figure came running to meet me. In an instant I recognized the oval, purposeful face, with faintly humorous gray eyes and exquisite teeth.

Elna Folson—my firmest feminine friend, companion of my early adventures with Jelfel, and incidentally daughter of the President of the Time Liner Corporation of 20,000 A.D. (In each Age, I must make it clear, there was a replica of the Time Liner Corporation Building of 2004—right up to the Age of Intelligence, the Last Age.)

"Sandy!" Elna exclaimed, using as ever, my nickname. "A stroke of luck, indeed! I took a chance in coming to see you; I know you're off tomorrow. So I chartered a fast time machine from 20,000 to reach you. There's something very important I must discuss with you." She looked at me with unwonted seriousness, which rather surprised me, for I knew her gay spirits and engaging ways.

"Oh, what is it?" I enquired, with blunt masculinity. "Not serious, surely?"

"I don't quite know," she replied thoughtfully. "It seems a silly subject, but it is important just the same. Briefly, Sandy—cramp, and bad dreams."

"Cramp and bad dreams!" I exclaimed. "Why, Elna, what's the matter with you?"

"Well, I— But come downstairs, Sandy. We can talk better there."

We descended to my apartment, and over glasses of ekrimar—the marvellous restorative fluid discovered by Handworth in 1986—she unfolded the story to me. And a remarkable one it was, too.

"Sandy, I'm not a nervous girl—you know that—and I don't think a girl of 20,000 knows the real meaning of fear; but something, oh, so terrifying, keeps me awake every night when I try to sleep. I haven't had a good night's rest for eight nights now... Honestly, Sandy"—her gray eyes were troubled—"I'm getting scared! Funny, isn't it?"

"You seem energetic enough," I remarked, surveying her face.

"Ekrimar makes fatigue invisible," she answered quietly. "I am dead tired. But, to get back to the point. I've been dreaming, vividly, every night about— Well, whom do you think?"

"How should I know?" I asked.

"Elnek Jelfel!"

My glass dropped from my nerveless fingers and fell to the soft carpet. I stared hard into her face. "Elnek Jelfel?" I breathed. "Elna, are you sure?"

"Do I look as though I doubted it?" she asked indignantly. "Yes, the old Jovian wizard himself, complete with terrible green eyes and biting cynicism. Every night it seems as though I can hear words, which say 'Reassembly through Elna Folson.' I feel as though I am then crushed by a nameless force, as though the very life is being strangled out of me. I awake shaking from head to foot, overcome by terrific fright. And all the time I see him, Sandy… Something is happening! It's just as though"— she laughed shortly—"as though I'm being killed by a memory. Of course, it's all so silly. Jelfel is dead."

"I wonder if he is?" I said, then detailed to her what I had learned from Anson and the President. Her face was startled when I had concluded.

"That does sound as though he's about somewhere," she muttered.

I nodded gravely. "Elna, I'm just trying to imagine what connection there is between your vivid dreaming of him, your feeling of cramp, and the sudden strange behaviour of time. He may be trying some of his radio-hypnotism on you. He did it to me once. You're strong-willed, though; even in sleep you offset him."

She spread her hands helplessly. "But why should he want to get at me? What have I done?"

"You and I are his sworn enemies, Elna," I answered quietly. "He may be trying to destroy you. Whether just as an experiment or genuinely, I don't know… But I'm going to sort out this mystery. Tonight, Elna, you'll try and doze in that armchair there, and I'll be here with Lan Ronnit. I'll get him to bring along his Brain Emanation Detector… You remember Ronnit?"

"Why, of course. The young chap with the inventive brain from 22,000?"

"That's right. This Brain Emanation Detector of his is a masterpiece. The brain, of course, emits force, impulse, invisible to the human eye. You know that?"

She nodded interestedly.

"Well, this invention of Ronnit's is for measuring brain power. By its use it is possible to tell the clever man or woman by the power he or she emits from the brain. That saves a lot of trouble. The needle on his dial shows immediately the force present—just like an old time voltmeter read a battery's force. Now, if we use that instrument tonight, it will detect great mental power, if such is present. You understand?"

"Perfectly. That's a fine idea; but then, Lan Ronnit is an ingenious fellow, anyhow."

"Truly. And there's something else he's making that may yet be useful somewhere. He calls it the Double Entity Machine. To pass the time away I'll explain it to you."

"Do! Anything like that intrigues me."

"Well, it's a trifle involved, but something like this. Light, as you know, is emitted because of the interaction between the atomic units of electricity, and the ether in which they are immersed. Ether, I hardly need to explain, fills all space—and, for that matter, every interspace. It is, in fact, the welding medium between atoms and planets throughout the Universe. Ronnit has worked from the basis of ether being electromagnetic in property, and also from the known fact that a wave of light consists of simultaneous electric and magnetic oscillations, at right angles to each other, advancing in a direction at right angles to both. You see, when the motion of an electron changes, it radiates energy into the ether… If there were no ether, there would be no light. That's logic. Similarly, the eyes of humans, animals, and so forth, are sensitive only to what is really ethereal radiation—called light. Now, normally, light waves radiate outwards from the source, becoming indistinguishable at varying distances, according to the strength of the basic output…

"It is possible, however, Ronnit finds, by superimposing a radiation beam, several degrees above even Hertzian waves, to *bend the ether itself*—that is, turn its electromagnetic power from a straight line into a circle, his radiation beam performing the feat of what he calls reversed momentum—like the stunt of throwing a hoop through the air in such a way that it will roll back to you when striking the ground. So, with this method, the light from an object is turned back again onto the object—but, as the return back takes several seconds, the original object has had time to move in the interval. Apparently, though, the object is still there, by the light waves reflecting an apparently stationary image. Thus Ronnit has invented a very useful weapon. A person can move from a given spot—indeed any number of people within reason—and yet apparently not move, all because of the bent ether. A neutralizing beam, of course, puts matters back in order again…"

Elna smiled thoughtfully. "Somehow, Sandy, I have a vague feeling that we are again on the verge of witnessing more scientific miracles like those on our last mad adventure with Jelfel. I'm not afraid, but I don't like suspense—and bad dreams and cramp!"

"You'll be all right," I reassured her, rising to my feet. "I'll just let Ronnit know we want him."

I moved across to the television communicator. This apparatus, separated from the main television bands by a frequency of reversed output waves (absorption beams which collected all encroaching television waves that would intermingle with the private and public bands) was perhaps one of the handiest devices that ever came to 2004. One push of a button started up the sound and vision machine; a turn on a dial tuned in the exact wave-length of the person you wished to call, the numbers being prearranged in the same manner as telephone numbers had once been... So it was that Lan Ronnit's lean visage presently appeared on the screen.

"Hello, Lee," greeted his voice. "What's the trouble? That Elna there, with you?"

"Yes. Now, Lan, listen carefully. This is important..." And I outlined the circumstances. His face was serious when I had concluded.

"Jelfel again, eh? That's tough, Lee. All right, I'll bring along the Detector this evening—about seven-thirty."

"That's fine," I nodded.

"Right you are, then. Goodbye."

* * * *

Seven-thirty that evening found Lan Ronnit duly with us, and we spent half an hour erecting his Brain Emanation Detector. Afterwards we sat for a time and chatted, then, as darkness began to spread its mantle over the crazy bulk of New York, I drew over the curtains, switched on the light, and motioned Elna to the armchair.

"Do you think you could try and sleep?" I asked her.

She nodded and yawned prodigiously. "After the nights I've had I could sleep on the edge of a time-line," she assured us; then sank down in the softly sprung upholstery and closed her eyes. I switched off the main light and connected up the small, pink-glassed table-light. My view became limited to Lan Ronnit's cadaverous face, bent over his instruments, and, behind him, the further vision of Elna crouched in the chair.

A pale green beam presently sprang from Ronnit's machinery and clung to Elna's hair... Instantly the needle on his recording dial registered 140—about quarter of the way around the dial.

"That's all right," he murmured. "Her brain emanation is about normal for a clever young woman... Ah, good! She's asleep, Lee." We listened carefully and detected her deep, steady breathing. In dead silence we stood looking at her, save for an occasional glance at the instruments…

Then… How am I to describe my sensations? There very slowly crept into the utter silence and half-light of my cozy flat the most terrifying fear I have ever known. A sense of icy presences, invisible yet ruthlessly potent, seemed to slowly group about me. I felt strange chills creeping up and down my spine, sweat began to roll down my face.

Lan Ronnit's profiled face was gleaming as though he had washed his face and omitted to dry it. Biting his lips to control himself he pointed with a violently shaking hand at the emanator needle. It was moving slowly—rising! 140—200—220—240— My eyes bulged in amazement. 360! Maximum! The needle became steady at that point. Mind force, terrific and colossal, was somewhere present.

"Look at Elna!" Lan Ronnit whispered with terrific effort.

I stared at her and beheld her slowly rising to her feet. Her eyes were wide open now, but staring with the most unnerving, fixed gaze into emptiness so that I felt my heart jump. She was dead asleep, yet wide awake—whether in the grip of some superhuman hypnosis or not I could not then determine. Gaining her feet, she took three faltering steps, then crashed over suddenly to the rug, to lie inert.

"Elna!" I gasped hoarsely. "Elna! What has—"

"Wait!" a voice commanded abruptly, from the air itself—a voice oddly familiar, that struck something in the recesses of my memory. A hard and metallic, faintly cynical voice.

Ronnit and I stood stupefied, unable to move to the stricken Elna, so overcome were we. There came a sensation of coldness—pure, streaming cold—the infinite cold of interstellar space. Then, it seemed, from Elna's inert body a misty figure rose up, took on gradual form, and at last became solid. A figure was standing on the rug before us—a figure of medium height with coal black hair, white face, and boring, implacable green eyes. A figure attired in dead black.

"Great God! Elnek Jelfel!" I gasped hoarsely.

He advanced slowly toward the table, and still Ronnit and I could do nothing but stare.

"Yes, Commander Lee—Lan Ronnit. I am Elnek Jelfel himself," he assented. "For a long time I have striven to overcome Elna Folson—to manifest myself through her body upon this childish planet. The reason for having a body through which to manifest myself is on account of Earthly conditions as compared to those of Ondon—and which process I will fully explain to you, at close quarters, at a later date."

"You seem as assured of yourself as ever, Jelfel," I said grimly, that strange feeling slowly passing away. "I thought you were dead."

"I know," he assented coldly. "I warned you that I should return. When you strangled me on my observation tower in the Age of Problems, I merely moved my own entity from my body into another dimension—there is no limit to mind force—and projected my mind back to Jupiter. There I took on another form—which I have now. I am, however, again in those earthly integuments which serve to make me earthly in appearance. Beyond doubt, Commander Lee, you have a lot to answer for!" He leaned forward, his face indescribably venomous. "You hurled Jupiter, my native planet, into the sun! You and Anton Frot, that mathematician. Fortunately, we realized what was happening, and migrated to another planet—Ondon by name. His Serenity Rath Granod, the All Wise, still rules the destinies of Zagribud, our principal city, which we moved piecemeal through the void. It is his will that the conquest of the earth be continued. Ondon is too inefficient. Only Earth alone will suit our purpose. The first batch of human beings will be shortly removed to Ondon, so that we may transfer our brains to their bodies."

"You're going to do all this without space ships?" I asked drily.

"Fool!" he returned cynically. "They will be removed from Earth by a process of which you at present know nothing—but which you will be fully acquainted with later on. You and Lan Ronnit, Elna Folson, that mathematician Frot—all of you, shall be the first subjects."

"Then—then Elna is not dead?" I said eagerly.

"No. I do not kill like that, Commander. Now, I must again return to Ondon before my time has elapsed. You see, I cannot stay here long in case I dissolve! The only reason I can appear in this earlier time at all is because I have never visited it before—but to obtain the entire human race it will be necessary to move time onwards to a point fixed roughly at 25,000—a little way after the Age of Problems itself. That will be done. I will no longer upset Elna Folson so much; in future I will make the materialization more comfortably. This has been an experiment to see if exchange of personality is really practicable. I have found that it is... Prepare, Lee, to match your tiny brains against the power of Elnek Jelfel and Rath Granod..."

Even as he spoke he commenced to become transparent. We had a last vision of his icy green eyes and white face—then the space where he had stood was empty!

CHAPTER 2

TIME AND RELATIVITY

Half an hour later Elna was normal again, seated in the armchair, her gray eyes scanning the strained faces of Ronnit and me as I told her of what had taken place.

"There is no question of it now, Elna—Jelfel has returned," said Ronnit grimly. "It seems that his appearance was purely to justify an experiment—to be assured that he could materialize on Earth through you. Later, maybe, he'll explain."

"I cannot see how time can be made to alter," Elna said worriedly.

"The only way, as I see it, is this," I answered. "Carreno's time band, as we have proved, extends right into the cosmos. Somehow, these Jovian scientists are going to alter it. We don't pretend to understand Jelfel's science, you know…"

"We must warn the people," Ronnit said purposefully.

"We can warn them," I admitted; "but we can't help them. Against Jelfel we're just babies! Let me think now…" I strolled meditatively towards the window, and pulling aside the curtain looked down on the blazing immensities of New York; and above, dim and obscure with the up-belchings of light from the city, the star-studded sky. My mind reeled as I tried to contemplate the nature of a mentality that could reincarnate itself through an earth woman after travelling through interstellar void; that could hurl its intellectual power across light-years of infinity…

And as I looked at the sky I beheld something strange; something that certainly was not a part of the normal heavens. Objects like shooting stars were falling to earth in the distance—perhaps fifty miles away. My mind revolved around a meteor swarm…then suddenly an amazing pyrotechnical display exactly over the city itself—a swarming mass of incredible colors. I stood open mouthed at the sight. Very slowly I lowered my gaze to the city itself, to realize that something must be amiss with my brain or else my eyes.

"Elna! Lan!" I commanded, in a low, husky whisper—and they came silently to my side.

"What's the matter?" Ronnit enquired in his cryptic voice.

"Do you see what I see?" I asked quietly. Perhaps my voice shook a little.

There was silence for a space, then an astounded exclamation burst from Ronnit's lips.

"Good God, Lee, the city's shifting or something! Changing... Looks as though it is being superimposed on itself! What on earth..." He stopped and clutched tightly at the curtains.

I too felt the same uncanny sensation that had stricken him at the identical moment. A feeling of nausea, an odd conviction that my body was going down and my brain up, as though the molecules of my being were in a state of disruption. I had a vision of Ronnit and Elna pitching helplessly sideways, then I suppose I must have followed suit. I struck the carpet and completely lost consciousness...

When I recovered it was daylight. Elna and Ronnit came to their senses almost at the same time, and we rose unsteadily to our feet in the shafts of the hot sun streaming through the window. For a space we stood looking at each other in dumb inquiry. Something was amiss somewhere; we could sense it. Slowly we turned around and towards the window. We stood dumbfounded, unable to believe for the moment the testimony of our own eyes.

"What on earth..." Ronnit began, staring hard and blinking. Then he pointed suddenly. *"Look!"* he gasped, and the gaze of Elna and me followed his rigidly pointing finger.

From our high perspective we could see the entire city before us, but it was a city that was at once familiar and yet mysterious. For a space I racked my brains to understand the mystery—then in a flash it came to me what had happened.

I clutched Elna and Eonnit with fierce compulsion.

"We've moved forward in Time! Don't you understand? This is the Age after the Age of Problems and immediately before the Age of Intelligence—the year 25,000 to be exact... Let me get this clear! In our last adventure we wrecked the Age of Problems, 22,000, completely, but the year 25,000 sees humanity well on the road to recovery again. I begin to get it. Jelfel has shifted all the people of 2004 to this Age of 25,000, so that he can be in a time where he has never been before."

"But why?" Elna demanded.

"For exactly three reasons," I answered grimly. "One, so he can be in a time he has never trespassed on before; two, so that he can get at us whom he hates like poison; and three, because the people of 2004 are more to his liking than the highly intellectual people who occupy this Age of 25,000. They might prove too good for him."

"But where are the actual people of 25,000—of this age?" Ronnit demanded.

"Presumably they have moved forwards twenty-three thousand years, just as we have," I replied quietly. "Whilst we were unconscious, then—whilst the entire civilization of 2004 was unconscious, we were moved from 2004 to 25,000. The change of time caused us to appear in your flat in 25,000? That is it?" Elna asked keenly.

"Exactly," I assented. "Since my flat, same as all New York buildings, including The Time Corporation Building, are identical in every Age, we hardly moved in space at all. In my visits here I've often used this flat. I—" I stopped and looked around at a sudden imperious hammering on the locked inner door. Opening it, Hilton, my man-servant, entered looking oddly bewildered… Quietly I explained the circumstances.

He moved about reiterating "Most extraordinary!" when I had made things clear to him, until presently he called my attention to the calendar on the wall.

"The 15th June 25,000!" whistled Lan Ronnit. "You were right, then Lee. Of course, that calendar, being automatic and controlled by the sun itself, is bound to be correct. Jelfel has succeeded this far, then—evolved us all into 25,000. Good Lord!"

"Lucky I have a flat in every Age," I commented. "For that matter, so have you, Ronnit—and I think Frot has, too. Shouldn't make much difference to us. We know 25,000 well enough, anyhow."

"So I've lost my Brain Emanation Detector, anyhow," Ronnit grunted. "It's in 2004… If you want any of my inventions at any time, I'll have to get them made here, from the records handed down from the past time. Some paradox!"

"It seems to me—" I began, then paused at a footfall. Two figures came through the doorway—President Templeton and Doctor Anson.

"You realize what has happened, Lee?" the President asked in his impartial voice.

"Certainly I do, President. Nor is this all. Jelfel himself appeared last night—"

"He did! For what reason?"

"Purely to justify an experiment, President." Briefly I explained the amazing manifestation, and Templeton's brows came down.

"Commandant, this sort of thing must be stopped before it becomes too great a task for us. You will take a fast time machine immediately and go forward to the Age of Intelligence—that is the population of the Age of Intelligence, which will be twenty-three thousand years beyond its appointed place—probably in the Last Ages of Earth. Learn from them how best to overcome our difficulty. If their brains cannot conceive a way we are in a tight corner indeed. After that—" The President paused and frowned as a young, dark haired woman entered, carrying a small object in a leather case.

"President, I have just flown from the T.L.C. building with this," she said quietly. "It's a Franton atom-destroyer. I was told you had flown to Commandant Lee's flat to see if—"

"All right, Miss Jeron, all right," Templeton grunted. "Take that thing to the arsenal. Very useful—no time to bother now. Hurry…"

The woman left and Templeton smiled faintly. "My secretary," he explained. "Well, Lee, I think that's all. Go with all speed, will you?"

"At your service, sir," I answered, saluting. He nodded and went out with Dr. Anson by his side.

"Literally, we are now in a position to be shot at," Ronnit said pensively, "Neither the obstacles of time or space are in Jelfel's way now. An absolutely open field—A ghastly thought."

"You'd better both come with me to the Age of Intelligence," I said quietly, and they nodded their immediate acquiescence.

We descended the building to the outside. It did not strike me as an unfamiliar panorama—merely an early edition of the Age of Intelligence. With my work, one Age was as familiar as another, as, to an old time engine driver, one state would be as familiar as another.

I found the housing sheds for the fast-time machines in their accustomed place, and silently the three of us passed inside.

Inside a machine, I moved to the controls, then to my surprise something held me rooted to the spot, my outstretched hand not four inches from the switches for releasing the exterior repellers. I shook myself, thinking for the moment some stray current of powerful magnetism had attracted the nails in my boots. I turned to make a laughing comment on the matter, moving only my head, when the laugh was stricken from my lips as though with a hand.

In the centre of the floor, facing Elna, Ronnit, and me was Elnek Jelfel himself, a faint smile on his ivory-white face.

"My salutations," he remarked dryly. "Forgive me if my arrival is a little starting, but then there are many things known to Jelfel that are unknown to the little-brained creatures known as Earthlings. You see, I am here now to start my campaign in real earnest. Sit down, the three of you, on that bench. It is rather a strain, even to my mental power, to hold the three of you rigid with mind force; the relaxation will be quite a relief." He smiled sardonically. "You thought, when you were up against me before, that you were competing with a scientific wizard, didn't you? You are now to face science of the *nth* degree. Power and genius colossal!"

"You ramble too much, Jelfel," Ronnit grunted. "Spit out what you've got to say—then clear off. You give me the creeps... I suppose you'll be telling us next that you came from Jupiter on a light wave, or something?"

"You know already that Jupiter is destroyed, and that we exist on Ondon," Jelfel answered bitterly. "Ondon—a miserable, barren planet with a yellow sun. We, of Zagribud, can never forgive the hurling of Jupiter into the sun... But, to the point. I am here as the ambassador of Rath Granod. At sundown, the first humans will be sent to Ondon, and I am here to supervise that work. You know already how, and why, I manifested myself through Elna Folson. Purely to see if duplicated personality could be achieved."

"We know you did it, but how remains a mystery," I answered, feeling again, unbidden, that admiration for the man's almost uncanny knowledge. Elnek Jelfel was the most compelling, insolently superior creature I ever came across.

"Ah, yes, I had better explain," he admitted. "You, Commander, are always so kindly and tolerant towards my expositions... To you, on Earth, the conversion of matter into energy is as yet an impossible feat. If energy disappears you expect to find generation of matter, and if matter disappears you expect to find evolution of energy. That so?"

"Right," said Ronnit laconically.

"Well, in the Ondonian laboratories, conversion of matter into energy is a simple task, by using the ether itself. The force of ether is so concentrated by our instruments as to change matter into pure energy. But, a person of even my slight size converted into pure energy produces, of course, an incredible amount of energy. You may know the elementary fact that one-tenth of a milligramme, a very minute weighable speck, moving with the speed of light, equals a load of six hundred tons falling one mile."

"That's a fact," I agreed.

"Splendid, Commander. I am indebted, indeed. Hence, the energy of a man, of the matter that composes him, is terrific! This energy, once released, results of course in the instant dissolution of the person concerned, as his energy passes into sealing tubes. Now, to convert that energy back into the original matter there must be a medium, and that medium must have exactly the energy equivalent of the matter that has already been converted into energy. The reason for this being that the energy of motion creates heat, but the intermingling of the two energies together causes the pure energy to resolve back into matter—hence it appears that one person possessing the exact energy equivalent of another, can evolve into matter through that person. Elna Folson is my exact energy counterpart, as we found by our detectors on Ondon—so I materialized through her. My energy was projected *via* the ether itself—for ether, as you know, projects energy at the speed of light—is indeed, the vehicle of energy. It was thus a case of fixing a movable force projector on Ondon to be exactly in line with the energy emanations of Elna. Wherever she went, however Earth changed its position, this straight line of force always followed her, so there could never be any doubt but what it was directly in line with her. The force projector was of course altered sufficiently to reach Etna although she occupied a past time…

"That line of force would affect her energy and give her a sensation of cramp, which effect, I read from her mind, she has experienced. So, when my matter form was converted into energy it was despatched from Ondon, walled in with sealed particles to prevent, any escape of energy, and propelled down that line of force in the ether—the perfect vehicle—just the same as a boat might follow a channel to the sea… Since the dissolution of my body also included the dissolution of my brain, Rath Granod and I devised a brain vibration absorber. Since every brain transmits minute electrical force, it stood to reason that this force could be attracted and held by a specially constructed magnetic device. The force of a concentrated thought, its electrical output value, could therefore be held steady on the magnet once the thought was emitted—and, electrically speaking, that brain emanation became a pilot-energy linked to the whole energy. Thus, my last concentration, before being converted into energy, was 'Reassembly through Elna Folson, on Earth'…

"Then I was in the blackness of pure extinction, but that trapped thought-impression remained, and was despatched with my energy through space. Arriving within proximity of Elna the electric power of that thought vibration sought its opposite in energy charge—Elna's brain emanations themselves. It so disturbed her she couldn't sleep, but it was some time before the force of it broke her own brain energy output, and simultaneously that thought vibration resolved itself back into matter, becoming again my brain. Instantly afterwards my body energy was retransformed in the same way—and so I came to Earth! The only known way to reach here. Now I am here the rest will be easy, for by this process Earthlings will be sent to Ondon."

"You could have come in a space ship," I commented.

"True—but this other way is the better. I can send hundreds to Ondon with the speed of light by this process, now I have proved it can be done…"

"Jelfel, I was ordered to come to this time machine to take it to the Age of Intelligence—to there consult a brain that could conceivably find a way of stopping your damnable plans—

"You can spare yourself the task, Commander," Jelfel intervened, his hand raised. "You have seen what Ondonian science can do—has changed the time of your world, even. Nothing can stop us now—you are powerless against us."

I resorted to sudden supplication. "Jelfel, intelligence is power, I know, but it should also beget mercy! Why not turn that glorious mind of yours to helping the Universe on its way, to uplifting the lesser intellects, teaching them to understand the immensities of time and space as you understand them…"

His cruel face set as hard as granite at that. "Commander, you will discover, if you live long enough, that as you increase in knowledge of material things your sentiment for them will proportionately diminish! Until at last you will see human beings, and all matter, for what they are—*chemicals!* Just evolved chemicals Commander, three parts water, walking about with puny intellects in a glorious young world, multiplying upon themselves—the affinity of one sex for the other, as positive will always attract negative… No, to be kind to such stumbling, groping intellects would be sheer futility… You think nothing of exterminating pests, if it is to your advantage—so it is with us. You had the brains to wreck our world, but only because you were given such brain power by a higher intelligence than mine—but that has passed. Jupiter was a miserable planet enough for brains such as ours. Ondon is, if anything, worse. An unpleasant world, Commander. We must have a young world, and that world is Earth! We cannot come in our own form, as you know—only I am the physical exception to our race, and even I have artificial arms and legs. We cannot come so cramped and uncomfortable as that, so the only alternative is to transfer our brains to the most healthy of your humans, and remove theirs for investigation—unless a better use for them occurs to us. To you, maybe, a horrible thought—to us, a purely scientific achievement."

"A scientific achievement!" I echoed in a hollow voice. "Good God!"

"And by the way," he went on coolly, "you were all removed from 2004 to 25,000 by a simple process of Rath Granod's. A Relativity Machine, which incorporates the actual position of time with your relative outlook upon it. Time is relative, when you understand it; hence, during your state of unconsciousness all the ages of Earth were made to move forward twenty-three thousand years, according to your state of perception. Our time being normal on Ondon we need no relative outlook. We have accomplished our object, moved the population of 2004 to where we can attack it. Mainly because I long to avenge myself on the three of you, and also because the actual people of 25,000 might prove dangerous with their knowledge. I take no risks. So long as the Realtivity Machinery on Ondon is at work, you will remain, to all intents and purposes in 25,000."

"That's some idea," Ronnit murmured, his inventor's soul absorbed.

Jelfel turned to him "True enough, Ronnit, yet quite simple. I have now a clear field to tread on, unhampered by the thought that I might find myself in a place where I have already been and so find myself on the brink of destruction... After I vanished from your sight last night, I returned to Ondon and had the Relativity Machinery set to work, and also projected my machinery from Ondon to Earth—which I believe you saw, Commander, in the form of shooting stars, if my reading of your mind is correct. I now have a fully equipped laboratory, and you shall be my first subjects..."

I looked at him grimly. "You know I'm not the sort of man to let you get away with that, Jelfel!"

He smiled amusedly. "My dear Commander, it doesn't interest me what sort of a man you are. You will do entirely as I say— No, don't move! It might prove awkward for you, and I am ever mindful of your comfort."

Held powerless by the nameless force he exerted upon us, the three of us watched in complete impotency whilst he walked slowly to the controls of the time machine. A few swift movements with the controls and there emerged from the silence the familiar hum of the exterior repeller motors. The machine began to rise upwards towards the time-band.

"What's the idea?" I demanded curtly, and he turned his pitiless, green eyes towards me.

"The idea, Commander? Why, surely you can guess? I am using the time machine as an air machine for a change, since it is equipped for both purposes. You will, I feel convinced, be interested in viewing my laboratory."

His slender artificial hand reached out and stopped the machine's ascent before it could actually reach the time line, then flinging in the switch of the propeller motor he set the vessel travelling forward, rising rapidly above the city of 25,000 and at length skimming the tops of the loftier edifices of New York.

During the time his eyes were fixed on the controls and dials, his terrific mental power was such that none of us could break it. We could only stand still and gaze at the hurtling changes of the city below—until at last, after a distance of perhaps fifty miles, we drew close to a little natural basin somewhere to the south of New York, sheltered around the edges with towering trees. It was to me a quite unfamiliar spot; whether natural or created by the forces of Jelfel and Rath Granod I could not even guess.

The time machine dipped slightly and commenced to sweep downward towards this depression in the landscape. The trees rose up to meet us. We dropped softly into the valley, and Jelfel switched off the engine.

"I believe Commander, I am what you would call in your Earthly language, a fast worker," he commented dryly. "You are now about to view my laboratory, underground, replete with its apparatus. I leave your brilliant mind to solve how I erected it all within a few hours of the apparatus arriving on Earth. Purely transmutation of elements and mind force... But, come."

He opened the time machine door and we stepped out on the soft grass. Not one hundred yards before us, in the valley side, reposed a peculiar type of triangular door, shining with a glow akin to that of burnished bronze. Towards this door we all moved, and I saw in the eyes of Ronnit and Elna a dawning wonder.

"Behold!" Jelfel said, in an almost needlessly dramatic voice, and stretched forth his hand. We stood perfectly still, following the line of his artificial fingers to the door. To our incredulous amazement the shining triangle slowly seemed to become brighter, transparent, became a nebulous mist, and then vanished—leaving a black and uninviting tunnel beyond. I rubbed my eyes and looked again to reassure myself that the phenomenon was genuine.

Jelfel lowered his hand. "Surely that doesn't puzzle you, Commander?" he inquired sarcastically. "That door is composed of solid light vibration, through which no being or object can pass. Light, as you know, emits vibration. Along the base of that opening is a tube-like machine which emits light-vibration, but is changed into solid form by an adjustment to the atoms of the vibrations. These atoms are, in truth, colossally magnified, to form a complete wall, and a similar light-vibration in the summit of the opening prevents the vibrations from escaping from their appointed place in the opening. At close quarters you would have found that glittering bronze door to be really a mass of swirling atoms and incipient molecules... Now, it is an accepted fact that one vibration can negate or neutralize another. In these artificial fingers of mine is that vibration, controlled by this little cap you see in my palm." He held out his hand and we beheld a circular piece of metal. "Pressure with my thumb on this cap releases a current which is contained in a little battery in my hand itself. The energy passes through my fingers and is flung at the door-vibration. Hence, the barrier at once ceases activity for roughly two minutes—time for us to pass—then it will reform—a barrier proof against practically every known force of destruction. You might try breaking a wall of atoms some time," he added dryly. "Now come…" and he led the way through the opening into the darkness of the tunnel. We followed him in that same condition of mental apathy, to start slightly as the atomic barrier suddenly reformed behind us, and we beheld the daylight outside through an odd, coppery curtain.

"This way," came Jelfel's voice from the gloom, and he brought out a radium torch from his belt. A remarkable instrument that torch; everlasting, gave the brilliance of daylight behind and before us, and emitted no heat… Everywhere, upon all sides, we had again the portent of impending disaster. The brilliance and cruelty of Jelfel was beyond Earthly comprehension.

CHAPTER 3

VIA ETHER TO ONDON

In dead silence we continued the journey through the perfectly formed tunnel, going lower and lower, it appeared, until at length we passed through another atomic screen and lastly into a vast underground laboratory that brought back to me vivid memories of the amazing Machine Rooms he had possessed in the Age of Problems...

Light gushed forth from above, sudden and dazzling—radium bowls that poured a blueish white effulgence on a wilderness of Ondonian complexity.

"I feel quite at home now," Jelfel commented, smoothing back his jet-black hair. 'Pray make yourselves comfortable, my friends. You are likely to be here a little while. Since you can't escape you can have your normal wills back again..."

Something seemed to release itself in my brain. I felt an influx of normal willpower. My tongue was freed.

Jelfel stood for a while looking at the three of us with mocking eyes, supreme in his knowledge; then he shrugged his shoulders and glanced up at the queer Ondonian chronometer on the shining wall.

"In a few more hours it will be nightfall," he remarked. "And sundown marks the end of freedom for the human race. In the interval you may be interested in viewing the planet you are shortly to visit. Here, my friends, is Ondon."

He pressed a switch and the radium bowls expired. The darkness of Erebus descended on the weird laboratory. Came a whirring, then a deep bass rumble. From above there suddenly poured a streaming white-hot incandesence of liquid fire—or so it seemed at first. We all three turned aside, arms across our faces.

"If you value your eyesight, don't look up," Jelfel counselled. "Look down—on the light-wave screen that reflects the image."

We moved forward and gazed into a sunken circle in the floor, some eight feet in diameter. Upon it there swirled strange, unimaginable shapes of the cosmos; the whole view conveyed the impression of falling through space. At terrific speeds misty nebulae and stars of every magnitude rushed up to meet us, dissolved and passed away. I became inordinately dizzy; my mind reeled in the awful gulf of this soundless rush through space. Then Jelfel's metallic voice steadied me a trifle. Elna seized my hand tightly and I shot a flashing glimpse at her drawn face in the reflected light. Lan Ronnit was staring fixedly.

"The light beam is transmitted by my machinery and at the moment is hurtling from Earth to Ondon, my friends—in the ordinary way a journey of more than four years. But, however, by linking time with the speed of light, the trip of the light-beam across the interstellar void occupies roughly four Earthly minutes. You are viewing what the light beam is passing—are stupefied by its stupendous onrush. Ah! You see a ball of dull yellow ahead? Growing slowly…? That is Ondon!"

We resumed our gazing into the light-wave screen and beheld the yellow world of Ondon, one of a system of four planets circling about a dim, sulphur-yellow sun… With the same incredible soundlessness we swept towards the planet, seemed to shoot through the scattered clouds that surrounded it, and still downwards into the dull obscurity of its craggy landscape. I felt Elna, standing close to me, shudder. I put an arm round her slim shoulders. I did not wonder at her reaction; there was something infinitely alien and inhuman about that dreary desolation…

Within, as it appeared, about half a mile of the surface, Jelfel altered his enigmatic controls and the view became rigid, focussed with uncanny clarity. Another control moved and we commenced, as it were, a steady air-survey of the planet.

We passed over awesome mountain ranges, reaching bare, gaunt crags and escarpments to the greyish-black sky—moved across stagnant lakes, amidst which there moved the most strange monstrosities dwarfing anything I had ever seen even in Earth's prehistoric times—swept steadily over jungles of sickly, yellow trees, across plains and inimical deserts—then at last to a mighty city, not unlike New York itself in appearance, but of far vaster and loftier proportions, a colossus of metal buildings, sprinkled with mighty, rearing towers, monster bridges of glittering metal, and latticed masses of outlook posts. In the exact centre there stood the highest tower of all, quite fifteen hundred feet high, overlooking the entire city.

The pedestrian ways were packed with insectile Jovians moving to and fro, and in the abysmal streets strange vehicles moved. Overhead shot air-machines of unknown power and design.

"Zagribud—Zagribud the Colossal, the Powerful—my home," Jelfel murmured with an unusually sad note in his voice. "I look upon it, my friends, with the feelings with which you look upon your beloved New York. To me it is everything. Well, I have said the planet is not prepossessing, but you've probably been interested in seeing what you are to visit…"

Came a click. The vision faded as the discontinued light beam hurtled into empty space and was gone. The radium bowls resumed their illumination, and we stood blinking after the darkness. I turned round and looked at my companions as Jelfel made final adjustments to his amazing telescopic machinery to ensure its safety.

"Here," Ronnit breathed, handing me a square of paper. "Take this. A map of Ondon, drawn roughly from the view we've seen. May be useful sometime…" He paused, and I put the map safely in my pocket as Jelfel turned and came slowly towards us.

"I am rather at a loss to know how to pass the time," he said smoothly. "The sixth dimensional body-stealer might interest you. It is the instrument by which I shall bring human beings here, prior to their projection to Ondon. You see this—" He pointed to a bellying cylinder lying in a metal cradle, to which were linked six stout cables. "This instrument is my sixth-dimensional Rotator. We know three facts, my friends. Time is allied to the fourth dimension; the fourth dimension itself is an angle in space; the fifth dimension is parallel to the fourth only in higher order, and the sixth dimension intersects the third, fourth, and fifth.

"Hence, it follows that direct transit can only be accomplished by the sixth dimension, for, being a vertical dimension in relation to its neighbours, it follows a straight track where the others do not. It may seem an odd thought to you, my friends, but when humans lie down they are in the third dimension and just under the fourth and fifth. When they stand up they are parallel with the sixth dimension, but never touch it because between it and them lies what is called hyper-space, and hyper-space is, literally, no dimension. This machine here simply presses hyper-space to nil with the result that the sixth dimension merges into actuality and any given human, or movable object is absorbed by it…

"Then, magnetism—which is of tremendous negative force and pulls upon the positive magnetism of the sixth dimension—causes the dimension to rotate, and, by calculating the swing of this dimension, or its arc through space, a human being caught within the dimension swings from one given space to another—the end of the journey being here. This machine accomplishes that. Also, it is automatic. If I stand within its radius and press a switch I am automatically placed in any predetermined place. That, as a matter of fact, is how I appeared in your time machine a few moments ago…"

"How do you detect humans, anyhow?" Lan Ronnit demanded.

"By the Emanation Detector." Jelfel's cold eyes turned to me. "I fancy Commander Lee has had some experience of that machine…"

"True," I admitted quietly. "One of your cleverest inventions, Jelfel."

"You honour me," he answered cynically. "Perhaps a demonstration of this Rotator will interest you."

He flung in the switches with the air of an expert and from within the cylinder came a sonorous droning. I fancied an aura of faint green light began to emanate from a circular metal disk supported on arms of chrome-steel above the cylinder. Within that area, I presumed, lay the sixth dimension. Jelfel looked at the manifestation pensively, nodded, then moved over to his Emanation Detector.

"We'll try a woman about twenty-seven, dark," he commented in an offhand tone.

"That will be…" He swung around the big pointer and looked at the screen above. A vision of New York appeared, rapidly changed to a main street, then slowly focused upon a young woman, carrying a neat, leather case, and walking slowly toward some unknown destination. There was something about her appearance that to me seemed vaguely familiar… Jelfel chuckled to himself and pressed a two-pole switch linked to the Rotator. In the Emanation Detector screen we saw the figure of the young woman suddenly vanish in a green mist. We caught a flashing glimpse of open-mouthed people staring, then Jelfel shut the machine off.

We waited intently. I stood with my fists clenched… Came a faint whistling from somewhere, a gust of cool air, and a wave of giddiness swept over me as the fringe of the rotating dimension passed near me… A thud.

The woman we had seen in the city was before us, standing, her eyes wide in fright, gazing about her. As her gaze fell upon Jelfel's ruthles face she caught her breath in sharply.

"So simple!" Jelfel commented with a shrug, snapping the Rotator contacts. "Now, my friends, you have seen how I shall accomplish the stealing of humans. Easy things to steal with their little brains. I might add I have only to widen the area of this Rotator dimension to absorb a crowd all at once. Then indeed will this laboratory be a danger-spot to outsiders, as it crackles with the energy I shall absorb from these captive beings before hurling them *via* ether to Ondon!"

"How—how did I get to this place?" the woman asked, taking a faltering step forward. "Who—who on earth are you?" She clutched her leather bag tenaciously.

Jelfel studied her, then bowed. "Your pardon, dear lady; you are the victim of a scientific experiment. Please be seated."

He pushed a metal chair in her direction and she sat down with a thud. It was then that I caught a full view of her face and in an instant I recognized her as the Secretary to Templeton, who had made a brief appearance in my flat a few hours before. In that case... My thoughts moved fast. In her leather bag was the deadly Franton atom-destroyer! She recognized me at the same moment, and would have spoken had I not, by facial expression, bidden her to be silent.

From then on I lived in fear that Jelfel would read her mind—but evidently he was not concerned with her, now he had brought her hither to prove his Rotator. I thanked the Fates that, by sheer fortuity, had led him to capture a girl of the Secretary's age and coloring.

"The next move to make is to take a batch of humans and then, by means of my radio, inform Rath Granod of their energy voltage," Jelfel said calmly, looking around. "It will then be his task to find the exact equivalents on Ondon to be the recipients for reassembly of Earthlings... Now, my friends, if you will pardon me for a moment I will inspect my energy-sealing tubes for the coming transit via ether. As you are to be the first travellers I must be assured of your safety! And, by the way, please do not tamper with anything. I should hate to find ashes upon my return..."

He turned and walked with his meditative tread from the laboratory into some unknown area of complication adjoining it. Instantly I turned to the Secretary.

"Miss Jeron?" I asked quickly.

"Yes. You are Commandant Lee, of course? I was on my way to the arsenal, following Templeton's instructions, with this atom-destroyer, and—"

"Never mind that," I interrupted her brusquely. "That atom destroyer. Give it to me, quickly."

She handed across the leather bag. I pulled out the small but deadly efficient atom-destroyer and slipped it in my pocket. The bag I hurled into a far corner.

Miss Jeron gave me a bewildered look. "Commandant, what is all this about? Who is this man? What are we—"

"This man is Elnek Jelfel—a fiend, a scientific genius," I answered grimly. "We are in deadly danger in this place. Do whatever you can to keep your thoughts jumbled up in case he tries to read your mind; leave everything else to me... Know anything of the workings of this atom destroyer, Miss Jeron? I'm a bit foggy on it. It's a new discovery, isn't it?"

She nodded. "It works on the friction system. It generates tremendous friction inside that little box by using tungsten rollers compressed one against the other. The little motor attached starts the rollers going and tungsten, being so tough, stands the heat but generates the friction. The friction is transmitted to a transformer which converts this enormously high percentage of energy into a current of repulsive electricity, which Franton claims will break down almost any known earthly atomic or molecular structure. It can also be opened and altered to become a repulsor."

"You know a lot for a Secretary," I murmured. "I think—Steady, here comes Jelfel again."

He came slowly into the laboratory again, and I watched him narrowly. "Not long to sunset my friends," he commented pleasantly. "Everything is ready. I see no reason why we cannot start now. I think we will despatch Miss Elna first; she is so adaptable with her particular amount of energy. You will come second, Ronnit; you third, Miss Jeron—I think I have your name correct according to your brain; the only thing I can read sensibly from your confused mentality—and you, Commander, will be last. I have so strong a desire to show you *everything* before you go!" And his green eyes blazed malevolently upon the four of us.

Instantly I felt again that terrific hypnotic power, but, try though I would, I could not overcome it. I realized the fatality of being so mentally enslaved; it rendered all my rosy ideas for escape useless... With quiet helplessness the four of us followed Jelfel into the adjoining apartment, and there beheld the amazing apparatus for projecting the hapless Earthlings through the void.

Jelfel paused with his hand resting lightly on the switches of his amazing contrivance, lined at orderly intervals along the side of an oblong table and directly beneath a wilderness of lenses and curious bulbs and tubes.

"I have communicated with Rath Granod," he said in his metallic voice. "It appears that, in the absence of myself from Ondon—for, as you know, I am Miss Elna's absolute energy counterpart—she will have to be materialized through an Ondonian named Lep-Nooze, who also possesses the same energy equivalent. Now, Miss Folson, lie upon this table, if you please."

With the quiet precision of one mesmerized, Elna did as she was bid, lying flat, gazing upwards into the very heart of that weird, many-lensed mechanism. I noticed for the first time that the apparatus was casting a bluey-white glow upon her recumbent form. Jelfel surveyed her, nodded silently, then moved to another switchboard littered with devices which I can hardly attempt to describe.

"The energy tubes," he said casually, and, as he threw in a master-switch, I fought again to reassert my will-power, but to my horror failed utterly. Ronnit, Miss Jeron, and I could only watch helplessly...

Of a sudden the great laboratory became alive with sound. Strange, gushing tumults came from the enigmatic engines beneath the projection table; electricity crackled and flashed from the engines controlling the energy tubes. Elna herself did not appear to alter in the slightest, beyond the fact that her eyes closed slowly, and her chin dropped with the coming of unconsciousness.

Jelfel threw a glance at a flickering meter-gauge on the wall, pulled another switch, and the noise ceased.

"Miss Folson is now no more," he said calmly. "Her energy, which is her life, is stored in those transparent cylinders. You see the dial reading... Now, that energy is finally broken from her body and hurled it to Ondon—so!" Came more quick movements amongst his machinery, more noises and further flaring of deadly electricity, then for a space the room seemed to dance with heat. The needle on the meter-gauge fell to 0.

I turned to look at Elna... To my dumbfounded amazement the table was empty!

I was still staring when the noise altogether ceased. I looked at Jelfel, feeling utterly strangled in mind and body.

"There you are, Commander," he said pleasantly. "Elna Folson has gone to Ondon, and will rematerialize into her original form through Lep-Nooze. Her brain emanations, as I explained before, followed her energy, and as the atoms of her body must be linked with her energy her body has gone as well—through space, to my own planet. You, Ronnit, are next."

The boring green eyes swivelled to the young inventor, and he moved slowly toward the table.

I felt, I knew, that the whole thing was devilish—yet what could I do with my mind so subjected? Elna had gone into the void, the first in a literal massacre of the human race. Again I struggled with enormous effort against the super-brain, and again came futility as the answer. I took one lurching step forward toward the table, but the eyes of Jelfel held me there. I could move no farther...

Then came the unexpected. Miss Jeron, overcome by the terrible strain and events, fainted clean away. She pitched forward into me, and I staggered beneath the impact, being unprepared for it. As she fell inert to the floor I flung out my hand to save myself stumbling—gripped a pole switch on the edge of the table. Instantly Jelfel shouted hoarsely.

"Don't break that contact, you fool! You'll blow us to hell—!" In an instant he was upon me, seizing my hand and tearing it away before I could pull the switch down beneath my weight. But in that instant I seized my opportunity. In his intentness to stop my action he had ceased to exert his mind force, and my own brain instantly returned to life. I struck him a resounding blow on the jaw and he staggered away from me on his heels.

Lan Ronnit, released also from his mental and physical apathy, slid off the projection table and joined me in struggling with the master-scientist. For a space we pitched about furiously on the shining metal floor—then Ronnit, lean and intent, whipped up a metal bar from the floor by the switchboard—a spanner of sorts I think it was—and struck Jelfel a terrific blow on the forehead. He sank limply beneath the impact and became still.

"Either you've killed or stunned him," I breathed. "In any case he's safer dead. Stand clear, Lan."

I whipped out the atom destroyer from my pocket and ruthlessly pressed the button. The motor hummed, but nothing else seemed to happen. Jelfel remained where he was on the floor, whereas he ought to have been radiated out of existence.

"The damn thing's no good," Ronnit growled. "Which reminds me, let's get that battery from Jelfel's hand to bust these doors." He dropped on his knees beside the unconscious Jovian, but to our alarm we found that the disk of the tiny machine within his hand had been smashed irreparably in the conflict.

Ronnit and I looked grimly into each others' faces.

"What now?" I asked gravely. "The Franton machine is no use, and Jelfel's 'doorkey' is useless. Any suggestions?"

He squatted in thought for a space, then slowly rose to his feet. "I've got an idea," he said in a peculiar voice. "Give me that Franton destroyer, will you? Carry Miss Jeron. You're the tough egg of this outfit."

I gathered up the limp form of the Secretary in my arms and followed Ronnit to the first atomic door. He levelled the atom destroyer carefully and pressed the button. Instantly the atomic door blasted into sudden, blinding incandescent fire. The air became thick with pungent smoke. In two brilliant flashes of light the lightwave tubes at the base and summit of the door ripped themselves asunder with terrific recoil.

I looked at the dark vista of tunnel before us, smoke curling around my nostrils.

"The machine worked that time all right," I muttered.

"Yes, and I'll tell you why," Ronnit responded. "It is attuned to all forms of earthly matter. Light is a universal property, therefore it comes under Earthly classification. But Jelfel is *Jovian* matter, composed of Jovian atoms and molecules. That is why he didn't disintegrate. This machine isn't tuned to his body frequencies... But let's get going whilst we're safe. We'll wipe up the earth along with this blasted lab once we can get some energized iralium" (the most powerful explosive known).

Our progress was hampered, so far as I was concerned at least, by the weight of Miss Jeron, and the pitch darkness, but at last we came to the second and final atomic door. This, too, we ruined and blasted into nothingness and found ourselves once again in the little valley, with the evening sky above.

"Thank heaven!" Ronnit breathed gratefully, wiping his brow. "There's the time machine, too—just as we left it. Come on…"

Increasing our pace we rapidly crossed the little stretch of grassy floor and entered the machine. Laying the Secretary carefully on the wall-couch, I threw in the air-plane switches whilst Ronnit sealed the door…

In another moment we were in the air, turning about, and heading toward the misty immensities of New York's weird skyline far down on the western horizon.

CHAPTER 4

THE SHRIEKING PUFF-BALL

The moment we landed back in New York we made for the Time Corporation Building. Miss Jeron, thanks to the ministrations of Ronnit, had recovered during the trip, and accompanied us to the Building. We entered the Debating Room with a rush, just as the President was preparing to depart.

"What's the matter, Commandant?" he asked sharply, divining from my expression that something was seriously amiss.

Hastily I related the details of our weird experience. "Elna Folson has been hurled to Ondon—she is the first of hundreds—thousands!" I panted. "Something has got to be done right away. Jelfel means business, unless by a lucky chance Ronnit has killed him with that bar, but I don't think so. When he recovers trouble begins in earnest. What must I do, sir? Your orders?"

Templeton considered with that calm, mental research for which he was remarkable.

"Elna Folson must, of course, be rescued from Ondon," he answered at length. "But before you start for Ondon, Commandant, you will head a raiding party to this hideout of Jelfel's and try by every known means to exterminate him. You are at liberty to use whatever methods you choose... That is all."

"Very well, sir." I stood back and saluted.

"About the Franton atom destroyer," Miss Jeron remarked. "Is the Commandant to keep it?"

Templeton nodded. "Certainly. Better in Lee's hands than in the arsenal. I will see that Franton receives notification."

Lan Ronnit and I left the Debating Room and shortly afterwards had reached my flat. In one stride I had reached the televisor and was speaking to Benruf, leader of the Military Force of New York.

"...every known device," I concluded. "Ray guns, energized iralium, everything. And instruct your men to be armed with Franton atom destroyers. You can have them made very quickly at the arsenal. Get plans from Franton. Be ready at the ninth hour. I will join you at the Military Grounds."

I switched off and turned to the waiting Ronnit. "Lan, that Double Entity Machine of yours, which you had to leave in 2004 when time changed. Can you have others made right away?"

"Sure I can," he responded readily. "I'll get several made right away. I have the plans with me, fortunately. I'll be here tonight at half past the hour of eight. That suit you?"

I nodded, and the door closed behind him.

Deeply troubled, I sat down to think things out. My mind was solely concentrated on Elna, my closest and dearest friend. I tried to picture the unnamed horrors that might befall her on the world of Ondon. I was consumed with a sudden desire to rush out, into a time-space machine, and start for Ondon right away. Then I controlled myself. Elna's life was certainly valuable, but the fate of all humanity was even more to be considered... I got up and walked to the window.

Night had completely fallen now and the view of light-drenched New York was before me.

It was.as I stood at the window that I became the spectator of most peculiar happenings.... Out of the darkness of the eastern horizon there gradually crept a green tentacle of light. It hovered for a space above the main street immediately below me, packed as the street was on the pedestrian ways with people—then suddenly it swept downward.

I watched, my jaw lolling stupidly. People began to melt and vanish before my very eyes, seemed to melt into the air. Within five minutes a great section of the pedestrian way was almost empty. The green ray re-curled on itself in an amazing manner and abruptly snapped into extinction. Then came the din of alarm sounds, whistles and hoots, as remote controlled armored cars, aware of the occurrence, came speeding into view.

"Jelfel's Rotator," I muttered, biting my lip. "He cleaned up nearly five hundred souls at that sweep. Good grief, where is it all going to end..." I looked again, about to turn away, when another occurrence astounded me. A ray of pure white light this time, blindingly brilliant near the horizon, then fading toward the zenith, was projecting into the sky at a sixty degree angle. I did not need to think fast to realize that it was ether tube machinery at work—the energy beam itself hurling the helpless Earthlings to Ondon.

I swung around and looked at the electric clock. An hour yet before Lan Ronnit was due. An hour and a half before the attack on Jelfel was timed to commence! I clenched my fists and took a step forward, overcome with indecisions—only to realize I could do nothing but wait.

Accordingly I turned back again to the window, taking heart very slightly as time passed and there was no repetition of the green Rotator beam. The white energy beam, however, still projected unerringly into space, directly in line, I presumed, with the unknown world of Ondon. That fact began to take hold on my mind. Directly in line with Ondon... Without something to guide me, I could never even find Ondon! I might search all the immensity of space for a lifetime and be no nearer. After all, why should I delay...

Was ever a man torn more between the love for his friend and the duty to his planet? Then suddenly I made up my mind and set off to seek Templeton. He had left the T.L.C. Building, but I found him at his own private flat, standing at the window gazing out with troubled eyes over the city. At my entry he turned sharply

"President, I have come to ask your permission to leave for Ondon at once," I said earnestly, standing before him. "Nor do I want any molestation of Jelfel for a few hours. In that time I hope to reach Ondon. Unwittingly, Jelfel will guide me to the planet."

"How?" Templeton asked curtly, his face none too reassuring.

I outlined to him, emphatically, the guiding nature of the energy beam.

"Let Lan Ronnit take charge of destroying Jelfel on the earth, and I will attack from the Ondonian end," I urged. "I only want one companion—Anton Frot, the mathematician."

"You will go without weapons?" Templeton asked incredulously.

"Not altogether. I'll call on Ronnit and get a Double Entity Machine from him. That, and a few Franton atom-destroyers, are all I need. Will you grant me permission?"

The President considered for a space, then to my intense satisfaction nodded.

"Very well, Commandant. I know your resourcefulness in danger. You may go, and Heaven grant that you'll succeed. You obliterated the menace once—but unhappily only temporarily. May you really win this time. Until I see you again, goodbye and good luck."

He shook my hand solemnly. I saluted and hastily departed, making my way instantly in the direction of Lan Ronnit's abode...

During my journey I found the main street in a condition of terrific confusion... Police, ordinary people, and scientists were all together in a jammed mass, searching, explaining, and baffled. Some were crying out for their lost ones, others were cursing the police for their slowness... One incident stood out predominantly, to me, as I made my way through the throngs— A little boy, standing isolated from the main surging of humans, was weeping copiously for his lost mother. At that moment the heinous side of Jelfel's plans came home to me more vividly than ever before…

Then I was through the jam, walked almost at a run down several side streets, and at last reached Ronnit's flat. He was in the act of packing up a Double Entity Machine even as I entered.

"Hello, Lee! What's the trouble?" He looked up sharply.

"You know what's happened, of course? The pedestrian-way tragedy?" I demanded.

"Certainly. Jelfel's Rotator; but what—"

As fast as I could I made the details clear to him.

"I'm leaving at once for Ondon with Frot. You're going to wipe out Jelfel, if you can, three hours from now. That's the arrangement. The time is later because I want Jelfel left free long enough to project that beam of his into space. I also want one of those Double Entity Machines."

I picked up the machine from the table—it was not large, and slung it over my shoulder with the straps provided for the purpose.

"I don't know when I'll be back, or what I shall do," I said grimly. "If it's within human power I'm going to give the Ondonians something to think about!"

Ronnit smiled faintly. "As for Jelfel, leave him to me," he said, tightening his lips. "My own ambition in life is to get the better of him—and perhaps this is my chance. Good luck, old man…"

I shook hands and hurried away. Ten minutes later I had picked up Anton Frot, the mathematical genius who had once belonged to the Age of Problems and who was directly responsible for the destruction of Jupiter. It did not take long to make things clear to his active brain, and presently we were in a fast air-machine heading for the space grounds.

A digression here is necessary, I find. Before my first experience with Jelfel, space travel before the time of the Age of Intelligence had been impossible—but thanks to Jelfel's own inventions—which had come into our possession at his vanquishment—we were now equipped with space-time machines. These marvellous vessels, whilst incorporating all the necessities of a time-travelling machine, also possessed the power of emitting *their own substance* at either end of the vessel—the substance being ejected into the ether by powerful electric currents. This substance, infinitesimal in amount, created reaction by pressing on the dense ether, and the recoil at maximum hurled the vessel through space at the speed of light. The idea would, undoubtedly, have been in possession of all later times, for all Ages to use, had not Jelfel effectively kept his secret until his almost individual war with me. Hence, it was not until the year of my second battle with him that space-travel became really possible. Time and time-space machines at this period were also equipped with

"Instantaneous Time Switches," making any length of time trip almost immediately. Thus, interstellar travel was made possible since, travelling at the speed of light, a ship could cover a light year in distance by moving ahead a year in time.

Hastily alighting from the air-machine we made with all speed to the flood-lit time-space machine hangars. An army of mechanics hovered expectantly as we appeared on the scene.

"Make way for this machine to leave instantly," I said sharply, and entered the bull-nosed vessel with Frot close behind me. In a few moments the massive door had closed and the lights were on. I turned to the familiar controls and watched through the window for the departure signal.

Three minutes later it came. I pushed over the lever to start the engines and we rose steadily into the air.

Anton Frot looked through the window with his keen eyes.

"Jelfel's ether beam is directly ahead," he said. "Are you making for it?"

I nodded, and started the engine again. We shot toward the north with rapidly mounting acceleration, then as we neared the blinding beam I slackened speed.

"You'll never be able to follow that beam," Frot said dubiously. "See, it fades above. What are you going to do?"

"Once we're in its path we can chart a straight line from it," I answered. "That is why I brought you along. Your mathematics can do it. It involves a high order of computation—to compute the bend through space, the movement of Earth in relation to Ondon, and so forth.... Just a minute, I'll move the ship into a straight line, then you can get busy."

As I operated the controls we moved slowly toward the beam of light. Far below in the gloomy abyss we could discern the tiny dark spot that marked the valley where lay Jelfel's domain, and from it was rising this immense beam into the infinite—sheer energy.

"How I'd love to blow the damn lot to Hades!" I breathed, looking down.

"You mightn't manage it," Frot answered calmly. "It wouldn't surprise me if that place isn't shielded with vibration or something. Don't forget we're up against a mind of super-proportions... Ah, we're approaching the beam—"

He became intent and earnest at the window, staring over my shoulder as I guided the vessel toward the blazing mist. We touched the edge of the beam, and.... I can hardly remember what happened afterwards. The entire time-space machine suddenly swung around dizzily, started moving forward at stupendous velocity, and flung Frot and me to the floor. We lay helplessly clutching the legs of the instrument board, striving vainly to get to our feet. But the more we tried the more a frightful, squeezing pressure bore us down, as though a massive, invisible vice were closing in upon us. Fire-balls burst crazily before my eyes, my ears were roaring...

I awoke with Anton Frot's arm around my shoulder. The light in the metal roof was still burning, shining on his lofty, almost bald head. The piercing eyes regarded me with intense anxiety.

"All right again, Lee? That's fine." I tossed down the glass of ekrimar he handed to me and felt fresh life surge within me. "Just the acceleration," he explained. "For about the first time in history we've had a free trip through the void. The ship got caught in that energy beam—and besides hurling the energy of human beings to Ondon at a speed far ahead of that of light, it hurled the ship as well. At any rate we're being taken in a direct line, just as you wished. See ahead, there. That must be Ondon itself."

I walked unsteadily to the window—our floor gravitators were, of course, in action—and looked ahead.

The usual vision of interstellar space met my eyes; the familiar awesome sight of supernal blackness, studded with stars and suns. A vision of changing time—of systems about to be born; at their zenith; and decaying... And ahead a system of four yellow planets grouped about a sulphur-yellow sun.

"Pity we've no means of identifying the system," came Frot's impartial tone. "It may be the Ondonian solar system—and it may not. We'll have to —well, take the energy-beam's word for it, so to speak."

"No; I've seen Ondon through Jel-fel's telescopic stuff," I answered quietly. "That is Ondon straight ahead the largest in the group, not far short of the size of Jupiter. Of course, Jovians would choose a planet similar in density, I suppose...That is the quickest trip we ever made!"

Frot nodded. "The beam evidently incorporated time travel dilation, so that to us we travelled faster than light and covered several light years to reach this system. A different system, a different sun. H'm, I'm none too much in love with our speed, Lee. We'll crash at this rate unless we can turn aside..."

Even as he spoke the Ondonian system had become perilously close. Awaking to sudden activity I turned to the controls, but all the efforts of the Particle Disintegrators at either end of the vessel failed to move it from the energy beam. I looked helplessly at my numerous switches, at the vision of the hurtling world upon us, then back at Frot. He thought for a moment deeply, then a gleam entered his eyes.

"Throw our time machinery into commission," he said quickly. "By computation, it seems to me that the equivalent of sheer energy to the speed of time balances as equal. Anyhow, it's a chance. Put on the time machinery and move forward exactly twelve hours."

Puzzled completely by his mathematics but willing to try anything, I obeyed. I adjusted the dial to the hair-degree necessary for only twelve hours' movement. Incontinently the machine seemed to careen through a wide circle. It lurched slightly; the view through the window shifted and blurred; space seemed to interweave on itself: It dissolved, changed miraculously, and slowly merged into a mountain range with a vision of sickly yellow trees in the foreground. The time-space machine was steady.

I stood blinking doubtfully and Anton Frot took a deep breath.

"I was right," he said impartially, crossing over to the wall couch and lying down at full length, as was his custom when theorizing. "Quite right." He placed his fingertips together, and it seemed the little veins at his temple pulsated more noticeably. "You see, Lee, energy at its maximum must have a mathematical numerical value. The energy content of Ino Carreno's time-band is 186,000 frequencies per second—the same number as is the speed of light in miles per second. So, as the time-band frequency moves at the speed of light, the equivalent of one divided into the other—if one uses algebra to assist one's calculations—produces unity. Hence the chances of dissolution in trying to move from one condition to the other were also even. You understand? Carried by our momentum we still moved forward in space, but in time as well. Hence we struck Ondon really this time yesterday, but shifting in time we arrive at this point quite safely. In that time Jelfel has shut off his energy beam, which has given us a safe landing. Our normal repellers have worked and saved us from destruction—there no longer being the energy beam present to hurl us forward."

"I don't pretend to understand your calculations, Frot," I answered. "You're quite right, though. The automatic repellers have given us a soft landing..." I paused and looked out of the window again. "That view I had in Jelfel's headquarters showed me all this," I murmured. "Which reminds me, Ronnit made a map."

I pulled out the piece of paper from my pocket, upon which were roughly scrawled the details—the mountain ranges, the lakes, jungles, deserts, and the approximate situation of Zagribud itself. As I looked at the map an odd thought came to me.

"Frot, since the time-space machine has kept to a straight line we ought to have landed very close to, if not in, Zagribud itself, since that is what the beam was directed to."

Frot languidly rose from the couch. "For a time-liner pilot you amaze me," he commented with refreshing candor. "Ondon has turned on its axis; hence we're at a different point on the surface. We can perhaps follow our course from that map. Let's arm ourselves and start…"

We partook of a hasty meal, then proceeded about the task of equipping ourselves with provisions and arms for the first sojourn on this uninviting-looking world. I took the Double Entity Machine on my back, and both of us kept ray guns levelled. Into a back section of my belt I slipped the Franton atom-destroyer and only wished I had another one with me for Frot.

"It's better to explore on foot," I answered, when Frot inquired why we didn't use the time-space machine and fly over the landscape. "This old bus may get stolen, and if it does it's all up with us… Come on."

The air of Ondon was exceedingly dense. At first it over-supplied the lungs, but by taking shorter intakes of breath we overcame the difficulty. Sound seemed to be triplicated. The clank of my ray gun as I slipped it into position sounded like a chain being dropped on concrete. Anton Prot turned and spoke, but so violent was his voice he had to resort to whispers, and even then every sibilance of his breath noticeably whistled.

With heavy, dragging footsteps, for the gravitation was tremendous in comparison to that of Earth until one became accustomed to it, we set off toward the distant mountain range. If, as I hoped, the map was fairly accurate, we were making in a straight line for Zagribud, though how far ahead it was we had no means of knowing.

Three quarters of an hour of hard progress beneath the hot, sulphur-yellow sun brought us to the edges of the yellow jungle. At close quarters the trees were the most unpleasant creations of vegetation I ever saw. Bilious yellow-green in shade, with perfectly oval leaves of razor keenness along the edges. Our first encounters with them resulted in so many cuts we had to steer a very careful course through the evil-smelling growth. Then suddenly Frot paused and pointed.

"What's that thing?" he asked in amazement.

I stared in the direction he indicated and beheld something akin to a mammoth puffball rising from the vegetation. It expanded even as we watched it, then presently it began to emit the most extraordinary noise. A shrill, piping whine that increased rapidly with the moments, until we were forced to clap our hands to our ears to shut out the awful row in the dense air. Even then the sound increased until it came through our stopped ears—distracting, head-splitting. Our brains swam before the intensity of it.

Frot made dumb motions with his face and at last I understood. I looked down at a branch at my feet, took a step back, and then kicked the branch as hard as I could against the powerful gravitation. More by luck than judgment the branch hit the puff-ball, and instantly it disintegrated. The noise ceased.

I unstopped my ears and wiped the streaming perspiration from my face.

"Great guns, what a row!" I gasped. "What on earth was it, Frot?"

"Nothing on earth," he answered somberly. "An Ondonian creation." His keen eyes became thoughtful. "Death by sound, Lee. That's how things work in this jungle—and why not? Nature always adapts itself to the surrounding conditions. Gravitation here is a hindrance to speed, so Nature makes use of another property, amongst plants anyhow. The dense air—magnifies sound. If sufficiently powerful, sound can kill! Let's look at that thing. I've got an idea."

We went over to the disintegrated puffball and found it to be apparently only a similar species to its earthly cousin. A closer examination, however, at last revealed two minute cups in the heart of the thing—the seed case—which had been split asunder by the blow of the branch I had kicked. Nearby lay a very thin but amazingly tough oval of skin-like stuff. Putting the whole thing into position again—the two half cups with the oval between, we were rewarded by a repetition of the ghastly row, which ceased the instant we let the halves fall apart.

"Lee, a great idea is forming," Frot murmured. "We have a weapon here—and a deadly one if properly handled. Sound seems to be the one thing Jelfel hasn't dabbled in yet. You see, these puff-balls grow very fast—the same as on Earth—and as they grow, instead of giving forth a flower and then dying, they tighten up until they shriek by these halves tightening up. This noise vibration results in them falling to pieces and so scattering their seeds to the wind... Very interesting! What do you know about sound?"

"Precious little," I grunted.

"Too bad. Evidently you don't know that the greater the number of vibrations to the second, the higher is the pitch of the sound, and that the lowest sound a human can usually hear is thirty vibrations a second, and the highest twenty-five thousand a second?"

"After all, we didn't come to Ondon to discuss sound," I answered testily. "All this time I'm thinking of Elna—and the human race. Come on…"

"In a moment," he replied calmly. "If I have an idea that can help the human race win this battle against Jelfel I'm going to mature it. In ordinary air, Lee, sound waves travel at one thousand and ninety feet a second, in sea water at fifteen degrees Centigrade at four thousand nine hundred and thirty-six feet a second. We may assume that the air here is between the two velocities… H'm. Yes, Lee, a great weapon. I think, with a little computation and something that will make good magnetism, I can make a sound machine. I'll go into the details later."

He picked up the core of the shrieking puff-ball and placed it in his pocket, tied inside his handkerchief. Then we started off again through the jungle, to come almost immediately face to face with an object like a nightmare diplodocus, only far and away larger. To this day it remains a mystery how such a mighty creature moved with such ease on so strongly gravitational a planet.

Two immense saucer-like eyes transfixed us with a baleful glare. Somewhere back in the poisonous undergrowth a mighty tail, twitching with anger, snapped down saplings and small trees.

Frot and I stood for the moment, as though paralyzed…

CHAPTER 5

ZAGRIBUD

Suddenly Frot gripped my arm. "Lee, the Double Entity Machine! Take it easy!"

I moved the nozzle-like projection end of the machine around to the front, flicked the button, and instantly covered Frot and myself with the amazing beam. This done we jumped to one side and made our way across to the undergrowth. Looking back we apparently saw ourselves standing, just as we had been when I switched on the beam.

The monster beast did not hesitate longer. Imagining us easy prey it charged toward the two images, blundered clean through them, and crashed into the underbrush beyond, emitting a bellow that made the very ground shake. I pushed over the negative button and the images vanished.

Frot grinned. "That brute will puzzle over that for eternity," he chuckled. "Come on…"

We continued our progress with heavy footsteps. Several times we came across those rapidly expanding puff-balls, but as they began to shriek Frot walked quickly forward, broke them apart, and put the cores in his pocket. I saw no reason for this action at the time, but knowing the brilliance of his mind assumed he had a good reason for them.

About an hour later we broke free of the jungle and into the light of that sulphur-yellow sun again, with the gray-black sky above. Here and there faint, unknown star-clusters twinkled. I began to appreciate how lovely a planet the Earth really is.

In all my wanderings through space and time I never came across a world so replete with natural beauty… The weirdness of this wandering on an alien world, surrounded by unknown and unprecedented things, never occurred to me—or to Frot. I think my experiences with the strangeness of Time had robbed me to a great extent of the emotion known as Fear.

Fear, after all, is only ignorance. Where there is no ignorance, there can be no fear… My main worry was Elna. It was purely for her sake that I insisted on pressing forward, and Frot, lean and wiry despite his sixty years, assented to my energetic decision without a word, scarcely speaking, his mind centering all the time on the puff-ball cores lying within his pocket…

At length, as we neared the edge of a stagnant lake, fatigue began to overtake us. We seated ourselves on the bare, rocky shore and sat for a long time looking out over the unfriendly expanse, realizing, for perhaps the first time, the incongruity of everything.

At that point it seemed that we fell asleep. The next thing I knew, I was getting unsteadily to my feet, my eyes half closed. When I opened them to the full I received a stunning shock. I was not facing a lake, or anything resembling one…

Before me, arranged in groups in tiers, were countless queer beings resembling centipedes. Innumerable green eyes set in earthly-looking faces stared down on me in implacable concentration. Arms, forming into two at the elbow, making four to each being, were folded—as were also the six legs supporting the weight of the short, heavy trunk. In an instant I recollected the vision I had had of Jelfel when I had been possessed of X-ray eyesight in my first fight with him—the same vision of a natural Jovian—made such to bear up under the terrific gravitational forces.

I swung around and found Anton Frot, apparently as calm as ever, by my side. He shot a glance at me then looked back again at the tiers of Jovians, around the enormously wide, softly lighted room, to the patterned floor at his feet, then back to the central figure seated a little in front of his unprepossessing fellows.

This central figure was usually heavy in build, and had, if anything, larger eyes and better cranial development than the others. He spoke at length, in a meaningless, high-pitched jabber.

Frot and I shook our heads. This being so the creature made a signal to two distant servants, and they came forward along the shining floor with a machine on a rubber-wheeled tripod. Standing three feet high, with their many legs and earthly faces, the two Jovian servants were as revolting as their fellows—like nightmare travesties of Earthlings.

The machine was switched on and as it began to hum something happened to the minds of both Frot and me; we became capable of understanding two languages simultaneously—our own, and Jovian. As though the performance was perfectly natural, the servants took the machine away and we faced again the central figure.

"So you are Commander Lee?" he said, in his high pitched voice, and although using his own tongue I perfectly understood him. "I have long been anxious to meet the man who is pitting his tiny brain against the strength of myself and Elnek Jelfel, my Ambassador. I, my friends, am Rath Granod—Master of Zagribud. His Serenity—and the All Wise."

"That leaves little to our imagination," Frot commented cryptically.

"Rath Granod—the devil who is upsetting Earth, eh?" I demanded grimly. "I'd like to tear the heart out of you."

The All Wise ignored my hostile remarks. "Only once did you ever become cleverer than I," he proceeded, leaning slightly forward. "That was when you flung Jupiter into the sun. You were too slow—we all escaped, as no doubt Jelfel has told you. You have come to Ondon to stop the stealing of Earthly bodies for the furtherance of our intellectual pursuits on the Earth. Do you realize, you poor fools, what you have done? Do you, Anton Frot, with all your childish mathematics?"

"My childish mathematics pushed Jupiter into the sun, anyhow," Frot replied coolly, and at that Rath Granod's face became a study in controlled passion. After a space of the most deadly, snake-like staring I ever witnessed, he resumed.

"You were both located near the Ri-Pud Lake. The Light Wave Trap, of which you have had an earlier experience, Lee, revealed where you were. You were transferred here by a sixth-dimensional Rotator, exactly similar to the one Jelfel has on Earth. Now you are here, I shall use your body, Lee, for my brain. You are a good, very healthy, strong man. Just what I need for earthly conditions. You, Frot, will also become the brain-carrier of a Jovian. The trifling five hundred sent from Earth last night are now in our laboratories, and the work is progressing apace."

I caught my breath in at that.

"You mean the massacre has begun?" I demanded hoarsely.

"It will begin at sundown," Granod answered steadily. "You will be removed to our laboratories for examination by our experts—and tonight I will take on your form! You should feel honored, Commander Lee. You yourself, until we decide otherwise, will be, as it were, a disembodied entity. Quite a fair brain yours, Commander, but not so accurate as Frot's. The fact that you are so receptive to the Language Communicator makes it obvious to me."

"That machine?" I asked, and His Serenity nodded.

"Nothing very intricate about it," he responded, revealing the same willingness to explain everything that was so noticeable in Jelfel. "All languages are composed of a series of sounds, and, if your brain is attuned to the vibration of those particular sounds, they make sense to you. If you don't understand them, you, on Earth, would start the laborious process of learning the meaning of the vibrations—namely a fresh language. On Ondon we merely adjust the brain to be capable of interpreting the new sounds so that they form sense; hence you understand what I am saying because your brain-cells have been so altered."

I nodded and waited for the next. It was not long in coming. Anton Frot and I were seized by the two servants and piloted from the room, down a long passage—in which I noticed instrument rooms containing amongst other things an exact replica of the sixth dimensional Rotator I had seen on Earth—down a wide staircase, and finally into an immense prison cell—more resembling a great cage than anything, the walls being composed of closely-placed bars. Within this dimly lighted expanse we beheld a great crowd of Earthlings, from every walk of life, huddled together like cattle awaiting slaughter.

Frot and I were flung down the three steps and the cage door clanged noisily. Then we slowly got to our feet with the questioning eyes of the Earthlings upon us. For a space I did not speak. I looked beyond the bars and beheld the most amazing surgical laboratory I ever dreamt of, with white-garbed, stocky Jovians moving to and fro, filled with the industry of their craft. More than ever I appreciated how animalistic was the treatment of the Earthlings…

"Odd they didn't take our stuff from us," Frot commented, taking the Double Entity Machine from my back and setting it on the floor.

"Only because they know we can't do anything," I replied grimly. "One thing only is in our favour; all the stolen Earthlings are here. Elna may be amongst them. I'm going to look."

"All right; I've a problem to think out. I'll see you later."

* * * *

I wandered amongst the closely-packed men and women, calling Elna by name, until at last, to my intense delight, I heard her respond. I turned in the direction of her voice, fought my way through the press, and finally reached her side. She was filthy dirty and unkempt, but otherwise unharmed.

"Sandy! Thank God you've come!" She drew me down on to the floor and we leaned our backs against the bars. "This place has got the Black Hole of Calcutta—which we hear about from history recorders—beaten to a frazzle. I've been here heaven knows how long, herded in with these other unfortunates… I don't know when the massacre is to start."

"I do—at sundown," I answered grimly. "I've been having a talk with Rath Granod. I came here with a time-space machine—not by projection."

"You did! Anybody with you? Lan Ronnit?"

"No, only Anton Frot. He doesn't seem to realize the danger. He's absorbed in a problem of some kind."

Elna smiled faintly. "He would be—but he's a cheerful old dear all the same. He might even devise a way of getting out of here... Well, I materialized here through a Jovian called Lep-Nooze—a horrible-looking specimen, too!" She shuddered at the recollection. "All these other folks were materialized through the night. This lab. out here has fairly burned with energy, I can tell you. By the way, how did you manage to speak to Granod? Does he understand English?"

"No—the brains of Frot and I were altered to understand Jovian. Quite an advantage." I explained it to her briefly.

"Then you can understand all about Jovian?" she asked keenly.

"Of course. But what's the use of that? Like having a million dollars on a mountain top."

She shrugged, a thoughtful gleam in her gray eyes. "Somehow I feel your knowing the language ought to be useful," she said absently. Then suddenly she scrambled to her feet. "No reason why we should leave Frot on his lonesome. Let's join him."

We made our way through the crowd and at last came upon Frot, seated with his back to the bars, his head in his hands. He looked up with a start as I touched him on the arm.

"Oh, it's you, Lee! Hello, Elna, how are you...?" He paused and considered. "Lee, I've just been thinking things out. These puff-ball cores—if only I could find some magnetic force of some kind, capable of reproducing the original sound in an infinite volume—"

"Amplifiers?" I suggested.

"Bah!" he snorted, "I mean, to hurl sound through the void, and yet make it arrive in its original din on another world—from Earth to Ondon for example—and then increase the din to full volume and shatter Zagribud with sound waves. It could be done... Damnation! If I could only work out the right formula. It's all a matter of maintained vibrations as opposed to forced vibrations, Maintained vibrations can, of course, be obtained by the electrical energy in the three-electrode thermionic radio valve, but that isn't what I want at all Reflexion of sound, too, has something to do with my idea, because when a sound wave strikes an obstacle the wave is reflected in such a manner that the reflected ray and the incident ray are in the same planes, making equal angles on opposite sides of the perpendicular to the reflecting surface—hence reflexion must always occur at the boundary between the different media... H'm—a pity I cannot form the idea into proper focus. Magnetism is the solution... But I will do it; I will do it. Be assured on that, Lee."

"Look here, Frot, don't you realize that death is staring us in the face at sundown?" I asked despairingly. "Unless we concentrate on the troubles of the moment you'll never fix any ideas at all!"

He did not appear to hear me. "Atomic energy. Enough in two ounces of copper to drive a machine from Earth to Ondon and back to Earth again. The core of a puff-ball—enough sound to wreck a city, if one weighs the equivalent," he murmured. "By Heaven, yes! It's an idea! I must compute." He tugged one sheet from a writing pad he carried in his pocket and commenced to figure industriously with his electric pen, having for illuminant the glow of the radium bowls in the laboratory behind. Manifestly, he was oblivious to everything save the problem that taxed his brilliant mind.

I took Elna on one side. "The man's hopeless," I remarked. "He'll go on like that until he either gives birth to a brain wave or gives up the attempt. My task is to find a way of saving all these good people before sundown. Living death... Elna, for the love of heaven, help me think!"

She stroked her determined little chin thoughtfully. "I could think better with something inside me," she answered presently. "Brought anything with you, by any chance?"

"Why, surely! What an inconsiderate fool I am! Here—" I reached down to my pack on the floor beside the Double Entity Machine and handed her some of the tabloid provisions we had brought from the time-space machine. She ate in silence for a space, swallowed a water-tabloid, then daintily dusted her lips.

"Ah! Elna Folson is a new woman indeed! Now let me see what I can think up... I still can't help thinking that knowing the Jovian language ought to fit in somewhere, but, like Frot, I can't focus the idea."

"No more than I can," I answered.

"Try some hard thinking," she suggested, in her practical way.

I sat down on the stone floor, took my head in my hands, and tried to shut out all distracting noises. My position was such that my eyes looked into the laboratory beyond—at first absently as I meditated, then very gradually I became more earnest in my observation of a mild operation taking place at a nearby table.

An Ondonian—or Jovian—call him which you will—had evidently met with injury of some kind, for he was rushed into the laboratory on an automatic stretcher, taken direct to the nearest table, and instantly anaesthetized. From my vantage point I could see the operation being performed with amazing skill, to some part of his face. I caught a glimpse of a gaping wound in his cheek, of a flashing, bloodless knife performing amazing execution under the quadruple, tentaculate hands of the Jovian surgeons—then very gradually a *new face* began to form! The man's entire visage, even to his eyes, were re-modelled, as though removing a mask and providing another one.

Presently the restorative was administered and the man got up slowly from the table, felt his face carefully, and then dropped to the floor, walking slowly from the great laboratory on his six powerful legs. As he passed close to me I took a good look at him. His face, even his eyes, were new! The eyes were now darker, and the face more refined. Mentally I placed him as a worker, judging from his powerful legs... He went slowly out of sight, and my mind revolved around amazing possibilities.

The sixth dimension Rotator—I knew its situation. Jelfel was dressed in the guise of an Earthling. This face-changing business... Suddenly I snapped my fingers in the air in decision.

"Got it!" I breathed. "Elna, we're going to take a chance, and a hefty one. But it has just got to work. I must get Frot's advice..."

CHAPTER 6

THE ARC THROUGH THE VOID

We moved toward him.

"…thus it follows that the media of the one might exchange with the other," he was murmuring, when we reached him. "A given quantity divided by that vibration— Yes, what is it?" he asked impatiently, as I commandeered his attention.

"Frot, a problem for you to work out. In that laboratory out there are six Jovian surgeons, all highly trained minds. In here are roughly five hundred Earthlings, all of good intelligence. Now, is it possible for five hundred Earthlings to hypnotize six Jovian surgeons, so that those six Jovians will do the bidding of one man, myself?"

He stared at me in amazement. "You are not mentally unbalanced are you?" he asked in concern.

"Of course not, man! I mean it! You know the power of a Jovian mind—its frequency, or whatever you call it. Can five hundred Earthlings render those surgeons incapable, for a time, of using their own minds?"

"I'll compute!" Frot replied, and delighted with the new problem tore another leaf from his notebook and figured hastily. I caught a glimpse of weird algebraic formulae over his shoulder and scientific symbols; then he looked up intently. "Providing the five hundred Earthlings rigidly and unwaveringly concentrate on a fixed thought, it can be done," he answered. "But they must not let their minds wander in the least. It works out at 9 divided by 9."

"Thanks, that's all I wanted to know," I answered grimly.

I moved to the nearest of the people, who were watching intently, and in a low voice took them quietly into my confidence. When they learned their own lives were at stake, they became willing—more than willing—to assist. Briefly their instructions were, when I raised my arm as a signal, to concentrate all their mental forces upon the six surgeons beyond. The vibrations of their minds upon the highly sensitive, easily receptive brains of the Jovians would do the rest, I conjectured. It took me some time to arrange the details with the whole crowd, but word of mouth from one to the other was a fast carrier, and at last I was satisfied they all knew their tasks.

"And on no account cease concentrating until I give the word," I concluded, at which a lean, discerning individual, who had become self-appointed leader, nodded.

"But what are you going to do?" Elna asked in bewilderment. "Am I to concentrate, as well?"

"Certainly—you and Frot. I shall give orders to the Jovians in their own lingo, and if, as I hope, they are overcome, they'll mechanically do as I order. Briefly, I am going to get a fresh face!"

"A fresh face! What a treat that will be?" Elna remarked, unable to resist the opportunity for a friendly dig. "But, Sandy—why?"

"I'm going to try to pass myself off as Jelfel. I'll explain later in full. I'm now going to entice the guard in here. When he comes seize him—stun him—kill him—do what you like. But keep him quiet. Now, are you ready?"

"Right!" Elna exclaimed, and Frot nodded. The waiting people prepared themselves.

I moved to the cell door and motioned to the guard. He approached, his white face and green eyes framed in the door-grille.

"What's the matter?" he demanded in Jovian.

I did not reply. Instead I raised my hand and struck him full in the face with my palm. The sound echoed loudly in the dense air. Raining Jovian curses upon my head he levelled his ray gun through the door, but in an instant I had seized it, snatched it from him, and brandished it in derision in the air… Then he did what I hoped for. Unlocking the door he hurled himself inside, two other guards coming up behind him. The first guard I stunned with the butt of the ray gun, the second blundered into the crowd and was forced helplessly to the floor. The third I tripped up as he came down the steps and settled him for a space with a smashing blow on the back of his thick neck.

For a space I waited, but no further guards appeared.

"All set!" I breathed, raising my arm for the signal. "Now—*concentrate!*"

Instantly the crowd turned their faces toward the six Jovians, and dead silence fell.

Locking the cell door behind me I soon navigated the short passage around into the operating theater. For a space I hesitated, my heart hammering at my side. Then, as I saw two Jovians pass their tentaculate hands transiently over their brows, I took heart and strode boldly forward.

Again nameless fear sought to engulf me. Suppose the effort at mind control had been a failure? If so, I was walking into a death-trap….

I walked more deliberately as I approached the nearest surgeon. As I tapped him on the shoulder he moved slowly around, his deep green eyes meeting mine. To my overwhelming relief they were without recognition or interest. A glance about me assured me that all the surgeons had ceased to work; were standing about in the throes of mental enslavement. "You!" I snapped in Jovian, recognizing the surgeon as the one who performed the facial operation. "Can you alter my face?"

He nodded vacantly, and I still stared unwaveringly into his green, mysterious orbs.

"You will do so!" I ordered curtly. "You will change this face of mine into that of a Jovian—will give me green eyes and a face like yours. Proceed!"

Although I realized I was probably taking my life in my hands, I laid myself on the operating table and waited. Dully, the surgeon motioned his fellows and they came to his side. I heard the hiss of the anaesthetic and wondered if it was the last thing I'd ever hear this side of Eternity. Beyond, I saw Anton Frot and Elna, with the crowd of Earthlings behind them... Then I lost consciousness.

My return to consciousness seemed almost immediate, although actually, I learned later, it was some fifteen minutes afterwards. The surgeons were mechanically washing their instruments in a powerfully-smelling fluid. I felt my face circumspectly; it seemed but little different from what it was before, save that it was remarkably smooth. Turning over, I looked at my reflection in the shining surface of the operating table. For a moment I was utterly incredulous. Green eyes, coal black hair, square and unyielding features... Was this the Sandford Lee I had known since babyhood...?

Under the influence of the restorative I soon regained my normal vigor, and marvelling at the painlessness of the whole operation, slid to my feet.

The next task was to complete the first half of my audacious plan. The surgeons were again standing about, apparently struggling to reassert their normal faculties. I seized the nozzle of the anaesthetizer, switched it on as I had seen the surgeon do, and sent the fine spray aloft. Instantly a powerful odor drenched the air and the surgeons. I switched it off again, stumbling backwards as the strong fumes almost overcame me. I gulped at the clear air in the passage and looked back. The surgeons were slowly collapsing into unconsciousness. Revived, I moved into the cell again.

Those within, and particularly Elna and Frot, could only stare at me for a space.

"It *is* you?" Elna asked in wonder.

"Of course—with a Jovian face," I responded. "Now, we've got to get out of here. Follow me."

At the top of the cage steps I paused for a moment. "Friends, do exactly as I tell you, and ask no questions. That's all." I strapped the Double Entity Machine on my back once more, and led the way into the passage outside. The mob of people behind me made the most distracting din in the dense air, with all their efforts at silence.

We progressed safely along the passage, then came to a barrier of guards at the foot of the giant staircase leading to the comparative safety of the upper regions. Instantly I swung around, played the nozzle of the Double Entity Machine in the air, and rushed forward to the staircase.

The resultant confusion of the guards was amazing. They knew not which was real and which unreal. Whilst the crowd blundered up the staircase, the images remained behind. Several unfortunates were recaptured and taken back to the cage, but the majority got through to the upper corridor. With Anton Frot and Elna at my side I peered down the immense corridor, recognizing it instantly as the one which led to both Rath Granod's Council Room, and to the instrument room where lay my goal—the sixth dimensional Rotator.

"Wait—and do as I tell you!" I breathed, as two guards suddenly appeared in view from around the corner of a contiguous passage. "This is going to be ticklish. Look downtrodden—the whole lot of you. If any of those guards from below tries to get up, just knock them down again. With a bit of luck we may yet escape. Get ready...."

With those words I stepped forward with apparent casualness as the guards approached. They stopped, looked at me intently, then at the crowd at the head of the stairs.

"You and you!" I snapped, without giving them a chance to speak. "What is the meaning of this?" These Earthlings left below when they ought to be in His Serenity's laboratory? What has been taking place? I, Elnek Jelfel, Ondonian Ambassador, am unaccustomed to being treated thus. Explain it, fools!"

"Elnek Jelfel!" the two gasped simultaneously, then they suddenly came to attention as their odd forms would permit. "Master, we were not informed of your arrival. Rath Granod the All Wise did not inform us—"

"Why should His Serenity inform mere guards?" I demanded superciliously. "I came *via* the exchange of personality process. You know this Earth woman here, Elna Folson, is my exact energy-counterpart. Instead of merging through her in my laboratory, in comfort, I find myself amongst this Earthling scum in the operating theater. I am annoyed—angry. Better care must be taken of the future carriers of Jovian brains!"

"Master, your Earthly form—" began one of the guards.

"Silence! Is it so wonderful that I appear in the guise I affect for my Earthly-work? To the instrument rooms at once, and bring these people along."

"Yes, Master."

Thanking heaven for my knowledge of the Jovian language, and hoping that Rath Granod would not see fit to appear on the scene, I led the way to the instrument room I had seen, when being taken down the corridor on the first occasion. Once my comrades were within the room I turned to the guards. I read dubiousness in their faces.

"Retire! I have work to do!" I commanded.

They hesitated, uncertain. The mob, however, decided it. The two were seized, bound and gagged with strips of pliable metal, and fastened to the girders of a near-by machine.

"Now, Frot," I breathed tensely, closing the door and securely bolting it. "Everything now depends on you. We can win, if you can calculate. Is it possible, with this sixth dimensional Rotator, to alter the radius of its arc in space far enough to transport by batches, five hundred people back to Earth from Oudon here?"

"I'll see," he answered dispassionately, and again drew out his notebook and figured at lightning speed. I waited in dire suspense whilst he made calculation after calculation, thinking deeply at intervals, then working from a fresh angle.

"A difficult feat owing to the colossal length of the dimension's extension," he said finally. "It can be done by elongating the atoms that compose the sixth dimension. You know that the stretching force on a solid body per unit area is called stress, and the extension per unit length is known as strain. Within limits the strain ought to be in exact proportion to the stress, and on removal of the stress the body will return to its original length. The body is thus said to be elastic…"

"Be damned to that!" I replied frantically. "Our lives hang on this!"

"I'm coming to it," he responded in his unhurried voice. "If the strain is too great the increase causes increased attraction in the atoms. If one goes too far the molecules themselves are separated and rupture and collapse occurs.

"This sixth dimension, as I see it, is half solid and half gaseous. In gases, molecules are separated by fairly wide distances—they can also move through large distances between successive collisions, the average distance being called mean free path. So, it follows, that if the mean free path of the gaseous half of the sixth dimension can be made to equal the strain placed upon the atoms of the solid half, the extension in length should reach Earth. It may fall short and pitch us into the void. I can't be sure. It would take too long to fully enumerate. It stands to logic, if we do arrive back, that we will land in the same Age as we departed from. Nor will the Earth have moved far enough out of its orbit to throw us out of true…"

"How do we extend the sixth dimension?" I demanded.

"By using the Rotator with four times its normal swinging force. Thuswise the dimension will be momentarily extended by the pull of outward force from the center. In that split second, if we set the Indicator to the farthest extension, 4556, which the dimension will reach, we ought to fall to Earth—then the dimension will resume its normal length. Like swinging a rubber ball on the end of an elastic thread. The thread will stretch on its farthest point then return to normal. I'll go first and test the idea."

"It's death here, or a chance to reach Earth," I answered grimly. "Right, Frot, take your stand.

Even as Frot stood within the range of the Rotator, imperious hammerings came upon the door of the laboratory. I flung in the switches with desperate haste, set the Indicator, and released the power with its energy quadrupled. Amidst a booming roar Anton Frot vanished from view. There was no time to consider whether I was hurling everybody to their doom or not. I herded the crowd at top speed into range, and sent them off in batches one after the other, one eye cocked anxiously on the slowly collapsing door, melting with the force of a battery of ray guns.

At last only Elna and I were left. I pushed in the automatic switch, and even as I did so the door collapsed and a party of Jovian guards, with Rath Granod himself urging them on, rushed into the laboratory… But they were too late.

The view vanished as the dimension rotated. A terrible feeling of nausea followed as we performed an invisible arc through the void—the center of the dimension being in hyper-space. So rapid was the transit the air of Ondon had not time to escape from the dimension before it rotated around to strike the Earth. Even so we experienced a tightness of breath, a sensation of deadly cold, and a feeling of sinking. The whole thing was akin to an intensified falling dream. Then suddenly we were rolling over and over on the ground, bruised and shaken, as the end of the dimension struck the third-dimensional plane with four times its normal force, and pitched us free. Instantly the automatic control on Ondon must have worked and the dimension ceased to be.

Unsteadily I got to my feet, clutching Elna by the arm as she rose to her feet. About us, on a peculiarly familiar hill, were all the Earthlings I had sent forth, and Anton Frot. He came slowly forward.

"I think I've got it, Lee," he said thoughtfully. "It will have to be amplified and then projected. The sound will therefore be open to infinite amplification—"

"Don't you realize what you've done, man?" I demanded, seizing his lean shoulders. "We've beaten Rath Granod! Look where we are! On the side of the valley in which are Jelfel's headquarters! Down there is where he is working... That dimension must have been permanently fixed in this position... Frot, you're a genius!"

"Compared with this sound problem, that was simple computation," he replied worriedly. "H'm, a difficult task, indeed."

I turned to the waiting, somewhat frightened people. From their expressions in the starlight, they seemed to be under the impression that they were vividly dreaming.

"Folks, return to your homes at once," I ordered. "And go quietly. With Jelfel close at hand we're none too safe. Tomorrow, war with Jelfel will start in earnest. We will carry the battle right into the enemy camp! You've been saved from a ghastly death, so thank the Gods for it. The city is over in the distance a long way. But we've got to make it. Come along."

So we set out resolutely but wearily for the distant glowing masses of New York... It was dawn before we did at last straggle in, worn out by our experiences, despite rests on the journey. In the city the rescued Earthlings broke up into units and moved homewards. I accompanied Elna to a hotel—for she had no flat in this Age, thanks to the changing of time—and then went on with Anton Frot.

He was still deeply thoughtful even when I left him, and bidding me a perfunctory "Good night," as though we had been out for an evening's walk, he went into his apartments muttering incomprehensible remarks about "shifting fields of energy."

For my own part I crawled back to my flat, dead beat, fell on the bed, and instantly was fast asleep...

CHAPTER 7

THE SOLAR GRAVEYARD

I awoke the following morning consumed with vivid energy. I am inclined to think that the atmosphere of Ondon contained a far greater percentage of oxygen in its content than earth did, which made it a remarkably healthy place for the lungs, if for nothing else. I thought Hilton, my manservant, would have dropped dead from shock when he saw me for the first time after I had arisen and appeared for breakfast. He took one look at my jet black hair and green eyes, swallowed hard, and set down the breakfast with a thud on a side table.

"My Heavens!" he exclaimed dazedly, genuinely shocked out of his senses for once.

I smiled faintly. "All right, Hilton; I'm still your master, Sandford Lee. This make-up is for a very special reason. There are some remarkably clever surgeons on Ondon." I told him of my experiences, and he listened with his customary, detached attention, slowly recovering his normal urbaneness as I proceeded.

"Remarkable, sir! Again you have outwitted this devil Jelfel at his own game. What is the next move, may I enquire?"

I considered for a moment. "Hilton, I think you can help me a little. Were there any disturbances after I left last night?"

"Last night? Three nights ago, sir—pardon the correction."

"Three?" I repeated. "H'm, I never will be able to understand the relation of time to space. Well, what happened?"

"Nothing, sir. There have been no more sixth-dimensional thefts, or whatever they are. Looks as though Jelfel is biding his time."

"What happened to Lan Ronnit's raiding party?"

"As a matter of fact, sir, I don't know." A shadow passed over Hilton's face. "From reports, it would seem that Ronnit and his men completely vanished! They set out to destroy Jelfel's headquarters, and—haven't been heard of since."

I jumped to my feet in horror. "What! Why didn't you tell me this before?"

"In the general shock of seeing you thus, sir, it slipped my memory... More coffee, sir? Or more toast?"

"No, man—no! Good heavens, this is disastrous! I've won one trick and Jelfel has won another. Lan Ronnit must be found!"

"Indeed, sir, I agree."

Hilton watched me with a contemplative eye as I hastily scrambled into my uniform coat and departed. Shortly afterwards I was in the presence of Templeton. For a space he sat in grim silence, looking at me—then his cold eyes flashed to the guards, and back to me.

"President, forgive the illusion created by my appearance," I concluded. "I am still Sandford Lee, but with a new face... Don't forget you once misjudged me, and very nearly lost a population because of it. Don't, for heaven's sake, make the same error again."

He hesitated, debated in silence, then to my intense relief nodded.

"I have infinite faith in your ability, Commandant," he answered quietly. "Certain little mannerisms alone convince me that you are Lee, otherwise I would have you imprisoned as Elnek JeJfel himself—though, if anything, you are a trifle bigger than he is, I believe... Have you anything of moment to report?"

I told him of the saving of the five hundred Earthlings, and his face came as near to genuine admiration as I had ever seen it.

"Commendable work, Commandant... For some reason, at present unexplained, Elnek Jelfel has ceased his activities. Either he has met with an accident; been killed, or something, or else he has returned to Ondon. I don't know. There is a doubtful peace hanging over everything. The only flaw is the mysterious disappearance of Lan Ronnit and his raiding party. I followed your suggestion and some time after your departure the other night sent a fleet of forty air machines, led by Ronnit, to attack Jelfel's headquarters in the valley. Since then, nothing has been seen or heard of them. I have sent scouts to search, but they also have not returned. Have you any suggestions?"

"I'll explore for myself," I answered grimly. "In any case, I have a plan to put into operation; that is why my face is altered. If you will allow me, I'll leave at once."

"Assuredly," Templeton nodded. "The sooner this trouble is cleared up, the better. Headquarters are deluged with enquiries concerning the stoppage of our time liner service."

"Better stoppage of the service than death to all concerned," I replied; then I saluted and left the chamber. The next hour I spent in gathering in Anton Frot and Elna. Whilst Elna was as practical and active as usual, Frot was still vaguely absorbed by his sound problem... In his flat I made my plans clear.

"What I have to do is to try and convince Jelfel that I am an agent from Ondon, in the body of Sandford Lee," I explained keenly. "He must do as I bid him; explain whatever I demand him to do. In that way, as I see it, he ought to be under control…"

"Suppose he reads your mind?" Elna enquired, "He's an adept at that, you know."

"I'll only concentrate on what I want him to read," I responded. "That ought to serve to convince him I really am an Ondonian in Sandford Lee's body. My one desire is to get him back to Ondon on some false pretext, and then wreck his laboratory here. Then he won't be able to get back."

"Unless by the sixth-dimensional Rotator," Frot returned steadily.

"Not even by that if his machinery here is destroyed. That Rotator is somehow linked to earth by Jelfel's machinery; I'm sure of it. We can rest assured he'd fall in the void if that's gone."

Frot considered in silence for a while. His reply was not reassuring. "An idea that has all the qualities of feebleness, Lee. He'd manifest through Elna again, or something. I tell you the damn man's a genius— an impossible enemy!"

"I still insist we can protect ourselves if we get rid of him," I said stubbornly. "This time we can stop him building more machinery here, if by some chance he gets back to earth. Those lights in the sky—which I saw when his first machines came to earth just before time changed—if we see them again we can stop him getting any further. We have the advantage of knowing what's happened before."

"Curious you saw that machinery *before* time changed," Frot remarked pensively.

"Not altogether—that part of the landscape probably *was* in future time at that second," I replied. "A few seconds afterwards the alteration in time reached us. But that's of no consequence. Once I'm rid of Jelfel from earth I shall feel free to act. Then we can think out a really feasible method of destroying him and his devilish companions."

"Mebbe," Frot agreed. "Personally I would sooner try commanding the moon to break in half. It would be easier. Still, I'm with you. What's next?"

"I'm heading for Jelfel's place now. Come on."

Shortly afterwards we were skimming in a time-space machine across the intervening landscape between New York and Jelfel's headquarters.

"The only way to make a satisfactory entrance into Jelfel's laboratory is *via* the time apparatus," I remarked. "My idea is to go fifty years ahead, then drop down into the exact position where Jelfel's headquarters once were. Then, reverse back to the present time, and hence we'll merge inside his laboratory—probably burst the walls apart. That doesn't matter, though."

"How do you know you won't merge inside a solid?" Frot asked, coldly incisive as ever.

"I don't—but the chances are we won't. Anyhow, we'll have to chance it. You two will be captives that I've brought back from Ondon. This machine is the one in which you two and Lee went to Ondon. Understand?"

"Proceed," Frot nodded, and gave himself up to thought.

I set to work with the time controls as we dropped down towards the depression in which lay Jelfel's laboratory. I felt assured it was the safest method of getting inside his mysterious domain. It would have been possible to enter with the Franton atom-destroyer again, of course, but I could hardly picture an Ondonian being so clumsy in his entry. Hence the time-machine idea. With a smile I pushed over the time-band switches.

To my horror, however, the machinery refused to respond! The gaseous time-band seemed useless. The vessel continued to hurtle downwards with breakneck speed, instead of gently rising up.

"Hurry up, Sandy!" Elna panted frantically, staring through the window, then with wondering eyes back to me. "We're going to crash at— Whoa! Look out!"

She flung herself back from the window, Frot raced to the opposite end of the chamber, and I still hung like a helpless fool to my switches. With a sudden stupendous concussion we struck something of incredible hardness—not the soft ground of the hill beneath which lay the laboratory, but an invisible wall. The time-space machine rebounded like a rubber ball, pitched crazily through the air, and fell with numbing force to the bare earth on the valley floor itself...

It became still.

Dazedly I staggered to my feet and helped up Elna and Frot. They looked at me in silent indignation, rubbing rapidly merging bruises on their foreheads.

"Some pilot you are!" Elna sniffed. "Commander of Commanders! Huh!"

"Radiation or vibration, or something, shielding the laboratory," I muttered. "And the time-levers were useless, too... We'll have to try and enter with the atom-destroyer after all. No other way. Come along..."

"My dear Commander, I shouldn't trouble if I were you."

The three of us spun round at that metallic voice. The figure of the Jovian master-scientist was standing behind us.

"I have always known you to be courageous, but I never knew you were a fool," he said coldly. "Your playful efforts at disguise distinctly amuse me. You see"—he smiled cynically—"you reckoned without my superior mentality. When you explained your plans to Frot and Miss Folson I heard them all by mental sympathy—namely, I attuned my brain vibrations to yours. The rest was simple. A careful following of your machine from New York—*via* the Light Wave Trap—the arrangement of atomic repulsion from the soil of the hill, a blocking of the molecules and interstices of the time-band—and you were powerless! Then, my arrival here—just the Rotator again. Nothing in it at all..."

He moved forward slowly, his eyes upon me. "Really remarkable how handy the soil of earth is for atomic repulsion," he murmured. "Just conceive, my friends, the unimaginable force that lies within each grain of soil! I split open those grains with electric current from my laboratory below, used a fan-shaped current-beam. This had the effect of releasing the energy of the soil atoms in a steady stream. As one atom released its energy another took its place—almost infinitely. As force usually moves the same way as it is propelled, the force went upwards, forming a screen of repulsion on the hill. You struck it, and, I imagine, found the result a trifle—er—shall we say, uncomfortable?"

"Jelfel, I came to get rid of you," I panted. "I've failed again—but one day I'm going to get you. I mean it! You—you devil!"

He laughed faintly and revealed his artificial teeth. "This battle really interests me," he commented lightly. "I must confess you did well to transport those five hundred Earthlings back to earth. So well, indeed, that I realize another system will have to be used. The sixth dimensional Rotator is too clumsy. It lacks the finesse for which I am remarkable... Mainly for that reason I have ceased using the Rotator these last few days whilst a better system is evolved... By the way, I've been combing the brains of young Lan Ronnit—"

"You've what?" I shouted in murderous fury.

"Patience, Commander, please. Your manners indeed are not what they were! Ronnit, along with an army of men in forty air-machines, tried like a collection of infants to rout me from my lair with such devices as ray guns, energized iralium, and similar elementary material. I was more than a match for the whole batch of them. I destroyed thirty-nine of the ships and their crews—they were useless to me for projection to Ondon—and kept the fortieth ship containing Lan Ronnit. Once I had removed him to my headquarters the fortieth ship went the same way as its fellows. So did all the scouts who buzzed round inquisitively."

"Destroyed the fleet?" Elna asked in horror.

"Certainly, my dear young lady. You will probably know—you will, Frot—that there is a slight division between molecules; that they are *almost* in contact? It was a simple matter to generate a beam composed of the same energy as the molecules in the air-machines. Hence, as like repels like, the division between the molecules was widened to such an extent that all the ships blew asunder, Like that!" Jelfel snapped his artificial fingers in the air and looked at us in amusement.

"You swine!" I exploded, feeling once again that utter hopelessness now I was in contact with him. I have spoken before of his uncanny personal magnetism and impeccable manners.

"The time is nearly up for the automatic switch on my Rotator to take me back to the laboratory," he said presently, glancing at a queer instrument strapped on his wrist. "Please be good enough to stand here with me."

"I'm damned if-—" I began savagely.

"It would be as well," he persuaded in a voice of ice, his eyes glowing

I shot a helpless glance at Frot and Elna. We moved to Jelfel's side with resigned footsteps; hardly had we done so when we seemed to perform that almost familiar arc in space and found ourselves beneath the Rotator apparatus in the laboratory. In the ceiling the radium globes glowed with their customary snowy effulgence.

At our appearance a haggard figure rose from a metal chair at the far end of the chamber and advanced unsteadily. I was shocked to behold Lan Ronnit, incredibly changed—a sunken wreck of his former lean, active self.

"Ronnit!" I seized him by the shoulders and looked into his face intently. For a space he studied my new features dazedly, but in a few swift, well-chosen words I made matters clear to him.

Jelfel, standing to one side, smiled faintly. "It is a source of unending mystery to even my capable brain why humans indulge in so much needless sentiment," he remarked. "You fawn over each other, love each other, pity each other. Your sexes do the maddest things for each other.... H'm. I once said the human race was the most motley, bigoted collection of self-righteous, narrow-brained, non-intelligent idiots I ever saw from cosmos to cosmos—and what I have seen since has done little to prompt me to amend my opinion. Consummate fools! Prostrating yourselves over chemicals!"

"There's such a thing as love and kindliness, which you have been born without!" Elna retorted hotly. "Love is the foundation of the Universe, Jelfel."

"How diverse you are, Miss Folson! *Power* is the foundation of the Universe. The greater the brain, the greater the power… But enough of this! Ronnit will be soon in good health again, if he lives long enough. From him I've learnt one or two things of interest—a Double Entity Machine and Brain Detector. Do not attempt to use such machines again, Lee. I know all about them now." He smiled grimly. "Two more weapons you are now to be without! Even if I don't use such inventions, I'll stop you using them at every turn."

He paced steadily about as he spoke, and presently resumed in a detached voice.

"I am working on a scheme now by which earth itself will be taken to within easy flying distance of Ondon itself! I have experimented, and have found that atoms can, by proportion in size, be brought close to each other without undue disturbance, and as planets are nought but giant atoms I see no reason why the feat cannot be accomplished. Rath Granod has approved the idea, and is even now concentrating all his activities in having the immense gravitational machinery built that will spread a field of magnetism through the void to shackle the earth…"

"Jelfel, this is the limit!" Ronnit muttered.

"I may rise to greater heights yet," Jelfel answered, unmoved. "The feat will be done by utilizing the earth's own lines of force, those natural magnetic properties which you Earthlings arbitrarily define as the Poles. The Earth's own magnetism, and its slow changes in a cycle of roughly 600 Earthly years is a mystery to you—but not to Ondonians. That magnetism is the outcome of absorption of magnetism from the ether, occasioned, one may say, by friction during the Earth's endless journey through that medium. Now, all the planets possess this natural magnetism in a greater or lesser degree. Earth has it; Ondon has it. What easier then than to build machinery to link the two magnetisms together? This Granod is doing. Gradually the two planets will come together… That is the outline of the idea. Later the full details will be in hand."

"For the sake of getting the Earth you will wreck an entire Solar System?" I demanded.

"Admittedly there may be disturbances," Jelfel confessed, "but so long as this fine world of Earth is untouched, what matters it? The Earth will be kept steady by the attractive force during its journey through the void. No harm will befall it, beyond the freezing with cold as it passes beyond the radius of action of the sun. During that time all Earthlings will be placed in a state of suspended animation—to revive when the warmth of our own Ondonian sun pours on the world. Then we shall remove the bodies as fast as our air-machines can do it. Thuswise we save an enormous amount of time and labor—and the transference of our city of Zagribud will present no difficulty—whereas to transport it from Ondon to here under the present distance would be extremely difficult. Just for simplicity, you understand. Once we have everything to our satisfaction, our brains and cities transferred, and so on— Earth will slowly be returned to its normal place in the void, and our work is over."

"Why don't you make a synthetic planet?" asked Frot coldly. "You're clever enough."

"Truly, but it would never equal Earth's fair beauty.... And now, my friends, I come to the most important part of the proceedings…"

Jelfel ceased his pacing and faced us squarely.

"I have decided to be rid of you all," he said slowly. "I owe you a debt for your savage attack on me recently. It took me some time to recover from that blow on the head from you, Ronnit! I would have been rid of you all before, only I thought your bodies might be useful—particularly Miss Folson's, with her energy counterpart to mine. It is essential now that you be wiped out. My plans are too immense to brook interference. I could radiate you out of existence, could even kill you with mind force, but I feel that something more elaborate is called for." His green eyes smouldered. "Lee and Frot, you threw Jupiter into the sun—you planned for me an unholy death. I have decided to do the same for you. But the difference will be that you will not escape, where I did."

"You're going to what?" I asked dazedly.

"I startle you, eh? I am given to such penchants, my friends. Yes, you are all going to your deaths—in the sun! I shall feel content that you have followed the planet you destroyed. Further, your time-space machine, in which you will make the journey, will be completely uncontrollable, both for time and space navigation, as, until you hit the sun, I shall immovably lock your switches with radio waves! As you hurtle towards your day-star, think of Rath Granod—and me. Goodbye, my friends.…"

Even as he had been speaking he had forced the four of us into the area of the sixth dimensional Rotator. The button flicked, and an instant later we found ourselves within the time-space machine again. The door had, of course, not been opened, and all our efforts now to shift the bolts were unavailing.

"I speak to you by beam radio," came Jelfel's voice from the air, sudden and startling. "By the same system of radio propulsion I control your machine. Thus… Until you strike the sun."

Dazedly we watched the switches on the control board jumping as though pushed with unseen hands. Another moment and we were shooting into the air, went round in a wide circle, and then turned directly towards the blazing orb of the sun.

"Best wishes, my friends." The voice of Jelfel ceased, but remote control remained...

For a space we stared at each other in blank dismay. Already the Earth was falling away beneath us as we shot headlong into the infinite. I switched on the floor-gravitator— Jelfel evidently had no wish to deny us that—and looked about me.

Elna laughed shortly. Hurry! "Four perfectly good Earthlings heading for the King of Ovens," she commented grimly. "Trust Jelfel to think of something picturesque."

"Diabolicial, you mean," Lan Ronnit growled, hands in pockets, staring out on the utter blackness of space. "We're thoroughly in the cart now!"

"It might be mathematically possible to—" Frot commenced absently; but whatever he had in mind didn't materialize. He shook his head doubtfully and joined Ronnit.

Jelfel's remote controlling apparatus, perfected to an almost incredible degree, guided our tiny, helpless time-space machine presently into direct line with the blazing, prominence-edged sun. I took a flashing glimpse at the blinding photosphere, and shuddered. Ninety-three million miles from Earth, and we were hurtling towards it with ever mounting speed, and would finally attain a maximum speed of that of light. I moved about and bit my lip in frantic concentration.

"We've about fifteen minutes to do the most desperate thinking we ever did," I said presently, suddenly unaccountably calm. "You know how we stand. How do we get out of this?" I looked at the chronometer on the wall. It read 11-15. At 11-34, approximately, we would strike and enter the sun... We were fortunate in having vacuumed walls to our machine; neither heat nor cold could reach us.

Frot took a seat and buried his high forehead in his hands. Ronnit stared at the growing sun through black goggles and wiped perspiration from his face with his sleeve.

Suddenly Frot looked up, his eyes gleaming. "Lee, this time-space machine.... Is it not made into a space machine by covering the Carrenium alloy with negative metal sheets?"

I nodded. "Yes, Frot. Ordinarily, but for the negative plates, this machine would instantly float into the fourth dimensional time-band. Why?"

"I have a great idea." He jumped actively to his feet. "That Time Indicator, for setting the period you wish to visit. Is it held by remote control?"

"I don't suppose so," I replied, moving to it. "This only sets the time; useless without the machinery in work." I swung it round the dial. "Yes, that's all right. What about it?"

"Think hard, Lee. When, in your early experience, you were flung into far futurity, at what period had the sun become a dead star?"

I thought deeply for a moment or two, then gradually I remembered the amazing number of years. "Three hundred and twenty billion years was the reading," I responded. "That is the maximum the indicator will take. As I was unconscious in that period the sun might not have become extinct until some time after that."

"We'll chance it," Frot responded. "Our momentum through the time-band will help to carry us forward as well. Set that Indicator to maximum."

I did so, then looked at him curiously. "What's the idea, Frot?"

He seized my shoulder tightly. "A chance in a million of getting free," he said tensely. "Several of these plates on the outside have got to be taken off—torn off. Anything! The ship will then float into the time-band, and as the indicator is set for the machinery we will automatically move on three hundred and twenty billion years. Don't forget this machine is equipped with accelerators. The time will pass almost immediately, instead of dragging out. You understand—move on to the time when the sun is a dead star. Jelfel is only stopping you working the time levers; he hasn't interfered with the machinery. It will work if we can only get those exterior negative plates off…"

"But how?" I demanded. "In the name of sanity, how?"

"The Franton atom-destroyer," he replied complacently. "In your belt there. A super-priser…"

"By heaven, it's a chance!" I exclaimed. "Come on—all of you… And let's hope Jelfel isn't listening to us by radio."

Evidently he was not, for nothing untoward occurred. At top speed we raced to the emergency chamber and donned space suits—composed of rubber and springs with vacuum lining in between that negated heat or cold. To each helmet was attached a telephonic apparatus for speech, and in the inner sides of the suit reposed energy heaters of minute size, and upon our backs were oxygen cylinders. Thus equipped I flung up the manhole lid, muttering inward thanks that Jelfel had not seen fit to block the emergency chamber as well, and floated up through the opening to the surface of the ship, with Elna, Frot, and Ronnit, grotesque bloated forms in their suits, drifting behind me. Our life-line fastened to the deck was a security, although there was little chance of us floating away. We were, in a sense, four small satellites held by gravitation of the little mass of the space ship. The life-line we used to pull ourselves about from place to place.

The instant we reached the time-alloy section of the machine the full-bodied glare of the sun smote us—a flaming inferno apparently directly above us. Through our dark glasses the whole void seemed to be a mass of streaming, colossal prominences.

"Quickly! Prepare to move off the plates!" I said into the Communicator.

"We're ready. Hurry!" came Frot's cryptic voice.

So we hung there, keeping exact pace with the ship, lying full length in the sheer void with the hurtling day-star sweeping ever nearer. My hands shook with the terror of the moment as my thick gloves fumbled with the atom-destroyer. Silently I praised the gods that had led Franton to make his machine of a metal impervious to the cold of space.

The moment I pressed the button that stream of terrific force struck the negative plates of the machine. The rivets flew apart like dust. Like a razor-edge that merciless beam cut beneath the plate, tearing out the welded portions like a wood-knot before a super-drill. I had to exercise extreme care to avoid destroying the valuable Carrenium alloy itself; even as it was I dented it badly in places, but on the whole little damage was done. The instant the plate was free it rose up and stopped six feet above the falling flier, keeping exact pace. For an instant I thought of destroying it, then realising it might be needed some time to enable us to use the space ship again, we hastily anchored it to the vessel with hawsers...

Valuable seconds passed as two more plates were literally ripped up and floated to the same spot above.

The void was no more. Nought but the blazing, unthinkable effulgence of the sun filled all the universe. We could do no more. Even through our black glasses the glare was blinding. We closed our eyes. Either the vessel would now rise slowly into the regions of the time-band or else...

I realised, as I hung there, that once the machine entered the time-band, if it did, we would again pursue a straight line, but hit the sun in far futurity, if, as I hoped, the newly equipped device of instantaneous time switch functioned. On my previous adventure in far time we had of course not collided with any solid body, since to a great extent, time was mapped out clear of obstacles. Always, though, a time machine followed a straight line, so whatever lay in the way—unless it dissolved in the interval—would still be in the way in the future. There are no corners in Time!

As I thought this out I lay, in silent horror, in space. Dimly I beheld my colleagues likewise, motionless. A weird assortment! Four human beings deep in the depths of their impregnable space-suits, three anchored sheets of metal, and the space ship itself, all falling towards the sun…

I told myself it was no use. Our effort had been in vain. This was the end. Then a sudden thought struck me—a desperate one. I issued quick orders into the Communicator.

"Hang on to the space machine itself—otherwise, if we hit the time-line we'll be separated. Hurry, for God's sake!"

Instantly the four of us seized what projections we could and held ourselves there by muscular effort—a very slight effort, indeed. I closed my eyes again. Never have I known such horror. Those of you who have never lain in sheer emptiness with the abyss of the flaming sun beneath you, and the incomputable magnitude of sheer empty space above, can hope to realise our position. Then—

The machine jolted!

I waited for instant fiery death.… But nothing happened. All remained deathly silent. Very tardily I opened my eyes. For a second I beheld unthinkably black sky; then abruptly the vessel struck something with grinding force. I was flung clear, in fact torn from my hold, and instead of falling seemed to be literally thrown down. But for my rebounding space suit I should undoubtedly have suffered severe injury from the colossal concussion.

I lay as though chained to the ground—ground of curious black gleaming stuff. Staring upwards through my dark glasses, nothing was visible. With vast effort I flicked the button in my glove for shifting the dark lens, and then beheld, now through clear glass, an unfamiliar sky dotted with unknown stars. Again with terrific labour I screwed my head round and beheld my companions, fortunately unharmed by their rebounding space-suits, all lying flat. The time-space machine lay half buried, whether wrecked or temporarily out of commission I did not know then.

"Are you alive?" I said into the transmitter in my helmet, and only one voice—the calm, methodical tones of Frot, answered.

"I'm alive, Lee. Don't know about the others. You realise what's happened, of course?"

"Surely—this is the sun itself, isn't it?" I asked, hardly able to use my jaws for their unprecedented weight. "So far on in time that it is a dead star. Just as you calculated, Frot. We followed a straight line when reaching the time-band and hit the sun in dim futurity. That emergency switch made the transition through time immediate. This stupendous gravitation—mass, of course."

"Exactly. Know what this stuff is we're lying on?"

"Looks like—like coal slack," I answered.

"No, it's pure magnetite; powdered magnetic oxide of iron. When the sun was normal this stuff existed with all the other elements as a gas. Now it's cooled we have the solid stuff. Look, countless miles of it—a desert of magnetite, minerals of natural magnetism. Lee, along with my sound idea, this magnetite is just what I want."

"Maybe," I answered. "Our task, though, is to get back to the ship. How are we going to do it with a gravitation like this?"

"Try rolling," he suggested.

We endeavoured to do so, but each movement took so long a time, each effort such a colossal strain, that we progressed roughly only a few inches in thirty minutes and that at the expense of our oxygen cylinders, which would not last indefinitely.

"We can't do it," came Frot's wheezing voice. "The gravitation is too strong. We weigh enormously heavy here. Now let me think…" There was silence for a space. I lay breathing with difficulty, wondering if this was to be the finish—death on a dead sun, tens of thousands of years ahead of natural time? To lie forever facing the friendless stars. Then Frot's voice, practical and intense, aroused me from my gloomy lethargy.

"Lee, have you still got that atom-destroyer?"

"Yes. What's the use of it?" I asked.

"You told me a long time ago that that disrupter can also become a repulsor. It opens for the alteration, doesn't it? So Miss Jeron told you, I believe."

"Right enough," I answered. "But what—"

"An experiment," he answered, "Try and give it to me."

I did give it to him—about an hour and a half later! It took us that long to move the yard that intervened between us. With a hand like a ton weight he took the enormously heavy atom destroyer and proceeded with infinite difficulty to make adjustments to the tungsten rollers within. At last he had the thing to his satisfaction, turned the lens downwards, and pressed the button. To my astonishment he immediately rose from the ground and crashed over two feet away.

"It works!" his voice exulted. "I'm using this thing now as a repulsor. It is powerful enough to lift me every time. True, the pressure is terrific, especially on the lungs and brain, but it's the only chance. I'll try again. Hang on a while."

And so he commenced the most amazing series of hops and leaps I ever saw, resting between each movement for a long spell… After an interminable time he reached the time space machine, and his voice floated to me again.

"The ship doesn't seem to be much damaged, Lee—this magnetite is yielding stuff. The only thing to do—for of course Jelfel's radio influence on the ship ended some millions of years ago!—is to get the ship into the time-band again, then keep it stationary whilst we fix back those negative plates. We can do it in space. As you three are still fastened to the ship you'll be dragged along into space if I can get the ship's Particle Disintegrators going. If I quadruple their force it ought to get the ship clear of this damned gravitation… Before I do that I want a container full of these minerals. Only one way to do that."

His voice ceased altogether and he disappeared inside the machine—to reappear I knew not how long afterwards, rolling an empty container which he dropped over the side. It half buried itself instantly in the loose magnetite, and I dimly beheld a stout cable anchoring it to the time space machine. Obviously Frot was going to dredge his precious mineral, and in space the stuff would remain in the container purely by their own mass…

Another long spell followed. I felt my oxygen supply was slowly giving out. What with the stupendous gravitation and thin air in my tank I was only semi-conscious. Then suddenly I became aware of being dragged along the magnetite surface. I beheld the dull flaring of the enormously strained Disintegrators as they tore against the sun's mighty gravitation in order to raise us to the safety of the time line. Weight, crushing and strangling, bore down upon me…

Again I was only saved from instant death by the springs of my spacesuit. Dimly I had a remembrance of being dragged upwards, of seeing my companions acting likewise, then either my air gave out or I fainted. I do not know…

CHAPTER 8

THE PLANET OF SOUND

Glorious, life-giving air, surging into my lungs, brought a return to my normal functions, to a certain extent. A wonderful feeling of lightness after the maddening pressure of the extinct sun. I realised at last that I was lying on the wall couch in the control room, Anton Frot holding an oxygen cylinder near my mouth.

Little by little I commenced to recover. He peered at me in the light of the roof bulb.

"All right now?" he enquired.

"Yes, thanks. What about the others?" I looked up in some alarm as I beheld Elna lying full length upon the floor. Lan Ronnit, however, was standing some little distance away, his arms folded and a dubious look on his lean face.

"Elna will be all right," Frot assured me, and laid his cylinder on one side. "Being a woman her physique is not so powerful as ours; she's been laid out more completely. Your cylinder was faulty; that's why you collapsed as you did. In the interval Ronnit and I have been out on the ship and have put the space plates back, but—" Frot paused and looked at me dubiously. "In fusing the plates into position I melted some of the time alloy… We—we can now travel in space, but not in time."

I looked at him in alarm. "Good heavens, Frot, do you realise what this means?"

"Only too well," he replied in a sombre voice. "Out of the frying pan into the fire. I've got my magnetite aboard if we need it, and at the moment we are heading for just anywhere, now roughly eighty million miles from the dead sun, absolutely in unknown time and unknown space. God, what a fool I was…! Lost! It's a grim thought, Lee. To think that Jelfel, Earth, and Ondon died tens of thousands of cycles ago, yet actually we only left him about six hours ago. I never shall understand time." He shook his bald head worriedly.

"Are we moving through space now?" I asked, getting to my feet.

"Yes, but I've shut the motors off. No sense in using them, unless we approach a planet and need them to throw us clear… We've got to figure something out, Lee. I don't know how to repair that melted alloy; only Earth has the necessary stuff for the job."

"Before we do anything we'd better revive Ehia, have a meal, and then figure things out coldly and soberly," I decided practically. "Give me a hand, will you?"

Under our united influence we succeeded in reviving Elna into fairly normal life. The freedom from pressure and free air again worked wonders, and after doses of ekrimar we all felt our natural selves again.

"Only one thing is in our favour," Ronnit said, as we started our conference. "To Jelfel, it would appear that we indeed fell into the sun; he'll think we're done with. I don't expect he'll try to read our minds to make certain we're dead—ten to one he'll take our extinguishment for granted. That, if only we could get back on fighting terms with him, leaves us free and unmolested. It's a great thought."

"Glad you see some occasion for optimism," Elna remarked tartly. "To be wandering in unknown space and time isn't my idea of a celebration… Anybody got any really good suggestions to offer?"

"If only we could communicate with the Planet Brain!" I said reminiscently, "You remember, Elna—the Quintessence of Intellect? We encountered it in that other mad adventure when we were trying to overthrow Jelfel… The Planet Brain; I believe it existed somewhere about this period in time, too. A world of pure intelligence. It even invited us to return and visit it if we ever needed to. I wonder what one ought to do to communicate with it?"

"That's a dead and forgotten experience," Frot said impatiently. "What we have got to do—"

He paused, and we all looked up sharply as into the utter space-silence of the chamber there slowly crept a deep, powerful humming note—something alien to our knowledge, that certainly had no equal in sound in any place we had ever known. We all waited in mute concentration, desiring to speak, yet held unaccountably spell-bound. Then quite suddenly—

A voice—a profoundly deep bass voice, each word cascading down into the depths of unknown harmonic abysses.

"Great heaven, the Voice!" I shouted hoarsely, recollection pouring into my mind. "The Voice of the Planet Brain!"

"You're right," Elna panted, recognising it at the same moment.

"My friends, you desire to communicate with the Brain?" the unthinkably deep voice inquired, from a space and dimension incomputable. "You have but to think of the Brain, place the frequency of your brain cells in sympathy with mine—as you have unwittingly done by even thinking of me—and I instantly understand you.... You are adrift in time and space again, I see. Poor, foolish children that you are. Well, I promised you help once, if you ever needed it. You seem to need it now. What do you desire?"

"Help," I answered earnestly. "I need not explain to your all-comprehending intelligence; you know the position we are in, and why. Can you return us to our own space and time? We will not trouble you to do more—" I hesitated. "By the way, where is your situation at the moment?"

"Can that matter?" the Voice asked, its tones seeming to fill all space. "The actual situation of the Planet Brain is now forty thousand light centuries away from you, but to the impelling force of emission cells, upon which I once gave you a brief lecture, there is no limit.... So you desire to be returned to your own space and time? I cannot conceive a more elementary task. I take it the surgical operation I performed on your brain has long since passed away in its efficacious powers?"

"Four years ago I returned to normal," I replied. "The effect, as you predicted, lasted long enough to enable me to fling my enemy's planet into the sun—with the aid of Anton Frot, here. Even so, Elnek Jelfel has returned."

"Ah, yes, Elnek Jelfel—the troublesome Jovian. I could, if I so wished, transform the four of you into pure invisible intellect; or could change Jelfel into a planet and hurl him, an expelled world, into the furthermost reaches of the void. But, I have my own troubles; I do not desire to expend the effort necessary. Even a Brain has its problems, but with knowledge, my friends, comes pity. At first triumphant power as one gains a litle knowledge—witness Jelfel—but with great intellectual power comes kindness and compassion. I am compassionate to those who struggle for the right. You know that. For the second time in my existence I shall help you. I will replace you in your own time and space and make your machine air-and time-worthy, so that you may do as you wish. For myself, I may play a hand in this childish cosmic game. Briefly, I seek a mate..."

"A—a what?" I asked dazedly.

"A mate. You earthly—planetary beings—take a mate if you desire one. Is it so very strange a planet should desire a mate—an intelligent planet, that is?"

"It's incredible!" I said with assurance.

"That, man, is purely your personal viewpoint. Remember, my friend, I was created in the first place by an ambitious chemist—I grew finally into a brain-world. I am purely chemical, seeking a chemical affinity. I seek a similar brain with whom to match my gathering power. I have hurled forth intelligence through the infinite—searching and probing for such a world—and I have found it. It exists in another time, but what is time to such a brain as I am? Its situation is five hundred million miles beyond Ondon, the planet of the exiled Jovians. There, there exists another planetary brain. You would call it female; I call it opposite in intellectual power to myself, and opposite in chemical attraction. Hence we are reaching towards each other, and all the powers of time and space are set at nought. Already, the first communications have passed between us…"

"That, after all, is an affair of your own," said I. "All we seek is transportation back home. You of your own self will do anything else you wish."

"Assuredly," the Voice agreed. "But when your battle is ended you will remember my words. For the time, at least, I leave you…"

The Voice faded, and simultaneously the time-space machine seemed to move very slightly. Struck with a sudden thought I moved to the window and peered out on the darkness of space. My breath caught sharply in sheer amazement.

Directly in line with our vessel was the Ondonian solar system! Not more than a couple of million miles distant. We were progressing steadily towards it.

"Good heavens!" Frot exclaimed, looking over my shoulder. "You told me about that Planet Brain, but I never suspected it was capable of this sort of thing. We're heading straight for Ondon, back in correct Time again. What are you going to do, Lee? Turn back home?"

"No," I breathed. "I have a feeling that we can do more good here. That magnetism that Rath Granod is going to spread through the void—providing he hasn't done it already—to capture the Earth. We've got to stop it, on Ondon!"

"But that's crazy!" Elna protested. "We'll be caught and exterminated before we can do a thing!"

"On Ondon, yes," I answered, thinking swiftly. "But what about the other three planets? I don't see why we can't make headquarters—a sort of base—there. About three hundred thousand miles from Ondon itself."

"We have no provisions or anything," Ronnit complained.

"We've enough to last the four of us for two months in the provision chambers," I replied quietly. "If we run out we'll have to return to Earth for supplies, that's all. What do you say?"

"Why not?" Elna muttered excitedly.

"We'll do it," said Frot decisively. "Lead on, Lee."

I turned to the controls, functioning perfectly thanks to the astounding intellect of the Planet Brain, and steered our course more accurately. Scarcely an hour later we were plunging through the dense atmosphere of Ondon's nearest neighbor. Below us, we had an evanescent glimpse of a frothing sea, in the midst of which reposed a Titanic island, furrowed with colossal, gaunt mountain ranges and abysses of enormous depth. With extreme difficulty I guided the vessel in the highest elevation of a bottomless gorge, tipped her nose down slightly, then at last came to rest on a small, flat and shingly plain. With a sigh of relief I slipped in the anchor-brake.

"I thought Ondon was a cheerless sort of hole, but this is worse," Elna said, with a shiver. "It seems somehow to strike horror into you. Look at it!"

The view admittedly was not enchanting. The towering pinnacles and crags far above us were etched out of the grey black sky—and, further to the right, lay the massive globe of Ondon itself (largest of the four planets) half of its bulk notched out with the sharp summits and buttresses of the mountain range. Before us was only the plain of stones and abysmal canyon.

"Looks like a graveyard," Lan Ronnit commented with a sniff.

"A queer world indeed," Frot remarked thoughtfully. "A dead one, from the looks of it. Better move on, I think."

"I'm not so sure," I replied slowly, staring hard through the window. "There seems to me to be something very peculiar about this smaller world. Look outside—an odd, vibrating effect."

Sure enough the phenomenon to which I had drawn attention was noticeable. A very faint apparent shifting of the mountain range was visible—akin to the effect seen on buildings when heat waves radiate from a street on a summer day.

I looked at the exterior gauge—an instrument for registering exterior air pressure, if any—and found the air density to be practically the same as upon Ondon itself.

"Well, if it is a dead world, it will hold our sort of life," I answered. "Suppose we investigate this trembly effect?"

Carefully I opened the door; the denser air whistled inwards. For a moment we stood quite still, looking over the unthinkably repellent landscape, then an odd noise began to arrest our attention. A deep, strident roaring, remarkably similar to that of a pair of mammoth bellows at work.

"What the deuce—" I began; then immediately fell to the floor, flung there by the din of my own voice!

Sore and bruised, but completely mute, I got to my feet amidst the most unearthly row. Turning, I picked up a loose bar of metal from near the control board and hurled it outside. The instant the deafening whine of its passage through the air had ended in its fall to the ground outside, the space-time machine rocked as though with an explosion. Sound waves, colossal and overpowering, shattered through the air, nearly destroying our ear-drums with their incredible force.

"Shut the door," Anton Frot wrote down, on a leaf from his eternal pocket book—and I was only too willing to obey. Once the normal air of the chamber reverted—or at least, once we were shut out from the planet's amazing atmospheric properties—normal sound reverted again.

"Did you ever in all your life—" I began, dumbfounded.

Frot's eyes were brightly gleaming. "Lee, I've got it!" he panted. "Sheer chance that we came here, I know, but it's the final link. And not an impossible cosmic occurrence, either. A planet of sound, we might call this world. I thought when we went to Ondon there was something more than the dense air causing such remarkable sound effects. Evidently the entire Ondonian system is affected that way—this planet is steeped in sound radiation, and, mathematically, I can explain it to you."

"But—our breathing at first!" Elna exclaimed in amazement. "It sounded like bellows! And when Sandy spoke—it flung him over. That metal bar you threw, Sandy—"

"Exactly! Exactly!" Frot answered tensely. "Listen, all of you. The amplitude of a vibration denotes the extent of the excursion of the particles of a medium from their mean position. The energy per unit volume, the intensity of the sound wave, is always proportional to the square of the amplitude. On this planet the high mountain ranges hold the sound vibrations—the dense atmosphere, too, hurls them back again. Besides that, the atmosphere must be highly energized to cause the amplification—or else, which is feasible, the sound particles themselves are larger! That problem I will solve later. The fact remains, it is no more unnatural for a planet to have natural acoustical properties than for the Earth to have hot-water springs… But we've got the very thing I've been looking for! Those magnetite crystals, the cores from the Ondonian puff-balls, and this planet's properties, being so near to Ondon, too, are all I want… What we have got to do is to use these puff-ball cores as our fundamental, use this planet as a natural reflector—its sound properties anyhow—the magnetite crystals for magnetism to hurl the sound waves to Ondon—and there we have it."

"Have what?" asked Lan Ronnit, rather hazily.

"A sound vibration machine, of course. We must make this world a reflector."

"Reflect sound?"

"Certainly. Concave reflectors bring sound to a focus—you know that, and at the same time they concentrate the energy. You know, back on Earth, how we detect lost air-machines by detectors, which pick up the distant sound of the engines... If this planet were of porous material the intensity of the reflected sound would, of course, be far less. The energy would be lost in the production of irregular molecular vibrations—transformed into heat, in fact."

"I grant you all this," said I. "But sound won't exist in the vacuum of space."

"You have me wrong," Frot replied patiently. "Not sound *itself;* sound *vibration.* That will pass through the void."

"Ah, I see. And you really think it can wreck Ondon?"

"Not Ondon—Zagribud. It might even heterodyne the power of Rath Granod's magnetism that is shackling Earth and render it useless. We don't know until we experiment... I have a lot to calculate. Sound undergoes changes in the air—heat and cold affect it—sometimes obliterate it. I have to overcome acoustical clouds, zones of silence, lots of things. But before I'm through I'll make a weapon that will shatter Zagribud to dust!" Frot paused, his eyes still glowing with the light of discovery.

"For that, then, we'll have to return to Earth for equipment?" I enquired.

"I'm afraid so, but it's worth it. I shall want electric apparatus for setting up my machinery."

"All right," said I. "The sooner we get going the better."

I slipped in the controls again, and in another moment we were rising from that arid desolation towards the mountain tops. As we rose, the mighty globe of Ondon hovered into full view—a yellow world, a world of menace and destruction. I swung the ship around and moved towards it at right angles to obtain my bearings for Earth.

"It's certainly a good idea of yours, Frot," Lan Ronnit murmured. "I can give you a hand, I think. You'll want a sort of audio-frequency battery as well, won't you?"

"Split the atoms of the puff-ball sound core and release their sound energy particles, then amplify," the older man responded, and the two of them relapsed into a condition of quietly argumentative technical wrangling. I stood by my controls, Elna lounging at my side. Then as we swung nearer to Ondon a frown crossed my brow. Instead of drawing away from the planet with our Particle Disintegrators, we were heading towards it.

"That's infernally strange," I muttered. "We're going the wrong way!"

Frot and Ronnit looked up from the table; I saw a strange expression on the former's face. He came to my side and looked through the observation window long and earnestly, then gently snapped his fingers in the air.

"Damnation!" he said in alarm. "Lee, that attractive force hooking the Earth must be in action; we're being drawn by it now we've come into a line between Earth and Ondon! Being drawn.... irresistibly towards Ondon."

"Good heavens, you mean that—" Elna began in horror.

"Figure! Compute!" I shouted hoarsely. "Anything! We can't let this happen now of all times! It'll cook our goose for good. Hurry!"

With desperate speed both Frot and Ronnit set to work to figure the matter out—the square of the energy, magnetism that was drawing us compared to the propulsive force of our Particle Disintegrators. They looked up at last with hopeless faces.

"No good, Lee—we're outnumbered in power by ten thousand to one, figuratively speaking," Frot said. "It's we for Ondon, and nothing can stop it."

In helpless stupor we watched the massive planet of Ondon approach ever nearer to us; with every passing second of the wall-chronometer our chances of escape were petering out…until at last we saw the planet no longer as a globe, but seemingly a mammoth bowl. The sky changed to the familiar grey-black.

We were dropping straight down into the area of a colossal lidless cube—that is to say an area of about ten miles width, composed apparently of seamless metal and walled on four sides—walls perhaps two hundred feet in height. Close to this massive affair lay a squat powerhouse tower.

As the vision swept imminently near I sprang to the control board and threw in the retarding machinery. The Disintegrators instantly fought desperately to hurl us away from Ondon, and to a slight extent succeeded. At least it broke the violence of our arrival.

Falling into the shadow of one of the great walls, we presently struck the floor of the mighty magnet, were pitched helplessly sideways, our nerves and bodies shaken with the concussion. Dazedly we got to our feet.

"The most immovable anchor ever made," Elna said, rather incongruously. "We're fixed to Ondon more tightly than any chains could hold us. I suppose we'd better be getting out…"

"We might wait until the magnetism is shut off, then clear off," Ronnit remarked.

"At that rate we'd probably wait forever," Frot returned. "No, I'm in favor of an excursion outside."

"Nothing else for it," I said dubiously, and, a very dejected party, we flung open the door and descended to the shining metal of the magnet itself. Instantly I felt a most peculiar sensation come over me—a feeling that, although I could walk, I could not rise at all. I glanced up at the towering wall near which the space-time machine had fallen, remarked its perfect seamless smoothness, and then around at the remaining three walls in distant perspective. A tremendous distance away along the wall was a closed and, presumably, tightly bolted door.

"Great heavens, look here!" Elna exclaimed suddenly, her voice echoing in the dense air.

I turned towards her, and, to my amazement, she was standing at right angles to me, on the wall itself, her feet firmly anchored to the metal!

"Like a globule in a teacup!" she exclaimed with a laugh. "Now I know how an old time fly used to feel." She resumed an upright position and came clumping back towards us.

"Magnetism, of sorts—etherised magnetism," murmured Frot. "Does not electrocute, but makes human matter akin to drops of water on a smooth, quasi-absorbent surface. Cohesion—the law of forces—acting on humans owing to the magnetism's peculiar qualities, and also the nails in our boots. H'm, very instructive, I'm sure."

"What are we going to do besides being instructed?" Ronnit asked testily.

"Since we can't back out, we'll just have to go forward," I said worriedly. "We'd better follow Elna's shining example and—walk up the wall! Come on."

We did so, and the instant we were on the wall the gravitational force holding us to it changed our relationship with our surroundings amazingly. To us, the floor was then the wall, the time-space machine seeming to be hooked to it. Before us, apparently in the far distance, was a grey expanse—the sky! I do not recollect having so weird an adventure at any time before or since.

"Do you know," Frot murmured, as we progressed, "I'm beginning to think that this magnetized plating might have great possibilities. If only I could make some magnetized boots. Enable us to walk anywhere—anyhow. Darned useful, you know!"

I nodded. "We might find a chance later on. For the moment we have other things to face."

So eventually we came to the summit—or end—of the magnetized wall, crossed over the six foot edge, and down the other side. I was somewhat surprised to find that, at the vision of distant Zagribud and the horizon lying at right angles-to me, I experienced no dizziness. Obviously the magnetism acted on all parts of the body, including the fluid of balance within the ear. At length we came to the ground, and started forward for, we knew not what adventures. Each of us was equally decided to trust to Providence to help us in our intentions to somehow try and stop the activities of the ruthless Ondonians....

Then all our plans vanished abruptly into thin air, as, quite suddenly, a cordon of six guards appeared from behind the nearby power-house of the magnet. They advanced with their weapons, apparently ray-guns, levelled menacingly.

"Again, eh?" asked the centre-most, in Jovian—and I recognized him, to my alarm, as the one whom I had duped earlier in our experiences when I had rescued the five hundred Earthlings. "You must be lovers of death, Earthlings! This way!"

We had no alternative other than to obey. With weary feet we were escorted across the intervening stretch of rock-like plain, until at last we reached an isolated space at the exterior of a squat metal edifice. This space we found, upon closer inspection, to be nought but a barred expanse about ten feet wide, the bars themselves forming a complete frame—similar to a grid. Nearby, attached to the lock of this grid, was a peculiar, drum-like device.

The guard-leader looked at this steadily for a moment, and to our astonishment the catch on the grid lock flew back. Certainly it was not my first experience with a thought-wave lock—I had encountered them before at Jelfel's hands—but that the lowly guard should be able to attune his brain vibrations to release a lock rather surprised me.

As I was considering, the heavy grille was pulled up, and below I beheld a sheer drop of about twenty feet into a well lined with the metal walls, and possessing a floor smothered in metal filings and dust.

"A pit, Sandy," Elna breathed, peering down. "That doesn't bode well..."

A movement of a button converted one of the walls into steps, and to these the guard motioned. I led the way down the staircase, and at length all of us were at the bottom of the twenty foot shaft, watching the thought-locking grille being drawn into position above us. The staircase abruptly snapped back into a smooth-faced wall...

Lan Ronnit sighed despondently.

"If you can think of a bigger pickle than this, let's have it," he growled. "We—"

He paused and looked up as the guard's voice floated down to us. His face was framed between the bars.

"When His Serenity Rath Granod issues his orders, you will be re-moved—but until then you are only having the punishment vile Earth-lings deserve," he said in Jovian, then with a short laugh vanished from view.

Elna put her back to the wall and slid slowly down into a sitting position. Frot began to slowly stroke his chin, deeply thoughtful; Ronnit watched him a trifle irritably. For my own part I paced up and down the confined space, totally at a loss. Indeed, it seemed, all our plans had ended in the most mortifying debacle.

CHAPTER 9

THE STRUGGLE IN THE POWER-HOUSE

I have no idea how long we all pursued our own thoughts in complete silence. I continued to pace up and down, striving to see some light in the darkness, straining all mentality to conceive a way out of the difficulty, only to have to admit myself beaten in the end. Undoubtedly, so far, this was the most secure trap we'd fallen into!

"Well, we might as well make ourselves thoroughly at home," Elna said at last, with that calm, unshakeable philosophy of hers. "Here goes!" And she made herself more comfortable against the wall, stretching out her feet towards the opposite wall. I stood for a space absently regarding her heavy walking shoes, with the triple rows of metal studs along the soles—then presently they engaged my attention more closely. The metal sweepings on the floor were flying up to those boot-studs and adhering to them!

Struck with a sudden thought I lifted my own foot and planted it firmly on the wall. To my astonishment it adhered firmly to it, and I experienced the same pressure at removing it as I had done when walking down the wall of the super-magnet. Pulling my foot down again, I called the attention of Frot to the phenomenon.

Immediately he experimented with his own boots.

"Of course!" he exclaimed at last, looking up. "Magnetism! Even in the ordinary way a magnet imparts its magnetism, or some of it, to the object it magnetizes. As witness the magnetizing properties of a needle that has been adhering to a magnet for some time. The magnetism of that wall is on our shoe nails—far stronger than ordinary magnetism. By Jove, what a chance! If I can get a look at that thought-wave lock above, I believe I might be able to devise a means of opening it. Might at least compute the necessary mental formula."

So saying he again tested the power of his boots on the wall, found they held him quite steady, and immediately slowly walked up sideways to the bars above. Once he had grasped them, we breathed a sigh of relief. For a long time he was poised there, studying the thought-wave lock's intracies, then he came down again by the same odd method.

"Later I'll analyze why this magnetism is so powerful, and how long it is likely to last," he remarked. "For the moment, that lock interests me. It's of the most elementary type—that is to say, must respond to the most elementary thought-waves. Its wards are composed of solid iralium, and the actuating force is purely a series of fine mica squares, with a central pivot to each, and each square of a different thickness. In all there are three squares. These, when swivelled over by the vibrations of thought-waves, release the wards, and the lock is free. What we have to do is to compute what power of thought-waves are needed to swing over those three mica squares. Every thought-wave has a different rate of vibration, must have—so computation should give us the answer."

"Since there are millions of possible thought-waves that won't be easy," I remarked.

"Not altogether, Lee. To a certain extent, from our own earthly experiences, we know that the average of thought-waves is about 120,000 to 150,000 frequencies a second—that is amongst the highly trained, civilized beings. These guards are a lower type. I place their highest frequencies in the area of 100,000 to 115,000. Now, Ronnit, help me to calculate possible vibrations amongst those numbers that could swing over mica strips which are so thin as to be almost two dimensional..."

Instantly Frot's notebook and electric pen came out. Whilst he figured, Ronnit made mental calculations, and between them they built up the most extraordinary series of mathematical formulae I ever beheld... And as they figured, slow darkness began to creep over the face of Ondon; it was nearing sunset. With the evening the air began to become chilly; a dewy, misty quality came into the atmosphere—no doubt the condensation of the heat from the day-scorched ground in the cold air of the night. Whatever it was, little streamers of mist slowly began to swirl about the bars above our heads.

Then at last Frot jumped forward in the fading light, clutching my arm.

"Lee, I believe I've got it! A thought-wave series of frequencies lying approximately at 113,000 has sufficient power, according to the square of the area, to turn over those mica squares. That thought-wave series in letters would be R-A-N—ran. In thought, though, it is the frequency that counts. A silly word, I know, but do you know if it exists in the Jovian language?"

"R-A-N," I repeated thoughtfully, feeling sure I knew the word, apart from its natural implication of the past tense of "run." Then abruptly I remembered—a long past conversation with Jelfel in my early adventures with him.

"Why, yes, Frot!" I said at last. "'Ran' was the name the Jovians had for Jupiter, the name of their planet. I believe you've hit it! Let's see…"

I accompanied him up the wall to the bars. Once there we beheld the lock through the rapidly thickening mists. Together we hurled the three independent thought-waves R…A…N… upon the delicate machinery. For an instant nothing seemed to happen, then there was a dull click—the iralium wards slid to one side as the mica squares revolved rapidly like the flywheel fan in the striking mechanism of a clock.

"You were right, Frot!" I breathed. "Great work! This mist, too—a gift of the gods, indeed. Give me a hand to get this grille up. Heh! You two down there. Come on!"

Elna and Ronnit soon joined us, and under our united efforts the massive square of bars was lifted high enough to permit us of crawling out beneath the edge, one by one. When at last we were free, Frot went closer to the amazing thought-lock and we found that the impulse of R A N both locked and unlocked it. For a space we continued to watch the wards slide up and down under the impulse of our thoughts, amused oddly by the effect. Then, the danger of our position again taking hold of our minds we made our way into the thickening mist and darkness.

"Where now?" asked Frot, streamers of mist clinging to his thinning hair.

"We'd better—" I began, then I paused and whispered for silence as voices made themselves apparent—voices in the Jovian language, which Frot and I, of course, readily understood…

There came a sharp exclamation of alarm, a sudden babble of excitement, then a calm, high-pitched voice which I instantly recognized. Rath Granod himself!

"I might have known a guard could not be credited with such intelligence as to trap four dangerous Earthlings," he said bitterly. "Nard-Som, you are an idiot—you must be, or you wouldn't be merely a guard! This punishment chamber is empty, the thought lock is tightly fastened. Earthlings are solid, not gaseous beings; they could not float away!"

"But, Master, we did put them there! I swear it! Nal-Isal here, will bear witness!"

"It is true, Master," confirmed another voice, presumably Nal-Isal's. "We placed them here and hurried into your august presence with all speed, that we might engage your supreme attention the moment your communications with earth had ended. In the meantime, the Earthlings have again escaped us—"

"Silence, little brained fool! Elnek Jelfel himself told me the Earthlings have gone to their deaths—the four enemy Earthlings at least. They were flung into the sun. Our ambassador himself did it—saw them go. How could they have appeared on Ondon?"

"But, Master—" entreated the hapless, baffled Nard-Som.

"Silence! You have dragged me here on a false mission, a pretext. I am none too sure but what you have a rebellious motive in so doing; there are many rumors of unrest amongst the masses. The way of Rath Granod is to exterminate blunderers!"

"Supreme One! All Wise! I beg of you—come to the terrestrial magnet and see for yourself the time-space machine in which the Earthlings came. It lies there, immovably held to the magnet floor."

A cynical laugh escaped the ruler of Ondon. "Another fool's delusion, eh? Or else a trap! No, Nard-Som, your work is ended—yours too, Nal-Isal. I have no further use for such as you!"

The voices ceased, and in the darkness and mist something suddenly flashed into life and was gone. Followed the thud of two bodies falling to the ground, then the slowly retreating footfalls of the Supreme One, and, presumably, of his accompanying retinue.

"Heaven bless the dense air," I murmured at length. "And also Jelfel's firm conviction that we are dead. We're comparatively free at last… Come, let's see what happened to those poor devils of guards."

Cautiously we moved through the mist, until presently we stumbled ever the two bodies in question. In the faintly reflected light from the city shining through the mists we beheld the dead forms of Nard-Som and Nal-Isal, obviously destroyed by some deadly weapon or other.

"What a chance!" I muttered. "I believe I can make good use of my face again. See, one of these uniforms. The upper parts fit well—the lower part seems to be a sort of skirt, hiding even the feet. If I walk in a crouching position, I might pass as a Jovian guard. What say you?"

"It's worth trying, anyhow," answered Ronnit. "I'll give you a hand, Lee."

Rapidly we stripped the dead guard of his uniform, which I fixed over my own suiting to take up the slight extra shoulder bulk. To my satisfaction the skirt part fell well below my feet… Dropping into a squatting position my appearance was at least Jovian, if my intentions were not…

"You're wrong in the arms," Elna commented. "You've only got two arms—these adorable creatures have four—and tentaculate hands."

"That fact won't be noticed in the darkness," I answered. "I shall do all I need to do before that fact is discovered… Now, the next job is to drag this Jovian—the one whose uniform we have not taken, that is—to the power-house. I've got an idea. Lend a hand."

Between us we carried the dead Jovian, and left the stripped one behind in the dark. Presently we laid our burden down outside the door of the great magnet power-house. I hesitated for a moment, screwing up my courage, then knocked heavily on the portal, my three companions hidden in the mists behind.

Presently the door opened—a shaft of powerful light streamed into the vapors outside.

"What's the matter?" asked a Jovian mechanic, looking out with his baleful green eyes.

I nodded towards the dead Jovian.

"The Supreme One's orders—the Earthlings are abroad again—have killed Nard-Som whom you see there," I responded, in his own language. "I have been sent from headquarters to summon all workers to search for the Earthling scum. Come—every man of you. The magnet will look after itself…"

The Jovian nodded, looked down at Nard-Som, then re-entered the building. Obviously he was not in the least suspicious of me; nor had he reason to be. I kept my arms hidden in the gloom, and my appearance, sitting uncomfortably on my heels, was exactly that of a Jovian guard.

"That way!" I commanded, when at last the power-house engineers came into view and out into the mist. "You are to take that direction; I have a party to lead over here. Do not give up until the Earthlings are found, or you will answer, as will I, to Rath Granod!"

"Never fear—Rath Granod is too ruthless to disobey," returned the leading mechanic, rather enigmatically, and then set off resolutely into the mist with his band of many-legged colleagues.… In another moment I was inside the power-house with my companions, and had shut and bolted the massive, current-proof door.

"Stout work!" exclaimed Elna delightedly. "What's next?"

I straightened up actively. "We've got the power-house to ourselves; the place which generates the magnetism to shackle the earth. If we can throw it out of commission, we'll be able to stop the power—"

"You think you will," said a grim Jovian voice behind us, and turning in dismay we beheld a Jovian guard standing on the engine-balcony above us, his ray gun levelled. "Make one move, and you are atoms," he said menacingly, slowly making his way to the stairs. "You don't think this power-house is left absolutely empty, do you, fools?"

I thought fast. Once again we were in a difficult position. Surrounded by the wherewithal for stopping the doom of a planet, yet held from it by the power of an unthinkably deadly ray-gun. The four of us stood silent as he approached us, each, I think, using our wits to the utmost… Then suddenly I had an inspiration. It was courting death to test it, but it might work. Instantly I acted and hurled myself at the guard.

His ray-gun pointed directly at me, he pressed the button, but nothing happened.

Completely bewildered by the non-effectuality of his weapon it was a simple matter for me to hurl him mightily to the floor.

Even as I did so another guard and two electricians—or mechanics—appeared on the balcony above.

"Fight them!" I shouted hoarsely. "The ray-guns are useless—we're Earthly composition, not Jovian. Therefore we're safe—just as Jovian matter is safe from an Earthly disintegrator. Pile into them…"

It was indeed a fact. The ray-guns, tuned to Jovian atomic structure, were useless against us, and a battle royal began in the giant power-house, accompanied by the deep roaring of the colossal generators and magnetic transformers.

Although I had my hands full with my own particular guard, I beheld Ronnit, Elna and Frot putting up a most amazing display, overcoming the Jovians mainly by again using the expedient of the magnetised boots—which effect showed no signs of wearing off. On the floor, it being stone, there was no magnetism, but we had the advantage of being able to attack from the walls and pillars, from most impossible angles. I beheld Frot sideways seizing his aggressor's throat in powerful, sinewy fingers; Ronnit was in a similar position upon a pillar. Elna was up on the balcony, exerting all her force to overcome the guard who was gradually overpowering her by superior muscular power.

My observation of this fact lent me sudden superhuman strength, hampered though I was with the additional gravitation of the planet itself. I dodged one of my opponent's rushing charges and delivered a blow clean in the centre of his throat. The result was amazing; evidently I had found an unsuspected vital spot. The creature reeled about, gasping mightily, made a last clawing effort to reach me, and then sprawled motionless on the stone floor. A rapid examination revealed that he was dead. Instantly. I raced to Elna's assistance. I walked up the nearest pillar, gained the balcony floor, and prepared myself for action. Like a battering ram I shot forth my fist, and behind it was all the weight of my body, doubly heavy with the gravitation. The blow caught the Jovian under the chin… With a piercing scream he released his grip on Elna, toppled helplessly over the balcony rail and clean into the centre of a mass of glowing wire-wound mesh immediately below.

Instantly amazing things began to occur. Blue flashes sprang from unexpected points of the power-house. The hapless guard himself vanished in a sheet of liquid fire; his ashes cascaded down on the stone below. The wires that had held him warped like threads of cotton. With an ear-splitting report a curious square object in the distance—probably some type of super-fuse box—blew itself into fragments and bars of metal came sailing through the air.

Subconsciously I became aware that the noise of the machinery had ceased. By sheer chance it had been short-circuited by the guard's body falling into a vital part; we had come to stop the mechanism, and a fight had done it for us! But I was too busy then to think of the details.

Elna and I climbed over the rail and down to the floor again. Between the four of us the two remaining electricians stood but little chance. In the space of a desperate four minutes we had shackled them together with their own uniform belts. They lay on the floor, glaring up at us, and muttering dire Jovian threats…

CHAPTER 10

JOVIAN ALLIES

"Phew!" Lan Ronnit whistled, wiping his face with the back of his sleeve. "That was warm work while it lasted. Looks as though we've had everything done for us, Lee. Where do we go from here?"

I looked thoughtfully about me. "I don't see leaving things like this," I answered quietly. "This magnet will soon be repaired with such men as Rath Granod about. We ought to stay and either turn all this apparatus to our own account somehow, or else destroy it beyond repair… Then it will be re-built. It's a problem, you know."

"The point is, how long can we hold out against this lot?" Elna demanded.

"Wouldn't it be safer to get back to Earth whilst we have the chance?" Frot enquired.

"I don't see why, Frot," I returned. "We can't do anything by going back to Earth; all the damage is being done here."

"True, but I was thinking of material for my sound-projector."

"Well, can't you hunt up something in this place? There's enough electrical stuff about, surely?"

"Now you mention it, I do believe the place has possibilities," he conceded gravely, and proceeded to stroll amongst the mighty, but now happily silent, engines.

I turned back to the bound electricians, "Say, you two—any food on the premises?"

"We tell you that?" one of them sneered. "What do you think we are?"

"You can either tell me, or have it hammered out of you," I returned grimly. "Which is it to be?" I clenched my fist threateningly.

"Oh, tell him," growled the other. "What's the difference? We don't get much honour for our job, anyhow. You'll find food in that apartment there, Earthling—that doorway over there. We live on the premises."

"Good…" I was about to turn away from them, then a remembrance of the electrician's words brought me back again. "What do you mean— you don't get much honour?" I asked.

"Merely that we don't care what you do," was the growling response. "If we do anything clever, we are cynically applauded; if we do anything wrong, we're just killed—that's all. Such is the justice of the Supreme One, Rath Granod. The—" He added a string of scorching Jovian epithets.

"It is not the way of an Earthling to kill unless he is forced," I said I quietly. "The deaths of your two fellows were pure accidents. True, you have your duty to do, but so have I—to my planet. If, though, you choose to throw in your lot with me, you will not regret it so far as I can help it. At the least, you will not suffer the punishment Rath Granod is liable to mete out to you for allowing us to capture this place. What do you think?"

The two considered. As I have mentioned before, they were not brutal fellows like the guards; merely highly intelligent workmen, far above the cleverest Earthling born, yet all the same nowhere near the uncanny perfection of Granod or Jelfel.

"Well, since it means death for neglect of duty—that's what Granod will call it—there's no reason why we shouldn't help you and have a chance for our lives," the one who had first spoken answered. "What do you say, Rof-Elsor?"

"I agree. I never did agree with this vile plan to change our brains into other bodies! It is not science—it is massacre of the *nth* degree. All right, Earthling, we are with you—but only on the condition that no harm, so far as you can avert it, befalls us."

"You have my word," I answered quietly, and with that unfastened the belts that pinioned them. They stood up to their normal three feet of height and motioned me to follow them. Frot discontinued his thoughtful tour of the machinery to join me, and presently all of us entered neat, living quarters.

"If it's food you want, here you are," Rof-Elsor remarked, and placed before us on the low-built table typical Jovian fare… The two creatures watched us as we hungrily ate, then, finishing the meal with a draught of peculiar liquid more like black coffee than anything else, we turned our minds to the troubles that faced us.

"What particularly are your plans?" Rof-Elsor enquired.

I shrugged slightly. "I hardly know. We've stopped the Earth magnet—that's one good thing. What we need to do is to completely wreck it. We want also to destroy Zagribud and all the devils who run it—we must obliterate Elnek Jelfel—and wipe out the very name of Jovian science from the face of the universe."

"So it ought to be," Rof-Elsor muttered, much to my surprise.

He saw our somewhat sceptical expressions, smiled faintly, and drew up a special Jovian chair to the table, motioning his companion—who possessed the remarkable name of Zan-Kafod—to do likewise.

"That a man belongs to a race like the Ranians—the Jovians—is his parents' fault," he said grimly. "If your earth chiefs indulged in massacre of another world, you would not agree with them because you happened to be an Earthling, would you? Of the same race?" His big green eyes looked at each of us, full of appeal.

"Of course not," I answered. "Insane fools on Earth start wars—which bring ruin and desolation and destruction to a perhaps thriving community. Men join in these wars—nearly every one disagreeing with the very idea of war—but forced to fight because of the diseased brains of those that started it…"

"I see," Rof-Elsor said thoughtfully. "So indeed it is on Ondon here—Zan-Kafod and I are alike in our views. Both our respective parents have been murdered in the past for some heinous scientific experiment by this overpowering devil Rath Granod, and his ambassador and Adviser-in-Chief, Elnek Jelfel. I hate him—Granod—all the workers of Zagribud hate him. We have tried to rebel, and failed—"

"I have heard Granod make an allusion to that…" I murmured.

"We hated him on our own world of Ran before it was flung into the sun and this vast cosmic journey was made to Ondon here—and we still hate him and all his works! If you have any plan to destroy these devils, we will help—all the workers of Zagribud will help. Anything, that we may escape the villainies, the atrocities, and the murderous experiments of this all-intellectual monster, Rath Granod!"

Rof-Elsor paused, incensed by his own furious outbursts; then he was calm again.

"You have, for instance, suggested wrecking this power-house. That would be a silly thing to do. Better to use its almost limitless powers as a weapon of some kind."

"Limitless powers?" I repeated.

"Certainly. Don't you realise that this power-house converts every known etheric vibration into magnetism, and then increases the actual magnetism by millions of times its actual output by further inflows of what Granod calls space-energy?"

"No—I didn't know that," I responded. "Frot, you'll follow this better than me."

"I am doing so," he said methodically. "Proceed, Rof-Elsor."

"Rath Granod's machinery absorbs all the vibrations of ether—which include light, infra-red, ultra-violet, all the spectrum colours, and the energy of the electromagnetic ether itself. The atoms composing these vibrations are rendered deficient in some of their electrons—the result of which is to produce high electrical positive charges in those atoms. In the ordinary way such an atom would of course collect stray electrons and restore its equilibrium, but Granod's machinery is so constructed as to prevent that taking place; beams of force prevent the begetting of stray electrons and also the combining with other stray atoms, oppositely charged, which would result in a compound molecule."

"In that case then such atoms are called 'ions' on Earth," Frot commented.

The Jovian nodded. "You will know, then, that such an atom is easily guided and propelled. Hence, every scrap of magnetic energy we use—the converted vibrations I mentioned—are composed of highly charged unbalanced positive atoms—countless tens of millions of them. Now, upon Earth, Jelfel has erected a similar equipment, but all his apparatus draws the magnetism of Earth itself into a whole, which is a negative attraction. Hence, the positive atoms of our magnetism seek to unite with those of the Earth, and so terrific is the attraction the effect is palpable even across the gulf of space, and will inevitably result in finally dragging Earth to Ondon... For the time being that has been stopped, but I can't see why all this terrific positive energy can't be converted into other uses... Of course, our magnet is made so that it follows earth on its journey through space; I forgot to mention that. That magnet, though, ought to be used as a propulsor, by conversion, or something—"

"Great heavens, I've got it!" shouted Frot abruptly, his voice jubilant.

We looked at him in surprise, as he turned to the Jovian, his eyes gleaming.

"Rof-Elsor, you have supplied the solution to my problem! How to transport very heavy electrical equipment across space from here to one of your neighbouring worlds. We can't drag the stuff into space because of the terrific power needed to gain our initial start from Ondon. Jelfel, in his case, got his machinery from Ondon to Earth by some method best known to himself, but I can use another method—transport my machinery to this neighbouring planet by changing the magnet into a propulsor of sorts... Listen, I'm planning a sound-destroyer—to shatter Zagribud with sound. Is the idea practicable?"

"I don't see why not," Rof-Elsor replied. "Paliso, one of our neighbouring worlds, is a planet of natural acoustics. Is that the one you mean?"

"That's it! Also, I propose to convert the sound of some of your screaming Ondonian puff-balls into the ultimate of sound—that is, get from the sound the essence of noise-vibration, so to speak—as one can get pure energy from an atom of matter."

"Quite possible—quite possible," conceded the Jovian electrician thoughtfully. "And use Paliso for the purpose! Indeed a masterly idea! For that purpose, then, you will require an atom-splitter, a sound reflector, generators, and directional beam machines—all of which are in the powerhouse itself. We will set about calculating how to convert the magnetism into repulsion; it shouldn't be difficult. All electrical law can be reversed—especially with the ether as the medium."

"All this is very well," said I, "but how are we going to do it? I'm expecting the other power-house workers back any minute after searching futilely on the errand I sent them on. What's going to happen then?"

Rof-Elsor smiled reassuringly. "I have said that all the workers hate Rath Granod—wish more than anything else to exterminate him. I will talk with them; I have little fear but what I can win them over to your side. If I can do that, you will have a willing army of helpers in your endeavours…"

Rof-Elsor had scarcely finished speaking before there came a sudden mighty commotion upon the distant door of the power-house. He rose to his feet with a twisted smile.

"Better come with me, Earthlings. My colleagues have returned."

We accompanied him into the machinery-filled hall, then waited expectantly as he opened the massive door and admitted his fellows. Instantly, the man who I had first enticed out of the power-house, pointed an accusing tentacle at me.

"There he is—the Earthling! And his fellow-Earthlings. Rof-Elsor, what does this mean?"

"Hi-Tum, the Earthlings are our friends. They have told me much; they plan to destroy accursed Zagribud, and to obliterate the accursed Serenity who subjects our lives. I have thrown in my lot with them—me and Zan-Kafod."

Hi-Tum seemed uncertain; his fellows muttered amongst themselves, their green eyes upon us. Then presently Hi-Tum regarded Zan-Kafod.

"Is this true, Zan-Kafod?" he asked quietly.

The Jovian nodded. "We all have a grudge against Rath Granod, Hi-Tum. I seek revenge for my murdered parents—so does Rof-Elsor. You have a motive; all of you! This very power-house which we control is the disseminator of death and destruction. I say, into the dust with Rath Granod, Elnek Jelfel, and all their accursed minions and servants! Rath Granod leaves us in peace here because he knows we dare do nought but obey: with the coming of the Earthlings, it is different. We hold a master card."

Again Hi-Tum considered. "I must confess I would welcome a return of the Rasimov Dynasty," he commented thoughtfully. "That was a period when the Workers overcame the Intellectuals—unfortunately short-lived. We could again give our fellows their birthright." He stopped, then made a curious obeisance that I recognised as being a Jovian salutation of high respect "Earthlings, you have my allegiance!" he said quietly, raising his tentaculate hand. "What of you, my comrades?" He looked about him.

"Yes, make Rath Granod eat the dirt of his own hell planet!"

"So be it," Hi-Tum murmured, and with that the odd little ceremony was over. I breathed more freely. We had gathered together an array of willing helpers—not so much wishing to aid us as to avenge themselves.

"We had better lay our plans," remarked Rof-Elsor. "It is distinctly probable that Rath Granod may send a scout to discover why the magnet has ceased to function. We are now declaring open war on Rath Granod; those who attempt to interfere must be instantly destroyed." He turned to Anton Frot. "You, Earthling, are a mathematician. You can help me plan a force ray to withhold intending attackers from this power-house, whilst we lay our plans for the Paliso sound-projector. Let me show you."

We followed him through the wilderness of engines until we came at last to an instrument resembling, more than anything, a gigantic electric torch. It possessed no lenses—only two dull gray wires almost touching in the center of a sunken concave plate.

"I've been thinking, my friends, of a better way for sending your machinery to Paliso than using the magnet itself, converted," Rof-Elsor said. "This instrument here—a force-projector—has a twin in another part of the building; but first I'll explain this to you.

"You have heard of atom-disruptors, molecule shatterers, and so on…. This force-projector is the prince of them all. I have explained to you how Rath Granod absorbs the vibrations of ether—of space. This machine concentrates all those vibrations and turns them into one composite force of unthinkable power, which, in turn is projected into that transformer you see over there. When this machinery is working there exists in the gap between the transformer and this force-projector an invisible stream of colossal energy, which, upon reaching the transformer passes through various processes and is finally converted into magnetism. Now, there being two of these force-projectors, I propose we use them for a two-fold purpose. One, to project your machinery to Paliso for your sound-projector, and the other one for a defensive shield for the power-house itself. Thuswise we can continue with our plans uninterrupted. Nobody can get past this."

"At that rate you could shatter Zagribud with that alone," I remarked.

"Unfortunately no…Rath Granod has thought of that possibility and has an offsetting machine to destroy such effect. He prepared that in case we rebelled and made an attack on the city—but he has no safeguard against sound vibration. In fact, I do not think such a possibility has ever entered his calculations… However, this force propulsor is a perfect weapon. I suggest we place it on the platform of the tower."

"Excellent," agreed Zan-Kafod, and immediately the little party of experts set to work to release the mechanism from its supports—all save Hi-Tum. He wandered about with the air of a technician, pulling wires here and there, and tightening up bolts in obscure corners of the machines. He returned presently.

"The main bulk of the machinery is out of commission," he remarked. "I have, however, repaired the damage far enough to permit of the force-projectors working all right."

By this time the force-projector had been moved from its supports—supports that were easily unscrewed, yet as powerfully solid as the ground itself when in position. Rof-Elsor examined the long stretch of wiring leading to the instrument.

"The wires are in order," he remarked. "This length should extend up to the platform from here. Come, Earthlings, assist us."

We turned to commence the feat, when suddenly to our amazement the power-house door flew open beneath the impact of some terrific force or other. We looked round in surprise, then in complete alarm as none other than Rath Granod himself and a party of his advisers and emissaries entered, their ray-guns levelled.

"So, this is what transpires in the power-house?" Rath-Granod asked, in his softest and most deadly tones, walking forward. "Rebellion! The magnet has been stopped—Elnek Jelfel informs me that the stoppage of the power has resulted in the Earth falling back into its former position. There have been landslides, terrific storms, tidal waves—occasioned by the stress. Countless thousands of Earthlings who might have been of use as brain-carriers have been drowned, maimed and destroyed. Unthinkable fools! Why have you so ruined my plans?" His boring green eyes moved to we four Earthlings.

"Ah, of course, the Earthlings!" he commented bitterly. "The reason is now obvious! So that fool Nard-Som did speak the truth. You *have* come to Ondon! How you eluded my equal in intellect, Elnek Jelfel, I can barely conceive—but I do realize that you are all looking your last on this side of death. Ready—men! Destroy this group and have fresh men immediately set to work to remedy defects."

"So be it, Your Serenity," answered his nearest adviser, levelling his ray-gun.

I waited with a grim smile, knowing the ray-gun could not affect us four Earthlings—then suddenly with a lightning movement Rof-Elsor flicked a switch on the top of the force-projector, by which he was standing. Being almost hidden by my larger body, his movement was unnoticed.

That which followed was the most incredible, nauseating sight I ever witnessed.

That beam of etheric force, linked up with the absorbers of the space-energy, impinged directly upon the eight Jovians, They staggered slightly, but did not disintegrate as I expected. Instead they seemed to melt—run, is the only word for it—like figures made of tallow. They tried to move and could not. They were literally converted into *heat!* They glowed; their faces ran and smeared like wax masks. They uttered the most unearthly screams and yells. I began to feel oddly sick, hardened though I am to the unusual. I beheld the faces of my companions drawn with horror at the sight, particularly Elna, who was as pale as a sheet, cool and collected girl though she usually was.

Rapidly Rath Granod and his minions trickled, and finally actually boiled! They became standing, immovable effigies of frothing incandescence—white-hot entities. Then—disruption! A cascading shower of boiling fire shot into the air as the entire party passed into a gaseous state. We were flung over with the shock, and when we looked again the space was empty! The stone floor was slightly discolored—beyond was the open door.

Rath Granod had ceased to be. His amazing mind, his advisors, everything, had been completely destroyed.

"Great heaven!" Lan Ronnit whispered. "This *will* unleash all the devils of the cosmos! Rath Granod wiped out—the Master of Zagribud."

Rof-Elsor switched off the force-projector with a shaking tentacle.

"If it's war we must attack first," he said, in a slightly scared voice. "There is only one man to equal Rath Granod—indeed exceed him—and that is Jelfel himself. If he comes to Ondon he will leave nothing unturned to rout us out, destroy us, and carry on from where Granod left off... Quickly, shut the door. We must get this machine to the tower to ward off attackers."

The door could only be kept closed by a couple of force rays playing on either side of it. These, however, kept it effectually in position.

We accomplished the task of carrying the extremely heavy force-projector to the narrow platform of the power-house tower by means of levitators—curious vacuum suction tubes which exerted their lifting effect through the medium of circular shafts. The machine was rolled to the bottom of one of these shafts and the suction drew it aloft. Hence, when we arrived on the platform it was there, waiting for us to lever it into position.

The mists of the evening had vanished now and the still Ondonian night had arrived. I was impressed for a space by the view of Paliso itself, and Ramino, its neighboring planet, within close proximity. The other planet of the system, Famino, was below the horizon. Used as I was to seeing new skies, there was something different about that sky of Ondon. In some odd way, it was oppressive, sinister. The phrase "a cruel sky," does, I know, sound absurd—yet that was just how I felt about it… One particular planet, a considerable distance away, appearing something like an overgrown Venus as seen from Earth, arrested my attention off to the East. I mentioned it to Rof-Elsor as we turned toward the force-projector.

"Queer," he murmured, staring away at it. "I never saw that world before! Is it a planet or a star? Looks like a planet…"

"There's another one over there," said Frot dispassionately, nodding westwards.

We turned, and sure enough in the western sky, about the same size, lay another brightly gleaming planet.

Rof-Elsor shook his head dubiously. "There is something here I cannot understand," he said. "Two new-born worlds. Certainly I've never seen them before, and I very frequently survey the heavens. After all, what matters it?"

We turned to our task, the incident forgotten for the time being, and presently succeeded in securing the force-projector at the edge of the platform, so that we could turn it in any direction on the ground below. I looked at the wires leading back to the machinery-filled rooms below. With a grim smile I reflected that it would be distinctly unhealthy for any invaders who tried to storm the powerhouse.

As I looked at the distant mass of Zagribud, a gleaming wilderness of lights, a city of super-science, an idea occurred to me. I took hold of Rof-Elsor's shoulder.

"Rof-Elsor, do you know anything about the machinery with which Earthlings are held in a wrong period of time?"

He shook his head. "No, Earthling. There you are in waters too deep for my brain to comprehend. I only know that the machinery lies in Zagribud itself, along with the sixth-dimensional Rotator, and the radio-system for communicating with Jelfel. To get at it is impossible;"

I clenched my fist. "If only I could get at that machinery," I muttered.

"Forget it for the time being, Sandy," Elna said, taking my arm. "We may get a chance later on. For the time being let's concentrate on Frot's idea."

"You're probably right," I assented, shrugging; then, all of us satisfied that work was complete on the platform, we returned downstairs, save Zan-Kafod$_r$ who elected to stay behind to watch for possible intruders.

In the small living quarters again we gathered around the table, a little knot of intent conspirators.

"We have little more to do on this planet beyond projecting my machinery to Paliso," Frot remarked. "I have my plans fairly well laid, but I'll not experiment until I reach Paliso itself. Once there we can make the time-space machine, in which we'll go, our base. The magnet being out of commission our vessel will rise as easily as ever, of course. I propose starting the projection of the equipment tomorrow night. What do you say?"

Rof-Elsor nodded. "The sooner the better. The death of Rath Granod will soon bring a host of vengeful advisers down on our heads. I have a haunting fear, too, that Jelfel will return to Ondon the moment he knows what has happened—"

"Once that happens we can expect trouble with a capital T," I said grimly. "Rath Granod may have been the ruler of Zagribud, but Jelfel, in my estimation, is far more clever and far more ruthless. The sooner I have the ground of Paliso under my feet, the better I will like it."

"There is one saving grace about it, if Jelfel does come back," Ronnit observed. "He will have to leave his Earth headquarters, and incidentally his magnetizing device for drawing Earth to Ondon. That makes Earth safe."

"It *may* do!" said Elna dubiously, shaking her head. "Jelfel won't be so childish as that, I'm sure... We ought to do something with the magnet here, to stop it being used."

"There is nothing that can be done that would be effective," I answered. "Even if we destroyed it, Jelfel would rebuild it on his return. No, we'll leave that for the time being. If we can destroy Zagribud, the magnet will go with it—so it is as broad as long."

"And again, that magnet can only be operated from this power-house, remarked Frot. "Therefore, with the place guarded by a force-projector, the magnet in truth is nought but a white elephant."

"Truly...." I stretched my arms and yawned. "Well, since all that is arranged for the time being I'm going to have a rest. I'm about dead beat..."

CHAPTER 11

THE RETURN TO EARTH

The following day, curiously enough, passed entirely without untoward incident, so far as hostile visits were concerned. In relays, the Jovians guarded the power-house from the platform, but there was no evidence of attack. Either the advisers of Rath Granod had not learned of his death, or only suspected it—or else they had other and more subtle plans. I did not know… But I felt uncomfortable at the calmness. It presented the aspect of a trap somewhere.

We pushed on with all speed in erecting the second force-projector, this time on the floor directly beneath a clear stretch of the engine-balcony. Above the clear stretch on the balcony was a movable portion of roof. Frot had planned, therefore, that his machinery could be placed on the clear stretch of the balcony, and hurled through the opening in the roof by the force of the projector on the floor below—the force passing through the iralium of which the power-house was composed—and so to Paliso, which seemed to me a remarkably good idea.

So, whilst Rof-Elsor and his colleague, Zan-Kafod, spent the day, in company with Hi-Tum, lifting the necessary machinery to the balcony floor by means of the vacuum levitators, Anton Frot became immersed in his beloved mathematics, first charting how to throw his machinery to Paliso with accuracy.

"It won't be so difficult," he commented toward mid-morning, appearing in our midst with his inevitable notebook and electric pen in his sinewy hand. "The machines, which will hold in one bulk by magnets, will overcome the force of Ondon's gravitation in relation to the force expended upon them. Just a simple problem in momentum and inertia—h'm, most interesting indeed. The field of attraction from Paliso rapidly reaches into that of Ondon. So, we have a use for the giant magnet after all. Once the machinery has passed the dividing line in space and has fallen into Paliso's field of attraction, it must be slowed down by the pull of the giant magnet, otherwise my apparatus will crash into Paliso and be reduced to dust. The magnet must be altered to follow Paliso instead of Earth, and must be put into working order. Lastly, except for the final computations on the arc of the trajectory through space, my machines must be rendered proof against the cold of space. That bit bothers me." He shook his head. "273.1 degrees centigrade is no temperature for machinery! It will never stand it."

"Rof-Elsor might have a suggestion," said I. "He knows a good deal."

"An excellent suggestion, Lee." Frot turned and explained matters in the Jovian language, but it proved to be Hi-Tum who provided the solution.

"Your problem is easily solved, Earthling," he said. "Several of the machines here have to work at the temperature of space when collecting space-vibrations—that is natural, but they are rendered proof against its ravages by the use of what we call 'throw-back' energizers. These machines emit a liquid, at regular intervals, which sprays the space-vibration machinery, and the liquid has the effect of altering the molecules in the machinery so that they turn extreme cold into heat. You on Earth have surely accomplished that much?"

"Not altogether," Frot answered. "We know of no way to turn cold into heat, but we do know certain peculiarities affecting atoms. It is also possible, we know, for say a star to get hotter the more heat it emits! I suppose this system you've mentioned is something similar, only practicable."

"Exactly so," Hi-Tum assented. 'However, as I was saying, we have only to spray the machinery with this Inolan liquid and it will preserve it during the time it travels through space. That's your final detail overcome."

"Indeed yes. The only thing left is to get the magnet working again. That can be done?"

"Assuredly. To an expert a short circuit is trifling," Hi-Tum answered, and immediately assigned to Rof-Elsor the task of re-assembling the magnet's various power necessities, while Frot, absorbed again, put the finishing touches to an incredible formula on momentum and inertia...

The coming of the Ondonian night found us in readiness for our machinery-throwing activities. All of us gathered on the engine-balcony—save Rof-Elsor whose turn it was at the force-projector on the roof-tower—and Hi-Tum stood by the switches while Frot issued instructions. Zan-Kafod was present at the controls of the great magnet itself. Ronnit, Elna, and I had little to do but watch.

Lying on the balcony floor was the necessary machinery for Frot's sound projector, while below it, and calculated to be in perfect line with Paliso, allowing also for trajectory and orbital movement, lay the force-projector. Through the now open roof we beheld Paliso, world of sound, low down on the horizon in a cloudless sky. Purposely we had waited for the dispersal of the evening mists.

"Are you ready?" Frot enquired.

"Entirely," Hi-Tum answered, his tentacle on the controlling switches.

"One… Two…Go!"

Instantly the force-projector hurled its energy through the iralium floor and beneath the machinery. Like a shell from a gun the Inolan-sprayed equipment shot skywards and vanished almost immediately from our view, leaving no trail of light from friction with the atmosphere, since Inolan liquid turned heat into cold, and cold into heat.…

Frot watched the speck vanish in the night sky, then calmly surveyed his electric wrist chronometer. For a long time he stood silent and rigid, then raised his hand.

"Now the magnet," he said, and instantly Zan-Kafod below us moved the necessary buttons. The great powerhouse became alive with sound; its engines flared into life, blue haze rose into the air. The smell of sulphur and ozone drifted up to the balcony. I shot a glance downwards at the white-hot bed of the retractor, roughly repaired as far as Rof-Elsor had understood it—the mass of wires in which the unfortunate guard had fallen from the balcony. That mesh of power struck me as being the most impressive section in the whole scheme of super-intelligent machinery.

"That's about it," said Frot at length, lowering his hand and looking up from his chronometer. "Stop!" And incontinently the machinery ceased and we looked at each ether expectantly.

"My calculations show that my machinery should now be lying, unharmed, somewhere on Paliso," Prot remarked calmly. "It was impossible to calculate an exact spot. All we know is that the machinery was held within the walls of that force beam until it reached Paliso, which prevented it getting adrift in space. The magnet gave it a safe landing. Our next move is to go to Paliso itself—but while you, Zan-Kafod—and Rof-Elsor, who is up on the platform, come with us, you others must remain behind. You, Hi-Tum, we'll leave to guard and take charge of this place; you, Fa-Isanod, will take your place at the space-radio equipment and we will advise you how we progress. Is that in order?"

"Quite," Hi-Tum conceded, with a little obeisance, "Are you starting for Paliso immediately?"

"Right away," I answered. "It's the best thing to do. We'll keep in touch; our time-space machine has been equipped with space-radio during the morning, along with the provisions, a small telescopic-refractor and other things. Let's get going…"

"Yes, and while we are away keep that magnet off," Frot remarked. "Otherwise we will be caught in its field of attraction."

"You may rest assured," Hi-Tum responded; then Rof-Elsor appeared from the roof and joined us.

Ten minutes later, after entering the magnet floor through the open doorway—which had been opened by our colleagues during the morning for the work of equipping our time-space machine with necessities—we entered the vessel itself. The closing of the outer door, a few movements of the controls, and we were in space once more, and leaving the grim world of Ondon far below us in the void... And from this vantage point we again beheld that celestial mystery—the two bright, unknown planets. Once more frowns of puzzlement came to the brow of Rof-Elsor, and once more he dismissed the matter as obviously being of no consequence—

Some time later found us floating down through the sparse upper clouds about the craggy world of Paliso. Exercising extreme care I gradually brought us down until we came to rest on the floor of the valley. It was certainly not the same one we had visited before. Above the mountain tops the globe of Ondon hung before us.

"Nice work, Lee," Frot commented, patting me on the shoulder. "We'd better wait and rest until sun-up, then start searching for my machinery. We'll find it quickly enough with the detector." This latter instrument we had brought with us, to enable us to detect the magnetized apparatus without difficulty.

"Until daylight I suggest a meal and sleep," said Lan Ronnit, and set the example by disappearing into the adjoining provision room...

Dawn on Paliso was as cheerless as all other spectacles on that inimical planet.

The sun rose suddenly from behind the gaunt mountain ranges and shed its sulphur-yellow light on cliffs of frozen gray, and a valley-floor of stones. Again, as we looked out of the window, bestirring ourselves from slumber, we remarked the strange shifting of the air occasioned by the planet's remarkable acoustic properties.

For myself, I felt much refreshed by the rest, and so, I think, were the others. We had a roughly prepared breakfast, some of the revivifying ekrimar, then set off into the air, keeping as close to the ground as possible, in search of Frot's machinery. Frot himself kept his eye chained to the detector-compass, whose needle-deflection would instantly reveal the presence of his equipment.

It was as we progressed that I realized the planet was nothing more or less than a dead world—at least to intelligent life—with its abysses, crags and awesome gorges of sheer-faced rock. No place for headquarters! Yet it had to be done.

"Right, Lee—steady!" Frot said abruptly, his voice cutting in on my meditations.

I slowed down to a crawl, using the helicopter screws to keep up aloft. Elna was busy with the binoculars, and suddenly she gave a little whoop. "Immediately below, Sandy!" she sang out, looking up. "On the valley floor."

Under her instructions I brought the time-space machine to the ground and safely anchored it. Moving to the window we beheld the small black hill that comprised Frot's apparatus a quarter of a mile distant.

"Splendid! It is unharmed!" Frot exclaimed in satisfaction. "Now for space-suits."

"What on earth for?" I demanded. "There's atmosphere outside."

"Truly—but think of the sound. That sound-force can kill, Lee. Space-suits are the only protection against it. Come along."

We moved to the emergency chamber, all save the two Jovians who elected to stay behind because no space-suits would fit them, and donned our suits. Then, unharmed by the terrific din we must have made, we climbed out and dropped to the stony valley floor, moving, with the slow progress of rheumatics, toward the mass of machinery awaiting us.

"We'll be all right if we erect it here," Frot said into his communicator. "We have everything we need. A clear valley floor; and open sky lies up there, clear of the mountain tops. By using the telescopic-refractor on the ship we can see how things progress after our experiments."

Without further words we set to work with the portable beams-of-force machines, which had been sent along with the equipment, and connected them to the batteries on the space-time machine. Thus we had instruments as useful as cranes, and with their tremendous power it was not difficult to marshal the machinery into gradually forming order.

First came the force-projector to hurl the vibrations intact through the void, then the sound channeler—as Frot called his instrument for gathering the sound into one complete whole before its entrance into the final projector—then the atom-splitter, this being converted so that the core of the puff-balls, lying in the base of the machine, could be shattered to their constituent atoms at the moment of their beginning to emit sound. This, he had calculated, would result in the pure energy of sound, the splitting of the particles of the sound wave itself. He had reasoned that the sound-particles were really carriers of sound, but that within themselves must lie sound without limit. This unearthly ultimate of sound, magnified to a vast extent by the planet's sound-amplifying qualities would result in a mass of colossal vibration—for of course the sound would finally become pure terrific vibration,, in which form it would travel through space—and so to Ondon. Without the air of Paliso—or at least the air's curious powers—our efforts would undoubtedly have been very feeble. As it was the scheme seemed perfect, particularly as the magnetic crystals, which Frot had dragged along with him in their container from the ship, would also be split up by the atom-splitter and resolved into pure magnetic radiation, to further increase the mass of incredible force we proposed hurling at Ondon. I began to wonder, as we progressed, if this splitting up of so many components into their absolute of energy might not actually blow even Paliso itself clean out of its orbit with the recoil!

Frot, however, seemed confident enough, so the work went on. It was a long task, with frequent intervals in which we returned to the ship for fresh air, renewal of air-tanks for our suits, and a rest. But at last we had the machinery erected and everything in perfect order. We had only to wait then for Ondon to rise above the mountain tops…

"It's certain to work!" Frot declared, with rare enthusiasm. "Zagribud will just smash into powder under such frightful force. I've charted everything out to the last degree. That force will strike Zagribud dead in the center… Let's have a look at Zagribud."

He turned to the telescopic-refractor and adjusted the lenses, after fixing the high-powered object-glass in line with another attachment—the horizon-reflector. This curious device, of Jovian origin, made it possible to see a planet if it lay below the horizon by drawing to itself the emanating light-waves from the planet in question. Thus it was that, although Ondon itself was not visible to the naked eye, with the instrument, its blunt nose flush with the observation window, with its clear, non-distorting glass, we presently beheld on the reflecting screen a view of Zagribud itself, and to the right the isolated mass of the power-house, with a dimly discernible figure pacing to and fro on the platform.

"All's clear as yet," Frot murmured. "No attack—nothing. I can't quite unterstand it all."

"Yes, too much like the calm before the storm," Elna remarked dubiously, staring at Zagribud's mighty mass.

"We might radio and learn the state of things," said I, and turned to the space-radio apparatus at my elbow. Presently I had tuned in to our little outpost power-station on Ondon, and the voice of Fa-Isanod came in the headphones.

"Everything all right?" I enquired. "We've landed safely on Paliso, and have got all our equipment in order. Any signs of trouble on Ondon?"

"None whatever," came the Jovian response. "I never knew such quietness. I must admit that I—" He stopped, and I waited for him to continue. Then as the silence continued I spoke again. "Fa-Isanod. Give instructions to the others to get as far away from Zagribud as they can—to leave at once. Otherwise you may be destroyed by our vibrations. Go toward the Ri-Pud Lake; we'll come back and pick you up. That understood?"

Complete silence.

"Fa-Isanod, do you hear me?" I demanded. "Answer!"

Still the dead silence persisted.

"Fa-Isanod doesn't answer!" I exclaimed worriedly. "Wonder what—"

"Sandy, quick—look here!" Elna exclaimed abruptly. "Hurry!"

I turned around, headphones still clamped to my ears, and looked into the reflecting screen of the telescope. At the moment I looked I experienced a sudden, brief spell of dizziness; for an instant something seemed to numb my mind, and then passed. I stared intensely at the reflector.

A rolling white mist was apparently stealing over the face of Ondon, seeming to have its source in Zagribud itself. A billowing cloud of whiteness that gradually covered the whole planet...then, very slowly, the mist began to disperse again. Yet, in some odd way the view appeared changed. It was the same, and yet peculiar. I cannot adequately convey what I felt, nor did I realize then what the occurrence signified. I turned away again.

"Something queer going on," I muttered. "Fa-Isanod stopped in mid-sentence. He hasn't even answered my warning to him. I—"

"That's odd!" exclaimed Lan Ronnit abruptly. "There's no guard on the power-house tower now! Nor can I see the dark spot of our force projector. What's gone wrong?"

I sat biting my lip in perplexity for a space, then I shrugged. "I can't pretend to understand it. Zagribud is still there, so it can still be shattered. It looks as though the power-house has been attacked by some unknown force or other." I took the headphones off and disconnected the transmitter. "About thirty minutes before your experiment is due, Frot," I remarked, glancing at him.

He looked up from his chronometer. "Twenty nine and a quarter minutes Earth time, to be exact, Lee," was his unmoved response...

The twenty nine and a quarter minutes dragged back with irritating slowness, but at last the time did arrive for us to again don our space-suits and stagger out into the valley beyond. In the interval, Ondon had risen clear of the mountain ranges, hanging as a yellow ball in a gray-black sky. And again, I noticed, on either side of her, those two bright, enigmatic planets...

Frot, a weird figure in his bulging space-suit, made a brief examination of his magnetite crystals and puffball-cores, inspected the tiny apparatus for pressing the two halves of the puffball-cores together, and nodded in satisfaction. Then he took his stand before the switchboard. I watched my own chronometer, and to the exact second he had predetermined Frot depressed the four-pole switch of the atom-splitter, which synchronically set all the other machinery in action.

Never shall I forget that which happened immediately afterwards!

A blinding beam shot from the hollow space at the bottom of the atom-splitter. We heard nothing inside our suits, but before our eyes the very air danced like a thousand furies. The very mountain range seemed to warp and bend before it. Came a ground-shaking concussion and we were all four of us hurled through the air like stones from catapults, to crash, thanks to our suits, bouncing amidst the stones of the valley floor quite two hundred yards from the scene of the disturbance. Even then enormous radiating pressures held us down, and I am sure quite five minutes elapsed before the frightful disturbance eased up and slowly ceased...

With extreme caution, in case the force had not fully spent itself, we returned to our machinery. The whole issue had toppled over with the recoil.

"Never mind," Frot said into his communicator. "The sound vibration has been hurled forth; what happens to this stuff doesn't matter now. Come—we must view Zagribud right away..."

In silence we returned to the ship, removed our cumbersome suits, and entered the control room again. Rof-Elsor and Zan-Kafod were full of the story of how the space-time machine had nearly overturned with the concussion...

"Now, let's see what's happened," Frot breathed in a pent voice, and again as he adjusted the screws on the instrument I felt once more that odd, evanescent dizziness. I turned to the view in the reflector... We all of us, our two Jovian friends included, drew our breath in sharply at what we beheld.

Zagribud lay a crumpled mass of smoking dust, from under which the very ground itself had been blown away! Our power-house, too, lay a split and rended ruin, and the square mass of the magnet had disintegrated into powder! Yet nowhere could I see a sign of anybody—no evidence of people fleeing with terror, or any sign of panic. For some reason, then obscure, Ondon was a dead world. Yet somehow I had an odd conviction that something was amiss somewhere. Again I noticed something peculiar about the scene. Again I felt dizzy... I turned aside and Frot switched off the scene.

"Well, you've done it!" I exclaimed, patting him on the shoulder. "You have blown Zagribud to shreds—and presumably our friends in the powerhouse. Still, I tried to warn them; this is not a time for discrimination... The menace to Earth has gone. That leaves only—Jelfel!"

Frot nodded. He seemed remarkably cool and detached in face of what he had done.

"So Zan-Kafod and I are without a city, and without a world," Rof Elsor remarked. "I am glad to see the last of Zagribud, but where are Zan-Kafod and I to go? Earth?"

"Assuredly," I replied. "Our work here is ended. Earth now holds Jelfel, and he must be exterminated. We can return to Earth immediately. Fortune has indeed favoured us so far..."

I turned to the controls and set our course for Earth, computing it from the constellations which I had, by now, grown to recognize at sight.

Our journey back to Earth differed but little from other interstellar space-journeys. Presently attaining the speed of light, as our Particle Disintegrators reached their maximum recoiling velocity, and moving through time, we found Earth rising to meet us some ship-board hours later. I then moved the vessel back in time to coincide with our own time aboard the ship.

For my own part I felt supremely happy at the vision of New York 25000 A.D. below me. With swift easiness our space-time machine shot athwart the tops of the highest edifices, skimmed the massive dome of the T.L.C. Building itself, and so finally to the space grounds.

"Home!" I breathed ecstatically, flinging in the anchor-brake. "We've done it!"

From the position of the sun I judged it to be mid-day, therefore there was every chance that Templeton would be about his normal duties in the T.L.C. Building. The six of us—Rof-Elsor and Zan Kafod evincing extreme delight and awe at the constant surprises they beheld on the way, and occasioning no little curiosity in Earthlings too!—made our way to the Building, and were ushered into the Debating Chamber, We were fortunate in that the entire Board was present.

"Commandant Lee!" Templeton exclaimed in delight, rising. "Welcome! All of you! What have you to report?"

"I have to report the destruction of Zagribud, President—the wrecking of the city responsible for the enslaving of Earth; and the killing of Rath Granod, ruler of the City. That leaves only Elnek Jelfel, and as he is on Earth I have returned to wipe him out."

Templeton pondered for a moment, a strange expression on his face. "If you have indeed destroyed Zagribud, Lee, how is it that we are still in 25000?" he demanded. "That should have been destroyed at the same time—the unknown power that is holding us here should have ceased—since the initial machinery is on Ondon."

I started at that; it was a point that had escaped me in the general confusion. I shot a glance at Frot; his high forehead was wrinkled in deep thought.

"I—I am afraid I cannot explain that," I answered. "Maybe something to do with relativity. Being used to a thing we can't detect a change—"

"That is not scientific, Commandant—it's fantastic," Templeton answered grimly.

"Well, we saw Zagribud destroyed with our own eyes—and so did these two Jovians," I responded. "The time problem is something I cannot understand…" I paused, puzzled, as a sudden most extraordinary shaking and vibration made itself manifest throughout the great building.

A continued period of crescendoing vibration, then—

"Lee! President! Quickly!" shouted Ronnit.

We all raced to the window and looked out over the great mass of the city. That same strange change was suddenly before us that I had seen at the outset of these amazing experiences—strange shiftings and meltings—one city upon another. A sense of enormous acceleration and increasing dizziness.

Helpless, futile, we dropped down into a whirling abyss of unconsciousness, before we could raise as much as a finger to help ourselves…

CHAPTER 12

THE CLEVEREST MAN ON EARTH

When we returned to consciousness, we were still in the Debating Chamber, yet in some unaccountable way it was different. The position of the central table had changed; some of the furniture in the room, sparse though it was, had altered...

Very slowly we got to our feet.

It was night now, where formerly it had been mid-day, but the automatic lights of the Debating Chamber had functioned and illuminated the great room in soft white radiance. Through the window we beheld New York, but... I caught in my breath and stared intensely.

"New York—2004!" muttered Lan Ronnit, taking the words from my own lips. I held my forehead and tried to sort the problem out. Anton Frot looked up at the sky, then gave an exclamation.

"Jupiter!" he exclaimed, pointing. "You're right, Ronnit—this is the sky of 2004."

"But—but what's happened?" I asked dazedly, and we all looked at Frot intently, Templeton and his fellow-directors standing in a little knot behind us.

"We've gone back to our natural time—2004," Frot said slowly and pensively. "Either the time-altering machinery on Ondon took some time to release its effect after we destroyed Zagribud—or else something else is responsible. Everything below is just as it ought to be for 2004. The entire population is back. Paradox though it is, we are now about twenty thousand years prior to the time Jelfel was even born! There is Jupiter, yet to our own knowledge we flung it into the sun in the year 22,000. Whatever it may be...we're back to normal. So presumably, are all the other ages. All in their rightful times." He stopped and pondered the matter over.

Templeton came forward and seized Frot's arm tightly. "Frot, does this mean the end of Jelfel?" he demanded grimly.

"I don't know," Frot answered. "We don't even know why we've come back to normal time like this. Something must have intervened between Earth and Ondon and broken the power that was holding us in a false time. If Jelfel is still alive he will be…let me see…" Frot paused and thought, then a bright light entered his eyes.

"He will, of course, be still in 25,000—where we were. But here's the point. If he was on Earth when this happened he would be moved backwards with us—bound to be, and that might have meant his dissolution by traversing a time already traversed. On the other hand, if he were in the void, or anywhere away from Earth, he'll be still in the era 25,000, as I said at first. That's rather amusing really—he'll be faced now with the civilization which begins the Age of Intelligence—the one era he tried to avoid because of their knowledge. 30,000 is, of course, the actual Age of Intelligence, but the rightful people of 25,000 are brainy enough in all conscience, rising as they do from the shattered civilisation of 22,000—the Age of Problems—which we destroyed ourselves on our earlier adventure."

"His machinery in the valley. What of that?" Elna asked.

The mathematician shrugged. "So far as I know it will still be there in 25,000," he answered. "It is the law of time. There is only one real way to solve the problem—"

"Go to 25,000 and find out," said I; but to my surprise Frot shook his head.

"No, Lee, the way to find out is to go right forward to 30,000—the Age of Intelligence itself, and learn what has happened in what, to them, will be past time. Then we get along a bit."

"That is a splendid suggestion," Templeton remarked. "A pity we didn't think of it before. However, it is not too late now. I suggest you all leave for the Age of Intelligence tomorrow. Spend the night in your own quarters, all of you. I will have work found for these two Jovians, and tomorrow you can visit Valma, Master of Science of the Age of Intelligence. You know him, Lee?"

"Surely," I responded. "What time-liner pilot, in his travels, has not heard of him?" I smiled faintly. "A very true phrase is attached to Valma… They call him the 'cleverest man on Earth'…"

* * * *

The Age of Intelligence, 30,000 A.D. represented the Third Intellectual Cycle in the history of the Earth. Firstly came the First Intellectual Cycle—the Egyptians, 1700 B.C.—then the Age of Problems 22,000 A.D.—curiously enough controlled by Jelfel (which Age of course still occupied the same position in the time line, even though our particular dealings with it had long since ended) and lastly 30,000, the greatest Earthly civilisation of all… A civilisation grown up from the ruins of

Jelfel's own civilisation of 22,000 after the Earth had been blistered with solar fire from the hurling of Jupiter into the sun.

Jelfel had once told me that his own Age of Problems was the cleverest intellectual age in Earth-history, and at that time, bemused by his brilliance, I had been ready to believe it. But, during my visits as a time pilot, I had seen glimpses of the superb scientific powers of the Age of Intelligence, and also had heard the comments of scientists in other Ages who had sought the advice of the Age of Intelligence in their work. Always had Valma, Master of Science, provided the perfect answer—because, being at the end of Earth time, he knew all that had gone before him. He was a man backed by all Earthly knowledge…

So it was that we set off in a private time-machine for the Age of Intelligence the following morning—a newly attired, refreshed quartet, and the only trace of our Ondonian experiences being my own Jovian face and eyes.

Again we saw the normal world warp into the fourth-dimensional time line and vanish; once more we hurtled down the time-line, passing the Age of Problems on our way, until at last, thanks to our instantaneous time-switches, we merged out of the timeline into the Age of Intelligence, coming to rest upon the charted land ground at the rear of the T.L.C. Building, 30,000…

Being already accustomed to the vast city, I rapidly led the way to the chief research laboratories, and eventually, after some difficulty in explaining away my face, succeeded in gaining an audience for the four of us with Valma himself.

We were conducted into a type of consulting-room—an apartment of indescribable beauty, superbly furnished and delicately ornamented. Whilst we waited a system of colour vibrations played upon the opposite, smoothfaced wall, and for each colour there was a vibration that soothed our beings like the gentlest music.

Then suddenly Valma was with us.

How he came, he best was able to explain. Quite suddenly he appeared, through the solid walls and closed door, smiling in welcome. A neat white laboratory smock entirely covered his powerful, upright figure, whilst the amazingly deep-set blue eyes studied us from under arched black brows. The brilliant sunshine streaming through the sky lights illumined the essentially mathematical magnificence of his tall forehead… Valma, Master of Science—the cleverest man on Earth!

"Ah, Commandant Lee—Miss Folson," he smiled. "Indeed an honour, I am sure, to interview the Commandant of the Time Way. I observe your face is slightly Jovian, but after your experiences that is not to be wondered at. Good day, Lan Ronnit—Anton Frot…" He seated himself and regarded us with profound thought.

"You know all about our experiences in the void then? Of our efforts to overcome Jelfel? You must—mentioning my face," I said quietly.

Valma laughed softly. "My dear Commandant, there is such a thing as records," he answered. "Documents, sheets of pure gold have engraved upon them the history of the struggles of one Commandant Sandford Lee to outwit a Jovian menace; the story of how that Jovian, Elnek Jelfel, was once outwitted and his planet flung into the sun; then the even more remarkable story of his return, and of how he was at last destroyed, and of the small part I took in doing it—though oddly enough, by ordinary standards, I was not even born then! But as you know, as I know, there are two states of time, as you once explained to Miss Folson when you first struggled with Jelfel."

I was about to speak when Valma went on again.

"As you are perhaps aware, Commandant, my entire civilization has been living under the most trying conditions lately, due to our being pushed forward some twenty-three thousand years. Really, most amusing. We have been living like savages in a dead world, and only a few hours ago did we revert back to our natural time. All due to Elnek Jelfel, of course."

"It is about him I have come to talk with you," I said earnestly.

"Yes, you have come to seek my counsel," the Master of Science nodded. "It has been written in Time that you came to seek my advice, and I gave it to you—so I must do so. Indeed, no effort of mine can stop it. Time is always as writ… Now, explain matters to me."

As carefully as possible I made all the details clear to him, and when I ceased to speak he smiled rather grimly.

"As I read the cosmos," he said at last, "I see that Elnek Jelfel has again outwitted you, Commandant! You have been made a complete fool of!"

"What!" I exploded.

"Sorry—but only too true," Valma affirmed. "I can mentally see what has taken place… Upon the death of Rath Granod, Ruler of Zagribud, Krot, one of Granod's advisers, discovered the fact, and unable to decide what to do, radioed to Earth to Jelfel—Granod's successor in title. Jelfel's advice was to do nothing until he came to Ondon. Jelfel did arrive on Ondon, by his sixth dimensional Rotator—then he allowed you to go as far as you would, mainly because he was interested in the possibilities of Anton Frot's sound-vibration projector. But, before that sound-projector could be fired he shielded Zagribud—indeed all Ondon—with an atomic screen, and so deflected all your sound vibration away into the void. Each time you looked into your telescopic refractor the six of you saw the image Jelfel *willed* your minds to see—"

"Good Lord! The dizziness—the numbness of my brain!" I exclaimed abruptly, suddenly recollecting the occurrence. "Yes—yes. Go on, Valma."

"The vision of unharmed Zagribud, then afterwards the ruined city, were only figments of Jelfel's tremendous will-power. The white mist was genuine enough, being his curtain of atomic vibration—but actually the mist *did not clear away*. It only seemed to do so by his thought influence upon you. Further, the guards of the powerhouse were blown out of existence by yet another of Jelfel's remarkable creations. His sound-deflecting screen must, at best, have been a hastily conceived process, but at any rate it was effective. So that sound-vibration was hurled forth—but into the infinite. Ondon, however, was slightly shifted in his orbit by the colossal shock. The vibration, then repelled, travelled in a straight line from Ondon's surface, and finally it struck Ramino, Paliso and Ondon's neighboring world, also slightly shifting him in his orbit. Ramino partly absorbed the vibration, and partly, by its very composition, again reflected the vibration, until it suddenly struck the time-altering beams passing through the void from Ondon to Earth. Instantly that terrific mass of sound-energy exploded, and so also did the influence holding Earthlings in wrong periods of time. That was when we reverted to normal... So, Frot, your apparatus did some good after all..."

Valma paused.

"So you see, my friends, because Jelfel is on Ondon, he missed being flung back in time, and incidentally into death. And Zagribud is still standing—and the year he is in is still 25,000. He will know from his telescopic apparatus that the time deflecting apparatus is out of action— that people are normal again—and will immediately set to work to repair the damage. But, by the same method that doesn't solve our problem— and from our records it is not altogether clear *how* he was overcome. We know he has—and will—meet destruction, but it is left to us to do it. The past can tell us nothing. It merely says we were responsible in doing it..."

"His Earth headquarters will still be in 25,000," I remarked. "I suggest we set out to destroy those, first."

"I regard the endeavour as a waste of time, Commandant," Valma answered calmly. "If we do that, we accomplish nothing. It is *Jelfel* we must destroy—not his works. No, I can surely devise a better plan than that."

I shook my head doubtfully. "Jelfel is a brilliantly clever scientist," I remarked. "He is determined to have Earthlings, and before he's done he'll succeed."

"Undue pessimism, surely? It is written in time that he fails…"

"Records may be wrong," I grunted.

"Truly—truly," Valma confessed, arching his eyebrows. "Still, I am called the Master of Science because I am the only man on Earth who understands time and space exactly as it ought to be understood. I have to follow what is written in time—I cannot avoid it. Therefore I will fling my own challenge through the void to this master-devil. You shall see the scientific power of 30,000, my friends!"

I inclined my head in silent acquiescence. "Very well, Valma. Far be it from me to even try and understand the workings of the mind controlling the cleverest man on Earth," and he smiled faintly at the compliment…

CHAPTER 13

THE FALSE EARTH

The days that followed in the Age of Intelligence were a delightful relaxation after our varied activities in time and space—and with each passing day we began to apprehend the amazing powers of Valma, and realized it then more than ever when he was designated as the Master of Science, I had been willing previously to hand the palm for scientific genius to Elnek Jelfel, but those days with Valma, in our great campaign for the final—as we hoped—extermination of the Jovian menace, left me completely bewildered by the man's almost incredible knowledge of time and space...

On the fourth day, at his request, we accompanied him to the research laboratories—an edifice of amazing proportions, equipped with every known earthly scientific device, built through the accumulated knowledge of Earth's intellectual centuries. In Valma there was concentrated all the knowledge of the Egyptians at the bottom of the Time-Line, the Age of Problems itself, and centuries of achievement added to that knowledge again.

"I have decided upon the plan of action," Valma said quietly. "We can outwit Jelfel up to a certain point, then something else will intervene to finally obliterate him. It is not written in Time what that something is. My mind is blank when I try to conceive the matter. That being so I will not tax the delicate structure of my brain unduly. Our task, my friends"—he became gently impressive—"is to give Jelfel no opportunity for thinking that he has failed in his efforts!"

"But—but surely that is the wrong method!" I protested.

"Anything but it! Listen, my friends. Our calculations have shown that Jelfel knows of the collapse of his machinery for placing civilizations in the wrong time; he is, therefore, rapidly rebuilding another machine so that he can continue his efforts—for, now he is undisputed ruler of Zagribud, he sees glorious progress ahead if once he can get Earthly bodies for himself and his immediate intellectual contemporaries... It appears, from my mental researches, that the recoil from the explosion of his time-altering beams has blown his machine to pieces in Zagribud.

Now in roughly twenty-six hours the second machine will be completed and he will again shift Earth's civilizations forward twenty-three thousand years. If that happened you could—indeed you could have done so all along—go forward to another Age and escape him by being in a time ahead of his existence, but that is not the way to exterminate him. So, you will stay and fight, as I will...

"If that happens, it will mean that once again Earth will be dragged to Ondon—this time by remote control magnetism. You know the principles of his magnetism, and of how his machinery absorbs Earth's natural negative electricity and makes therefore a perfect attraction for Ondon's positive electricity? Well, his remote control system consists of a mass of machinery exactly duplicating that which he has on Earth in the valley in 25,000. Hence, he will control Earth's passage through space to his own world—and, he will be quite sure he succeeds—whereas actually he will do I nothing of the kind!"

"I'm afraid I don't understand," I remarked, puzzled. "Surely, if we destroy his headquarters in 25,000, we at least are sure of Earth being safe?"

"Certainly—but only until he thinks out a new system," Valma answered. "No, my friend, that is not the solution—besides to do that would kill my own idea. Listen to the plan I have arranged. Elnek Jelfel is going to be subjected to what we might call celestial juggling. He will capture a *mythical Earth* and draw it to Ondon; he will *not* really put civilization twenty-three thousand years forward—and lastly, he will find, when it is too late that the mythical Earth is really the shield of deadly weapons, which we will use to destroy him and Zagribud. The destruction of Zagribud may, or may not kill him—I forgot the unknown power that is destined to be his final master..."

"You have your plans well laid, Valma," I admitted; "even so, I don't follow how he is going to capture a mythical Earth, as you call it, or how it will be the shield of weapons—or how you'll stop him from altering time."

"I assure you it is not at all difficult," the master-man returned. "Step this way, my friends..."

He preceded us into his instrument hall, eventually coming to a halt beside an instrument resembling an enormous telescopic reflector—a great tower of pure, glittering gold, created by the ton by transmutation of elements. In my own time the value would have run into incalculable millions.

"This," Valma explained, "is the Time-Line Adjuster. Firstly, let me outline to you *how* Jelfel moves people ahead twenty-three thousand years. I have studied his methods, and it appears his system is this... By a compression band he forces down the fourth-dimensional time-line, which as you know flows as a steady river, with the result that Earthlings are caught up in it. That causes a sense of acceleration, and finally, unconsciousness during transit. Then, when he has moved them on twenty-three thousand years he allows the time-band to move back into position, *but* and here is the vital point, my friends, he generates a negative force which is in opposition to the time-band. Thus it is that the normal flow of time—which would instantly fling humans back to their rightful time the instant the time-line is removed—is held rigid—and so humans are kept in that advanced time. But, when that negative beam system was destroyed by the recoiling sound vibration, civilizations shot back to their normal places... That clear?"

"Yes," said Anton Frot keenly; but Elna, Ronnit and I looked on dazedly.

"Splendid. Well, this Time-Line Adjuster will thwart Jelfel's efforts when he again tries to move people forward twenty-three thousand years. My machine radiates a force exactly contrary to Jelfel's system of negative-beam and time-line depressor—and also it will react so as to be in force in 25,000 instead of here...that is, the time Jelfel is in and will attack from. So, his efforts will be useless I fancy. Is that clear to you?"

"Go on!" I urged eagerly.

Valma moved to another immense instrument before continuing—this time an apparatus similar to a box of burnished bronze, and containing many lenses.

"With this I shall create the false Earth," he commented, as though the task was a trivial matter. "This machine also, like the Time-Line Adjuster, incorporates the necessary mechanism for projecting the image back into 25,000. Allow me to explain it to you. Firstly the machine sends out what I call a recoiling light-frequency into space—into the sky of 25,000. That light-frequency absorbs everything it sees from the sky of 25,000—which will be, of course, the Earth itself as seen from the void. The light-frequency, bearing this image, returns to this machine and is reprojected into time—in the sky, above the *genuine* Earth of 25,000. The image incorporates all the actual colors and is rendered three dimensional—that is, a solidity. Thus, a false Earth lies above the genuine one in 25,000...

"Now do you see the idea? By timing this projector I can make it appear that Earth is very slowly approaching to Ondon—or so Jelfel will imagine, when he looks through his telescopic devices—for this image, being an apparent solidity, will hide the real Earth beneath. As my machine has an infinite power beam, reaching to Ondon itself if necessary—and also as my focussing lenses can be made to enlarge the image until it actually equals that of Earth itself—using the void as my screen for projection—the illusion will be complete…

"And behind that screen will travel space-time machines equipped with every known death-dealing device. Thus, when the image has reached a point near to Ondon—and Jelfel fully believes he's captured Earth, we'll turn upon him and come out from behind our screen. And Earth will be safe—for his time-apparatus will be useless as well. Your opinion, my friends…"

"Astounding!" I breathed. "I could never have thought of that in all my life!"

"I am the Master of Science," he said calmly, and without a trace of egotism. "In our attacking space-time machines we will carry improved Frot sound-vibrators, heat-rays—"

"Heat-rays!" Lan Ronnit echoed. "But they're ancient weapons for this Age, Valma!"

"In the old form, yes," Valma conceded. "My heat-ray system is the limit in efficiency. I gather the heat of the sun, store it, and then project it through crystals of what I call solidified water globules. Water globules are perfect condenser-lenses, my friends. These globules are petrified and embodied in hundreds in one great lens. Hence the stream of sun-heat passing through this lens produces a most terrific heat-ray… And now, my friends, to business…"

He turned and strode actively about the great laboratory, summoning his assistants to his side. With the swift conciseness of a man who knows every intricacy of his craft, he gave instructions and shortly afterwards, before our very eyes, the necessary apparatus for our interstellar contest began to appear.

"These machines are of course the fundamentals," Valma remarked, nodding to the Time-Line Adjuster and the 'False-Earth' machine. "The attachments have yet to be manufactured."

The process of the manufacturing was the most amazing thing I ever beheld in the Age of Intelligence. The mighty place became alive with curious beams and forces, the nature of which I could not even guess at. Bars of solid, shining gold seemed to rise from nowhere, enormous plates of pure copper arrived by the same startling process—until at last, after three hours of unceasing energy, the room was filled with orderly, tabulated machinery of infinite complexity.

"Quite in order," Valma commented, looking about him and rubbing his delicate hands gently together. "I think that is all for now. Everything is ready for use the instant I give the word. Now, my good friends, if you will come into the next apartment you shall see for yourselves exactly what is transpiring…"

In the next apartment he extinguished the daylight with metal shutters over the glass roof and switched on the time-televisor, such as were used on regular time-liners, only on a much larger scale. The apparatus functioned, of course, on the same principles as television, only that the images received could belong to past or future time as the operator desired... A few trifling adjustments and the vision of New York, 25,000, appeared on the twelve-foot screen. I realized after a while that the image was coming from a movable transmitter on the roof of the T.L.C. Building itself. Presently a voice spoke in the darkness in the ceiling.

"Is that as you desire it, Valma?"

"Entirely," the great scientist responded in his grave voice. "Leave it at that angle, Ronnit..."

"Yes, Master."

For a space Valma sat silent in his golden chair, gazing absently at the screen, its reflection casting his powerful, highly intelligent profile into sharpest silhouette.

"This, I hardly need to explain, is time-television, my friends; just the view that is collected by a transmitter. Presently you will see 'space-television'—which is television as it really ought to be. I— Pardon me a moment." He turned aside to an instrument in the darkness and listened intently for a moment. "He has just released it...? Yes. Excellent indeed. Release the machines."

The floor beneath our feet began to tremble slightly a moment later, as the monster machinery in the adjoining laboratory began to take on life and speed. Valma turned back to us again.

"My assistant has just informed me, according to his observations of Ondon in 25,000, that Jelfel has now repaired his time-altering machinery and is sending that beam to Earth to depress the time line and again send civilization forward. My machinery, now working simultaneously, should provide our friend with a complete illusion and render his efforts useless... Watch the screen."

Again we looked, and almost immediately our attention became riveted upon the view of the sky in 25,000. Strange, swirling shapes were becoming visible in the noonday light—a hazy, indeterminable formation that very slowly spread from horizon to horizon. The bulk of the city of New York became covered, by almost imperceptible degrees, with the image of the false Earth flung out from Valma's astonishing machines. Above, in a yellow pall, we beheld the dim vestiges of a city, amorphous, and quite without understandable formation. Through this dull saffron curtain the sun shone with an obvious decrease in light.

"It is possible to see through the image when the light of the sky is behind it," Valma commented. "But it is not possible to see through it and view a comparatively dull solid like the Earth itself—so I fancy the illusion, to Jelfel, will be quite complete. However, we will see for ourselves how things look to Jelfel... Come."

We moved to yet another apartment, again enveloped in the deepest gloom. I caught a glimpse of banks of massive insulators and coiled wires as I entered—then came a blue flash as Valma moved a switch into position and set into life several softly droning engines, immediately we beheld yet another twelve foot screen, which gave us a vision as soon from a spaceship—that of rapidly leaving Earth behind us. I caught in my breath in a startled gasp.

"Light waves," Valma said in a casual voice. "Almost similar to Jelfel's own telescopic device, the difference being that this is space-television. It will therefore pass through all solids and requires no transmitter. There you see the Earth below in the void. As this televisor is now receiving the light from 25,000, by being deflected from the time-line, you are actually viewing the false Earth I have projected over the genuine Earth of that Age. How does the illusion strike you?"

"Why, it's perfect!" I exclaimed in delight, staring hard. "It's impossible to tell the thing is a fake."

"So perfect, it looks as though something's gone wrong somewhere," Elna commented.

"Nothing has gone wrong, Miss Folson," Valma assured her, as the globe of Earth rapidly receded in the screen. "Beneath that apparent globe lies the real world of 25,000. Ah, we are now approaching the edges of the Solar System." Valma turned aside and, moving about a tiny red light, inspected meters, dials, and curious contrivances that glowed pale pink, then he turned back to us, as the view in the screen abruptly changed, seemed to swing round in space, then headed directly for a yellow solar system directly ahead in the cosmos.

"Just altering the light-receiving apparatus," Valma commented. "Hitherto we were catching Earth's light-waves—now we are tuned into Ondon's—going ever nearer as I increase the wave-length. Watch carefully. This promises to be most interesting."

Silently marvelling how this unguessably old, yet never dying, genius managed to catch the light waves of the time 25,000 and reflect them back on his own screen in 30,000, the four of us sat spell-bound...

With amazing rapidity we hurried towards the yellow planet of Ondon, straight down towards the invincible might of Zagribud, looking just as it had before our seemingly futile efforts at destruction with Frot's sound projector—and straight down towards the roofs of that Jovian-teeming city. I caught hold of the arms of my gold chair tightly; a sensation of headlong falling was upon me. Then the apparatus slowed down, we passed through the solid roof, saw all the formations inside the metal work, and at last, after much searching, arrived in a familiar apartment where a solitary figure in dead black moved silently and efficiently.

"Jelfel!" I exclaimed involuntarily.

"Yes, and he took a little finding, too, not knowing the exact whereabouts of his laboratory," Valma commented. "Watch again, my friends."

The focus of the almost uncanny space-television apparatus changed a trifle and we beheld a three-quarter length picture of Jelfel, entirely free from all tremor, standing before an apparatus similar to our own. He was gazing intently into a screen, upon which was a view of our own superimposed Earth of 25,000! This reflecting and sub-reflecting through the void was almost more than I could grasp...

If the cold smile on Jelfel's face was any guide, he was feeling particularly well pleased with himself. In fact there was an expression about his mouth, a suggestion of merciless hardness that inwardly troubled me. I had seen that expression before, and it always implied he knew of something which others did not. Yet what could he know? For once in his life of power and ruthlessness he had been utterly fooled...

Then presently he wandered away from our view towards a mass of machinery. I heard a noise in the almost dead silence, the snapping of a switch. The view faded, became transparent, and then vanished. Lights came up in the projection chamber.

"One day, maybe, I will find a way to link sound with this unique machine," Valma said thoughtfully; then becoming practical again. "Well, now we know how Jelfel sees things. We have him completely trapped, and his time deflecting has obviously proved useless, otherwise we would not be in 30,000 at this moment... The next thing to do is to marshal together our army of space-time machines and then follow the slowly receding Earth image, timed by my instruments, through space to Ondon."

"In that case, Valma, I suppose we shall have to go to 25,000 to make our start?" I enquired.

"We could start from here and alter our time-machinery to go back— but it would simplify matters to start right away from 25,000. Yes, Commandant, we will do that."

Later in the day—I use the word purely for convenience—we arrived in 25,000, and, having been there so much during the time-juggling period, we felt entirely familiar with our surroundings. The sky, we found, was exactly as we had seen it in Valma's televisor...

Immediately Valma led our little party to the quarters of Luvstrom, Minister of War for 25,000, and for two and a half hours we were in conference—planning, plotting, arranging, suggesting—until at last we had before us, mentally, a detailed plan of our *modus operandi*. It was decided that at the final word from Valma forty space-time machines would set off into space from 25,000, behind the three-dimensional false Earth, and launch the great attack for Zagribud's final extermination. I was to head one fleet of twelve ships, Valma another twelve, and Luvstrom sixteen... So it was decided. There remained nothing more to do but wait, until the timing device used by Valma revealed that, in relation to Jelfel's force, the image of Earth was sufficiently far away to permit of us going behind it—

The long awaited day came at last. Valma rejoined Elna, Ronnit, Frot and myself from 30,000—for we had stayed behind to await his instructions and supervise the equipping of the space fleet. His announcement was that Earth was now one quarter of the way to Ondon—the image was, at least. To us, the vision in the sky of 25,000 was a singularly remarkable one. We beheld an exact, seemingly solid counterpart of Earth itself, daily becoming smaller. As, by the same proportion, the view would become larger from Jelfel's end, the real Earth was never seen beneath, even the movement in the natural orbit having been carefully checked...

"Yes," Valma remarked, glancing up at the false Earth, "it only shows what a perfect liar light can be when you know how to turn it to account. Have you got everything ready, Lee?"

"Everything," I assented. "We are all set for departure."

"Then we depart right away," he decided firmly, and set off forthwith for the space-time machine grounds, arriving at length on the vast area where lay the forty glittering prospective destroyers of Zagribud.

Our actual departure was without ceremony or excitement. In 25,000 either war or peace were treated with equal lack of emotion. Calm detachment was the keynote of that advanced era. To bid a man "good cheer" when he set off to exterminate a planet would have been marked as a token of slight lunacy and a strong case for a brain expert to be summoned, because the individual concerned was revealing a "primordial trait." Again, as I stepped into our particular time-space machine, I wondered if the discovery of perfect time travel had improved man or spoilt him. As I write now, at the end of my adventures, I find I love 2004, my own Age, more than any other. But I fall into the evil of digression...

With Valma beside me at the controls, and Ronnit and Frot on the look-out post, I at least had able assistants. Elna, who was with us, merely watched with deep interest. Leading the fleet I swept into the upper air, through Earth's brief atmospheric belt, and then lunged into the depths of space itself, heading straight for the false Earth directly ahead. At our speed we rapidly began to overtake it.

"Slower—slower!" Valma counselled. "Don't go through the image, or you may be sure Jelfel will guess the idea."

"But, Valma, at this pace—" I began. "Why, we'll be ages crawling in the rear of this image! You forgot that!"

He smiled enigmatically. "The Master of Science never forgets," he replied calmly. "I have considered that point. That is why we came in space-time machines. The period taken for the false Earth to approach reasonably near to Ondon can be calculated. So, move forward that time—and give instructions to the entire fleet to do likewise."

I turned aside to the radio inter-communicator and relayed his orders to the remainder of the ships. With a simultaneous movement, at my word, forty time levers moved over and forty switches again removed us from the universal time-line. I looked outside.

The deeps of space were unchanged—save for one thing. The mirage Earth had gone!

"The false Earth is now near Ondon, and hence out of our sight," Valma remarked in his steady voice. "It was necessary to come into space first, in order to still be in space at this later time. We have merely to follow a straight line from here and we will find the false Earth again, near enough to Ondon to permit of us coming from behind it to attack. Full speed ahead, Lee."

Immediately I pressed over the machinery switch of the Particle Disintegrators and our flagging rate began to rapidly pick up.

"Say," Lan Ronnit remarked, turning, "Jelfel said he was going to put humans in a state of suspended animation, whilst Earth crossed the void. What rotten luck for him if he's using all that power on an image!" He grinned at the thought.

"Undoubtedly he will be," Valma answered. "Still, that is his affair, not ours."

Rapidly we gathered the maximum momentum and hurtled through infinity, out beyond our own Solar system and into the space beyond. Immeasurable emptiness, bridged by man's brains and ingenuity!

About an hour and half later the false Earth began to appear in the void before us, whilst directly to the left of it was Ondon—and, on either side of Ondon, and now very much nearer to it, those two strange planets that I had observed from the planet itself, and which still lacked an explanation.

"Splendid! Splendid!" Valma breathed. "Steady, Lee…"

Manipulating the controls with the dexterity of long practice, I manoeuvred the ship until at last that mighty mass of projected image filled all the void before us—a world, and yet not a world. An incredible paradox—a transparent solidity!

"Now for my penetrator," Valma said keenly, and switched on the instrument in question—actually a simplified form of his space-television, once again capable of passing through anything. The receptive beam passed through the image before us and revealed Ondon itself upon the screen, Zagribud lying still and somnolent, apparently, in the light of the yellow sun.

"Well, we've succeeded all right," Frot remarked with supressed eagerness. "What do we do now? Open fire?"

"Of course," Valma answered grimly. He switched off his machine. "We can fight *through* this mighty screen if need be—just as an army fights behind a smoke-screen sometimes, Elna—Ronnit, man the heat-rays. You, Frot, make calculations on the positions of our beams and check up on results. You, Lee, stand by for orders at the controls."

Rapidly Valma gave his instructions to the entire fleet of ships behind us, and they spread out into fighting formation in such a manner that their deadly beams would not disrupt one another by crossing. When at last everything was to his satisfaction Valma turned to give the order to fire, but before the word could leave his lips he stood as though struck with sudden paralysis, staring through the window.

"Great heaven above!" he gasped out at last. "Look!"

Immediately we all crossed to the window, and to our dumbfounded amazement, from the far distant edge of the false Earth, there was appearing a veritable multitude of cigar shaped machines.

"Attackers—and from behind the screen!" Frot shouted hoarsely. "Why didn't they come through the screen, I wonder?"

Even as Frot spoke the approaching army of spaceships suddenly began to bristle with deadly beams of force and destruction.

"Jelfel! He's tricked us!" I gasped out. Then suddenly I awoke to life. "Quickly, all of you, man the weapons. Attack! Fire!" I bawled into the space-communicator…

CHAPTER 14

THE INCREDIBLE OPERATION

Instantly our defensive weapons came into being, but to my horror I beheld, almost from the first, that we were hopelessly outnumbered—not only in the matter of ships but in the efficiency of our weapons. Valma's heat-beams certainly accounted for four of the opposing fliers in the first two minutes, but that was the only ascendency we had. Immediately afterwards the void became a mass of whirling vortices of light and glittering, darting spaceships.

Clutching my controls, I had every ounce of my skill thrown to the test in dodging the rays that sought to disrupt us into powder. With dazed eyes I beheld spaceship after spaceship burst into blinding effulgences of light, saw broken pieces floating aimlessly about in the abyss with void-frozen bodies drifting likewise, chained by the slight gravity of the shattered spaceships—but the whole mass slowly gathering speed in the downward movement that betokened Ondon's gravitational pull.

"Those beams of theirs!" Valma panted. "They're of a frequency I never heard of! You were right, Lee; I may be the cleverest man on Earth, but this creature Jelfel is far above me in his knowledge. What a brain the man's got! Incredible knowledge! Those beams just bring instantaneous disruption—but no melting, nothing. Pouf! And the ship is gone. Blasting of atoms.... But *how* did Jelfel know that—Look *out*, Lee!" I swung my control lever round and by a fraction of an inch we missed the full sweep of one of the rays.

"I'll get that beauty!" Lan Ronnit muttered, tight-lipped and grim, watching the ray amongst its fellows, and the ship that possessed it. "Watch!" and he set himself mercilessly before his heat-beam machine.

As our vessel swung round and came into the full view of that particularly persistent spaceship, Ronnit sighted it across the hair-line divider of his apparatus. Then, a faint but unholy smile on his face, he depressed the force button to its fullest limit. There was a faint ray in the blackness of space, then the ship in question turned blue-white, swung round in a giddy semi-circle, and went reeling away, uncontrolled, into the infinite gulf. I presumed the heat had burned the pilots to death—sealed them in a coffin of white-hot metal. Watching the ship I saw it crumble into boiling and dripping destruction a few moments later. Perspiration began to run down my face with the awful intensity of the moment.

Ronnit rubbed his hands with curious calmness. "That got 'em, Lee. Now let's try a few more!"

"It's no good!" I groaned at last "We can't do anything against all this lot! We are done for, Valma!"

"At least we'll try and do what we came for," he answered curtly, "Remember, it is written in time that we shall succeed. Go through this false Earth and we'll attack Zagribud itself. Hurry, man…"

Dazed somewhat with the circling beams, I performed an erratic and crazy revolution in space, swung round, and held my breath whilst we hurtled towards the apparently solid mass of the false Earth. As we gathered momentum, my brow clouded. This mythical Earth was undoubtedly a marvellous formation—so skilful, so incredibly life-like. It almost looked.…

"Wait!" Valma called suddenly. "Wait… I have just recollected—the opposing ships came *round* this screen, not through it. It must *be* the Earth. Turn aside! Anything! Great God, what's gone wrong?"

"I can't stop now!" I panted, tearing at my controls. "At least, I don't think so. I—" I wrenched the steering propulsor around with dangerous force. We swung around broadside and hurtled in somersaults through the void. Then abruptly there came a deep roaring from outside— Atmosphere! Then this supposed image was indeed the Earth itself! With reeling brain I saw the globe of 25,000 A.D. somewhere over to the left of us, from the angle we were at.

We pitched and twirled right and left, all thought of our other companions in space forgotten.

"To the right! To the right!" Valma thundered, perspiration wet on his face.

Again we twisted, and shot round at almost inconceivable angles. I saw the loftiest tower in New York hurtling to meet us—a second later and it was far behind, missed by the barest fraction of an inch. Try as I would I could not steady the persistent lurching of our space-time machine…

We quaked and vibrated our way out into the void again at last—a tiny stretch of void between Earth and Ondon. Indeed, all Ondon lay before us. Once in the grip of the sinister influences housed upon that planet, and the struggle would be useless. With complete helplessness we were dragged down to the borders of Zagribud itself, and came to rest at last, fairly quietly, upon the great magnet itself.

Mechanically I switched off our engines and turned. In utter dismay we looked at each other.

"Incredible!" Valma muttered at last. "It proves Lee, that records are not to be relied on. There is no mention in past time of this happening; the record of the incident either was never made or else was lost. Beyond doubt, amazing though it is, Jelfel has succeeded after all in taking the genuine Earth instead of the false one. I cannot understand—"

"You never will," a laconic voice commented, and turning we beheld Elnek Jelfel himself in the doorway of our machine. The sealed door itself had vanished!

"You pardon the intrusion, I hope?" Jelfel asked pleasantly, stepping forward. "Doors are really the most childish things to remove when you carry a force-ray capable of transforming solid metal into pure vapor. That was why you heard nothing—just soundless disintegration. A new discovery—remarkably effective... Well, Commandant, again our paths have crossed—if I may resort to the melodramatic! Entirely your own fault, you know. Ah, Miss Folson, my deepest respects..." He bowed cynically. "And you, Valma, whose calculations did not quite equal my own. I am indeed having much attention in my humble efforts."

"Cut all this out, Jelfel!" I snapped, going close to him. "What have you done? How have you done it? The Earthlings—the Earth itself—"

"Precisely, the Earth itself, he conceded coldly."Since you chose to absent yourselves from attack whilst you travelled through time, you have only yourselves to blame. I was waiting for that move, in fact. In that time I discovered your trickery, by the sheerest chance! Whilst observing what I took to be Earth, I saw a comet pass clean *through* it and emerge on the other side. I knew at once that that could not be a solid world. I set to work with my brains, concentrated, and at last was able, as I have done before, to read your brain, Commandant. Really, you have a most malleable series of brain frequencies, I assure you... After that, the rest was easy. I threw a power area through space, deflected it so that it struck 30,000, and destroyed your false Earth and machinery for spoiling the influence of my Time Band Compressor...

"Then, I had merely to again move civilization forward as before, set my magnets to work, and draw the real Earth here whilst you were absent in time. Perfectly simple... You have a stray and entirely unimportant comet to thank for your downfall, otherwise, I confess I should never have known the difference. It was simple to compute from your brains how long you would be absent, Commandant, so the arrangement of my space-fleet was singularly easy. Frankly, I never expected you would live through the battle, but here you are—and I see there are seven other spaceships surviving out of the fleet. Too bad, my friends—really it is!

And, by the way, Valma was quite correct when he explained to you how I deluded your poor simple minds into thinking you had destroyed Zagribud…"

"Jelfel, it is written in Time that you shall fail!" Valma said grimly.

The ruthless Jovian smiled faintly, "Surely, Valma, a man of your high intelligence—so called—does not rely on faulty records?" he asked sardonically. "If I were to do that I could never accomplish anything for fear of what is written! But we have wasted enough time here. Come with me!"

We followed him from the magnet floor, through the doorway in the walls, and then for a space were held in sheer amazement by the sight before us. Filling all heaven was Earth itself, semi-inverted to our view, the city of New York 25,000 plainly distinguishable. Upon a great stretch of clear ground, clear of the magnet, lay massive space-machines.

Even as we watched some rose into the air and vanished towards the nearby Earth; others came out of invisibility and landed, disgorging parties of stocky Jovians, pushing upon a conveyance of some kind a number of inanimate Earthlings.

"What—what is all this?" Lan Ronnit gasped.

"Earthlings were placed in a state of suspended animation during the transit through space," Jelfel answered quietly. "I told you that before… Of course, I am afraid the transit has killed all Earthly vegetation, and so forth, but that need not be a great trouble. I can soon replace it; indeed the buried spores themselves, with warmth again, will burst into life. The frozen seas will thaw— Yes, Earth, when she returns to her normal place in the cosmos again, will be as fair a world as ever."

"This means that you've wrecked Mars, Venus, and Mercury as well!" Frot snapped out suddenly. "You—you celestial butcher. The shifting of Earth from its orbit must have—"

"It has not made the least difference to your Solar System," Jelfel answered with supreme calmness. "I only want Earth. Mars is barren in this period, Venus is composed of worm-like objects; Mercury is naught but a blistered sepulchre. Earth's motion to Ondon has been counteracted by beams of force upon the neighboring planets, which have held them steady, for of course, when my operations are complete, I intend to return Earth to its rightful place in the void, and my fellows and I will go with it—in Earthly bodies; That is why I have kept a clear space in the void to return your—or rather *our*—planet to… I hope you notice I do not destroy worlds unless I need to?" he concluded drily.

"I don't pretend to understand you, Jelfel," I said grimly. "You spare Mars, Venus, and Mercury—keep them safe—which is a decent thing to do. Yet you murder Earthlings as though they're flies. You're a mystery to me!"

"True, I have moments of restraint," he replied coolly. "Further, I am not murdering Earthlings—that would defeat my own ends."

"At the rate Earth has travelled through the void, it's a wonder it hasn't collapsed into pieces," Frot remarked thoughtfully.

"Pressure on all sides has prevented it," Jelfel replied curtly. "In fact, the atmosphere of Earth is now so saturated with my different energies and magnetisms that even if by some remote chance Earth were to fall back to its normal position in space, I doubt if anything unusual would happen. Earthlings could continue to survive, I am sure... But come at once. I do not propose to stand here giving explanations. Follow me!"

We followed him perforce to the mass of Zagribud, close at hand. I wondered at first why he adopted so ancient a method as walking, but presently the subtlety of the idea became apparent to me. As we went we caught up with the unconscious Earthlings lying upon the square, many-wheeled conveyances. A Jovian stood on the back of these machines and guided them across the rough ground. Men and women, even children, lay in utter somnolence, all unaware of the grim fate that was shortly destined to overtake them unless I could by some miracle prevent it.

Everywhere I looked I beheld the same evidences of approaching disaster for a vast number of the human race—and even those that escaped would be slaves of the Jovians! And yet... There was no mention in Earthly history of Jovian control over the world. I took heart a little at that remembrance. At least it was a crumb of consolation.

Once in the precincts of Zagribud itself, I gained for the first time, an idea of its real power and might. Jovians came and went with fixed purpose in the ground pedestrian ways, queer motor machines shot up and down special vehicle tracks, amazingly swift air machines skimmed the tops of the almost immeasurably lofty buildings. And in the center of the city reposed one gigantic tower, which I had noticed before, towering to a height of close on two thousand five hundred feet. I wondered to what depth its foundations were sunk. Jelfel saw my gaze directed towards it, and paused, ready again to reveal that queer streak in his complex nature—explanation of the unexplained.

"The Cosmos Tower," he remarked. "From there I take all my astronomical observations. It also contains, just below the summit, what I call my Cosmic Detector—a very useful instrument for registering if anything of danger is approaching from the void which is liable to threaten the security of Ondon. You must see it some time... Now, we will continue..."

We proceeded on our way, and as I went I sensed the incredible powers and scientific knowledge of the race of Zagribud, dwarfing anything ever attained in Earth's entire life history. This set me wondering. What was the *cause* of such amazing knowledge? Why was the Jovian race so wonderfully clever? It seemed that the theory that cleverness merely is the outcome of years of knowledge was at nought here. No, there was something different in the make-up of a Jovian brain to cause it—that was all...

Reaching Jelfel's headquarters, his instrument rooms, we sat down at his behest and for a while he performed his usual action of surveying us before speaking. I am inclined to think he always did this to weigh up our thoughts before giving voice to his own.

"Not so very long ago, Commandant, you effected an audacious rescue of some five hundred Earthlings—or nearly that number—from my surgical laboratories," he commented softly. "At that time Rath Granod was in control; had I been there you would never have succeeded. My late Supreme Master knew nothing of your ingenuity... This time, you will not perform such a feat. Even you will find it difficult to save anybody this time—everything is against you... Since the fates have been kind enough to bring you all back to me again after my effort to destroy you in the sun, I will keep to my original plan and make you my first Earthly subjects. I have always admired your body, Commandant—so powerful, so earthly! Much better than this cramped, Jovian one of mine with its artificial integuments. Have you ever stopped to think what is going to happen to your brains, my friend?"

"You said you were going to pot them, or something," I returned curtly.

"Yes, I said that—but I also said a better plan might occur to me. One has done so. Your brains will be transferred to Jovian bodies—yours to mine, and mine to yours! Is that clear?"

"You—you inhuman monster!" Elna shouted hoarsely, her gray eyes wide in horror.

"I can hardly be anything else but inhuman, since I am not earthly, my dear lady," Jelfel replied, and dealt her a merciless glance of his green eyes. "I shall not forget you, Miss Folson, either! You will become a Jovian servant on Earth—my particular servant, and will have to tolerate a Jovian body until the end of your days! You, Frot—you, Valma; you Ronnit! None of you shall escape! Curse you all..." Jelfel paused and then shrugged slightly.

"At times, emotions of a past time are liable to overcome my innate gentility," he commented drily. "During the operation, Commandant, I will have your face altered to be normally earthly; frankly your Jovian appearance does not appeal to me, since I am to have your body!" He clenched his thin, artificial hand. "I have two thousand subjects awaiting treatment in four hours!" he said bitterly. "And you four shall start the brain transference! Now think your way out of that, you fools!"

He turned and touched a button at his elbow. Four heavily armed Jovians entered, seized us, and without a word escorted us to underground dungeons, contiguous to the great, surgical laboratories. Within the crowded space we found countless other unfortunates, revived from the suspended animation, lying upon the floor or propped against the walls. It was a far more noisome place than the previous cage we had encountered, and indeed much darker... The five of us were bundled over to a far corner, and there took counsel amongst ourselves.

"This is the end of the road, all right," Lan Ronnit commented bitterly. "If this is the best effort of the cleverest man on Earth, Valma, I'm not interested!"

"I did my best," Valma replied sadly. "Unhappily I have failed. Why? Because Elnek Jelfel is the cleverer man. Which proves he was right in what he once said to you, Lee. The Age of Problems *is*, *was*, and *will be*, the greatest Intellectual Cycle in Earthly history. The various tenses cover it from every aspect of Time, I think," he added with a faint smile.

"It is glaringly obvious that no amount of trickery can get us out of this," Elna said very quietly. "I know when I'm beaten..." She sank her chin on her chest, not dejectedly but thoughtfully. She was made of stronger stuff than a weakling...

So the hours dragged slowly by, hours crammed with suspense. I tried everything I could think of to outwit Jelfel, but it was useless. The guards paced rhythmically outside the dungeon door; from the dungeon itself there was no escape. Neither had we any weapons...

I have little recollection of how the time really passed; my really clear recollection was of being roughly hauled to my feet along with my companions and seven other Earthlings. Including Elna, there were four women and seven men in the party, counting in myself.

We were taken from our prison and marched down a short passage of metal, then into the already familiar laboratory replete with its super-surgical devices... For myself I did not fear the operation itself; I had already tested Ondonian surgery, and knew it to be a science passing all Earthly skill... It was the fate of Earth itself that troubled me. For the life of me I could not understand why no record lay in Time of Jelfel's conquest of Earth, for there was certainly no escape this time...

Then suddenly my meditations were rudely interrupted by my coming face to face with Jelfel himself. He permitted that icy smile of his to flit across his hard face.

"Good evening, Commandant," he said pleasantly. "And pray accept my regrets for having called you 'Commander' until recently. I have only just discovered—a little while ago—your elevation to the rank of Commandant. Commander of Commanders."

"I received that honour four years ago, for overcoming you!" I retorted.

"Ah, yes—the fight that failed," he commented lightly. "You were quite brainy at that time. Commandant; even brought Miss Folson back to life after I killed her. I must thank you for that, though; that very fact made it possible for me to return to Earth again through her. Naturally, I soon discovered she was alive again… But now, I think, we are coming to the end of this little interplanetary duel, interesting indeed though it has been. You observe…" With a wave of his arm he motioned to eleven broad tables, about two feet high, drawn up under powerful radium lamps. Upon each of the ten of the tables reposed a Jovian, obviously unconscious. The table nearest us was empty.

"For you and me, Commandant," Jelfel explained smoothly, indicating it. "A very high honour for you, I assure you! The next four Jovians are female, the remaining seven male. Miss Folson, would you be so good as I to lie down on the second table—there, beside your future brain carrier!"

"I—I— Never!" Elna shouted hoarsely, clenching her fists desperately.

"Look here, Jelfel—!" I began dangerously.

"I would warn you Lee that any false move will result in your instant destruction!" Jelfel snapped venomously, all the veneer of culture abruptly vanishing and the real cruelty of his make-up becoming obvious. "I require your body, so don't jeopardise it! Elna Folson, do as I command you!" His green eyes blazed at her with terrific power; she seemed to sway before their intensity, but, as Jelfel had found before, her mind was a strong one.

"I'll—never—obey," she answered dully; but it was obvious his enormous mental force was slowly overcoming her. To my surprise, however, he did not proceed further with his hypnosis. Abruptly he turned towards me, suave and cultured again.

"If I hypnotise Miss Folson into doing my bidding her brain may be awkward to manage during the operation," he explained smoothly. "I have appealed to her innate graciousness, and she will not respond. The only alternative is force!" He made a quick motion and in response two surgeons from an army of twenty-two, grouped behind us in readiness, came forward. In another moment they had seized Elna in their tentaculate hands, raised her rapidly through the air, and deposited her on the second table beside the unconscious Jovian. She struggled mightily, but futilely… An anaesthetic cylinder hissed, and she presently relaxed limply and became still.

"Such methods pain me with the gentler sex, but sometimes it is necessary," Jelfel remarked. "Now, Commandant, get on that table, please."

"I'll see you in—" I began furiously.

"Do as I say!" he thundered, and, realizing the pitiful futility of defying him, I slowly obeyed—climbed on to the low table and lay down. A moment passed then he was beside me. "I will see you later, Commandant," he said coldly—and that was the last thing I remembered, save for the hiss of the anaesthetic…

The brain operation must have been completely painless, for I experienced nothing but peace during the transference. I seemed, as on that previous operation to my face, to awake almost immediately afterwards. There was no trace of headache, or weakness. Only an odd, unaccustomed stiffness.

"Better, Commandant?"

I looked up at that with a start, only to start again with extreme violence. Before me, it appeared, stood myself! In my T.L.C. uniform! My face was again Earthly, and, although not resembling the face I had been born, with, was passably terrestrial for all that. This vision automatically forced me to look down at myself… Black clothing! Stiff limbs! I felt my hand—Artificial! My legs also… With clumsy effort I got down to the floor.

"You've—you've done it!" I shouted hoarsely; then paused amazed at the sudden strain on the artificial vocal chords with which this amazing body was equipped. I did not wonder, at that moment, that Jelfel was glad to be rid of it.

"Of course—I always succeed," Jelfel answered, in my own voice, flavoured all the same with his own biting intonations. "There you have Miss Folson—"

I swung round to behold Elna slowly getting to her feet. She looked at me without a trace of recognition, then turned to Jelfel. Queer noises emerged from her mouth.

"These transferred Jovians will have to be taught Earthly language, and the use of Earthly vocal chords," Jelfel commented. "You, Commandant, are looking at the wrong person. The Jovian behind us is now Miss Folson!"

My brain reeled as I looked at the squat Jovian seated on the operating table.

"Elna! Elna!" I shouted hoarsely. "In heavens' name, Jelfel, what have you done?"

He smiled cynically. "Surely no explanations are necessary? The body of Elna is now the carrier of the brain of my closest female attendant. Etna's brains are therefore in the Jovian. You have a saying on Earth, Commandant, that exchange is no robbery. This is a literal interpretation of the phrase. I am afraid Miss Folson will find it a trifle difficult to converse with you, having Jovian vocal chords and no knowledge of the language. She will, however, understand your voice quite well, having still her own mind... At last I have gained that which I have so long sought!"

I could only stare, dazedly and blankly, overwhelmed by the knowledge of this super-genius's complete success. Little by little the truth came home to all of us—we were possessors of Jovian bodies. Anton Frot, knowing the Jovian language, was the only one who could speak to me in the Jovian tongue. Valma, Ronnit, and Elna were mute; could only signal affirmative or negative answers by head movements...

"You will stand by for further orders," Jelfel said presently. "I now have my particular advisers by me, in Earthly bodies, ready for the great Conquest. The others have yet to be attended to. In the interval, now that I have gained my end, you will be treated with relative freedom and I will have every comfort until I need you..."

He made a signal to his guards and we were taken with the unfortunate 'transferred' Earthlings from the great chamber...

CHAPTER 15

ASCENDANCY

The passing days of hopelessness had only one bright point. We were all allowed the freedom of the great city of Zagribud. Jelfel, as he had said, had accomplished his purpose, and knew we were now powerless to stop him. Day by day fresh Earthlings were transported from the now stationary Earth in the Ondonian heavens, and the inhuman butchery went on. Helpless, we five looked on, metaphorically chained hand and foot.

Then, as the time went on in suspense and idleness, I became aware of strange and unaccountable changes coming over me. I found myself understanding a lot of things that had puzzled me before! In some indefinable sense I was actually becoming much cleverer! Once the condition commenced, this heightened knowledge increased day by day, until finally, puzzled, I confided in Frot—or rather in the Jovian who carried his brain.

"There is only one explanation," he said, in Jovian. "You are now reacting to the brain transference, and something is happening which Jelfel never reckoned with. The power of a brain always relies upon the quality of the blood-stream that feeds it. Thus, at last, I begin to see why Jelfel and his fellow Jovians are so brilliantly clever. The air of both Jupiter and Ondon is highly oxygenated—creates a blood stream different from ours, which results in intellectual power of almost uncanny perfection. The actual brains, I imagine, are no different from ours, but they are treated to a better blood-stream, which results in knowledge which Earth can never approach... But, here is the point! You now possess the body that was formerly owned by the most brilliant man in Jovian history; there is nothing to stop your brain finally becoming like his, fed, as it is, by that perfect blood stream. We others will get cleverer also—I myself feel as you do already—but we will never approach your perfection, since, in some way, Jelfel's body seems superior in some indefinable way..."

"Good heavens!" I breathed. "Then—then the very thing that Jelfel has looked for, fought for, even murdered for, is going to prove his undoing! If I am increasing in knowledge, it stands to logic that he and his contemporaries, who possess *our* bodies, will decrease with our earthly bloodstream!"

"Exactly," Frot assented keenly. "Lee, Jelfel is going to destroy himself in his finish… However, lie low for a while and we'll watch what transpires."

Communications by written word to Valma, Elna and Ronnit confirmed our hopes. All of us were becoming rapidly cleverer—were approaching that glorious perfection of knowledge that formerly had been the birthright of a Jovian. The possibilities opened up before me like a shining vista…

From then on we all practiced our mentalities as much as possible, exerting them to respond to new problems, and each time we found ourselves the masters! With remarkable rapidity I found myself ascending to the level of Jelfel himself. I wondered how he was faring.

We found out how he was faring very shortly afterwards…

Towards the close of one of the days we chanced to find ourselves in the vicinity of the power-house for the magnet, the one medium that held Earth near Ondon. The familiar mist of the evening enveloped everything, when suddenly there came from its midst the voice of Jelfel—or of rather myself, since he had my body.

"You fool! You say the Retractor is faulty, has been hastily repaired after that short circuit—that it isn't radiating power as it should? Well, repair it! Why drag me here for that?"

"But, Master, the repairs made before are not good enough," a Jovian voice replied. "Only you understand how to make a thorough overhaul of the defect… Since a guard fell into this machinery, it has never been properly right—"

"Very well, I will repair it—but your work for me is done!"

We heard the sound of footsteps as Jelfel entered the building, then, with infinite caution the five of us moved to the doorway and peered within. The Retractor was, fortunately, fairly close to the door—it was indeed the machinery composed of that ill-fated guard in the struggle to obtain the power-house. Jelfel paced about thoughtfully for a while, stroking his chin. I found again enormous difficulty at crediting it was my body he was using… At last he made a gesture of impatience.

"I cannot repair it tonight, Zal-Jafor. It requires thinking out. The energy is certainly escaping somewhere—somehow. I am bemused tonight."

"Bemused, Master!" the Jovian expostulated. He was actually a Jovian, by the way, possessing his own brain and body. "But, with every passing moment, due to the leak in power, which is becoming steadily worse, Earth is drifting further and further away from Ondon. You see, your magnetic machinery on Earth, which you remote-control, is getting stronger than this magnetic, due to pull from the Earth's sun… Master, you have got to stop the leak, or lose the Earth!"

"Who repaired this Retractor?" Jelfel asked abruptly. "Or, I should say, who attempted to repair it?"

"Rof-Elsor—but then, he is not so brilliant as you, Your Serenity."

"And where is Rof-Elsor now? He might stop the trouble."

"Rof-Elsor, so far as I know, is somewhere on Earth," Zal-Jafor replied grimly. "No, Master, this is a task for you alone—"

"Well, I cannot do it now," Jelfel retorted. "I will come in the morning and go into the matter. In the meantime, try and locate Rof-Elsor…"

"As you wish, Master."

We backed away into the friendly mist as Jelfel came striding out, to presently be swallowed up in the gloom.

"It's working!" Frot breathed. "We're winning—and quite unintentionally! A few more days and Jelfel will be cornered! With his brain power decreasing, and ours on the increase, he'll not stand a chance. Come—a little planning is called for."

We turned to depart, then with the peculiar suddenness for which it was remarkable, the mist dispersed into the upper air, revealing to our eyes the amazing sight to which we had now become fairly well inured…. But tonight there was a change! The Earth was noticeably further away in the heavens. Although it filled nearly all the sky above us, the view was not as distinct as formerly. Already the leakage in the magnet was having its effect…

"We've got to think things out as rapidly as possible," Frot remarked. "If Jelfel can't stop the Earth, it will slowly move back through the void, drawn by our sun, until it is drawn completely into the sun. At all events we must stop that—indeed we know we shall by Earth being in existence at all in later time! We can take it for granted that Jelfel will not repair his magnet; by tomorrow he'll be unable to compute how to do it—but that is not our point.

"We can let the Earth drift further and further away, and turn our attention to destroying all means of communication between it, save one. That one will be a time-space machine for ourselves to use the instant we need it. We can hide it somewhere; with his decreasing knowledge Jelfel won't be able to read our minds and discover its whereabouts… Yes, for the moment we must concentrate on saving any more Earthlings from butchery, and force Jelfel to give them back their own bodies."

"I agree—but we don't want *our* own bodies back yet," I responded quickly. "If we do that our brain power will commence to fail. Our bodies can wait awhile…"

"Right enough—but we must help the others."

And this plan firmly fixed in our minds we turned our faces once more towards the brilliantly lighted enormities of Zagribud.

* * * *

The following day we had our plans laid. I myself was to carry out the most important part in this gradually improving battle with Jelfel. And for this part I removed the artificial integuments that made me Earthly in appearance and became, of course, an apparently natural Jovian. Attiring myself in clothes borrowed from Frot—for he of course possessed a normal Jovian's attire—I set forth for Jelfel's own headquarters in the heart of Zagribud, leaving my four companions in the little domicile that had been assigned to us for the time being.

I felt enormously courageous as I made my way amongst the masses of Jovians in the pedestrian ways; my knowledge was equal to, and even superior, to theirs, since I owned the body of their Master…

Entering the great edifice that I had learned was his headquarters, I made my way through the various passages until I reached his instrument rooms. Two armed guards barred my path.

"An urgent message for the Master," I said, using my vocal chords as well as possible to simulate a Jovian voice. They moved aside at that, to my relief, and I entered the great instrument room and closed the door tightly behind me. In the distance, before his countless switchboards, stood Jelfel in my body. I advanced slowly, and he turned to face. "Well?" he demanded curtly, also speaking Jovian with difficulty with my Earthly voice. "What is it?"

"Elnek Jelfel, you have a lot to answer for!" I said grimly, in normal language. "Perhaps you have difficulty in recognizing me like this?"

"Ah, so it is the Commandant himself!" he said cynically. "Still pestering me, I observe. I shall have to hurry your transportation to Earth. Why have you risked your life coming here at all?"

"Just to have a chat," I returned steadily. "And also to use one or two of your very valuable instruments."

"Remarkable, Commandant!" He smiled coldly. "Anything else?"

I went closer. "Listen to me, Jelfel! I am gaining the upper hand— and you know it! You're not so clever as you were. You couldn't repair the magnet last night! Earth is slowly drifting away!"

"You know a lot," he answered slowly. "The magnet is certainly faulty, but I am going to repair it—"

"It's no good, Jelfel, you're losing ground—otherwise you'd stop that leakage *now*!" I intervened curtly. "Do you know *why* you're losing intelligence? Because your blood stream was the cause of your terrific mentality. I am now obtaining that benefit; you are becoming clogged—doltish!"

His expression changed; it was manifest the idea had not occurred to him before.

"Further, you're going to get worse!" I proceeded mercilessly. "I am going to get better. Your own villainy has proved your undoing!"

"I'll soon alter that!" he snapped out. "I will have my blood stream changed so as to be the same as yours!"

I smiled twistedly. "Yes? How, Jelfel?"

"Why, I'll—" He hesitated, and I realized how much indeed the mastermind was collapsing. Formerly he would have instantly reeled off some amazing and practicable formula; this time he paused, shot a glance at me, and then pondered deeply.

"You can't conceive it—any more than I could have done in my own body!" I said grimly. "You've been an inhuman devil, Jelfel—taken advantage of those with less intellect than yourself—have maimed and terrorized the population of an entire planet. But you're going to start paying for it now. Little by little... Until at last will come—annihilation!"

"Don't be a fool!" he retorted bitterly. "I will show you how Jelfel treats such as you—"

"Even your personality is changing," I proceeded inexorably. "You're half Jelfel—and half somebody else—maybe me. Something half-Jovian and half-Earthly. An interesting species—a cosmic half-breed! Your manner is different; you've lost that persuasive brilliance, your powers of mass-hypnosis—"

"You—" he exploded, taunted beyond endurance, and whipped out my own ray gun from his belt.

"Drop that!" I commanded fiercely, staring immovably into his eyes. *"Drop it!"*

But my mind was not then strong enough for that. He pressed the button on the ray gun, but instantly one of my two sets of right hands shot up and whirled the instrument from his grip. With one rush I bore him to the floor; then forced him up again using the ray-gun to my own advantage.

"You've evidently forgotten that that ray-gun couldn't hurt me in any case," I said sarcastically. "Earthly ray-guns are useless on Jovian matter, you know. You were going to solve that little problem—evidently something else that's too much for you in your present condition. Now do exactly as I tell you; I don't want to destroy my own body if I can help it—I shall want it back later. Issue orders immediately for the restoration of earthly brains to their natural bodies. Everybody—save me. I am staying this way for a while."

"You think you can do this?" he demanded savagely.

"I know I can," I returned calmly, "Hurry!"

He hesitated again, glanced at the ray-gun, then turned to an instrument on the wall.

"Not that way!" I intervened curtly. "You're coming with me—to the surgical laboratories. It's a safer way. And remember the ray gun. Don't dare make signals—"

With a sudden mighty backward sweep of his arm, however, he knocked the ray-gun from my tentaculate hand and hurled himself forward. In his anxiety to overcome me, however, he was a trifle too hasty. He stumbled over my smaller body, tripped forward, and, being still unable to fully calculate my five-foot-ten length, struck his forehead a stunning blow on the instrument board behind me. He reeled, clutching his brow, and in that moment I seized my chance. I gave him one huge shove and sent him stumbling dazedly into a recess. One clean movement and I had slammed the door upon him, ramming the bolts into position. A dull thud from within a moment afterwards convinced me that he had relapsed into unconsciousness from the blow.

At top speed I raced into the adjoining apartment and gazed hungrily around the instrument jammed walls. At last I beheld that which I sought and fully understood—the marvellous Emanation Detector, which by a process of vibrations and calculation recorded on a screen any person or any object within a distance of twelve miles.

Rapidly I calculated. Elna's emanation number I knew, from past experience, was 1016. Immediately I swung round the pointer to the required number, and adjusted the switches. Presently the screen blurred, then there came into clear view the Jovian female who was occupying Elna's body. I beheld her actually at the space-ship grounds, talking apparently to another 'transferred' Earthling, preparatory to entering a space ship... Another few minutes and my task would be extremely difficult—if she set forth into space.

I searched around and beheld the almost familiar sixth-dimensional Rotator. A snapping of switches and altering of frequency dials—I apprehended the device almost as clearly as Jelfel himself with my improved mentality—and that amazing movable dimension was pivoted in space, and calculated to exactly strike the spot where the bogus Elna was standing. Came a thud in the instrument room, and there she stood before me.

"What does this mean?" Elna's voice demanded—but it had none of her natural sweetness of tone. Obviously the Jovian female had been taught the Earthly language.

"You'll soon find out!" I responded tersely, and then I had a great inner struggle with myself to convince my mind that I was not actually hurting Elna herself in that which followed. I seized her by the shoulders, threw her with a crash to the floor, then rapidly gagged her and bound her to the massive pillars of the Rotator.

"You'll do like that for a while!" I barked. "You're going to give that body back to its rightful owner..."

I then set to work to calculate the correct emanations of Frot, Ronnit and Valma. Satisfied at last I set to work again with the Emanation Detector, and was fortunate in finding that none of the three had left Ondon. The sixth-dimensional Rotator soon brought them into the laboratory, one by one, and as fast as they appeared I overpowered them.

So far matters had gone fairly smoothly. Jelfel presumably was still unconscious, for no sounds proceeded from the locked recess in the adjoining apartment. Certainly the blow had been violent enough to occasion such a condition...

I next turned my attention to the radio apparatus—or rather television machine—and presently tuned in my own particular domicile in Zagribud. (All domiciles in the city were equipped with both transmitting and receiving apparatus).

Presently the Jovian face of Frot appeared on the screen before me.

"Frot, I've succeeded in getting back all the rightful bodies," I said quickly. "All of you go straight to the surgical laboratories; tell the surgeons Jelfel has sent you there. I'll fix the rest. Be with you in about ten minutes."

"Right—I'll attend to it," Frot replied in Jovian, and switched off.

The remainder of the time I spent in arranging my four captives in a neat "bundle," directly in the focus of the Sixth dimensional Rotator—and also in calculating the distance and angle of the surgeries. Then, glancing over my captives I pressed the automatic button. Once more that dizzy sensation of headlong falling through space, and the vision of the great laboratories materialized before my eyes. So much for Jovian mathematics; I began to realize how rapidly I was equalling Jelfel himself in intelligence....

Four Jovian surgeons advanced in amazement as I appeared and looked down interrogatively at the bodies on the floor. Behind me, I noticed my four comrades, anxiously waiting.

"Orders from Elnek Jelfel," I curtly said in Jovian. "Transfer these bodies back to their rightful owners—immediately!"

"You cannot give us orders in that fashion. Jelfel himself must speak," said the foremost surgeon: a remark which I had fully expected and the answer to which was cut and dried.

"Whom else but the super-intelligent Master could project these four bodies, and myself, here?" I demanded. "I have been given those orders; it is your duty to obey. This operation is to be performed because the brains of the accursed Earthlings are becoming clever by reason of the change. Hurry—fools!"

"Truly, only His Serenity could gather these Earthlings together so rapidly and send them here *via* the Rotator," the surgeon said to his colleagues. "The matter is in order. We will proceed at once…"

The main reason for them crediting my story was, I think, my own abstinence from being re-transferred to my own body. Otherwise I doubt if my ruse would have succeeded. Not for an instant did they suspect my identity; my complete detachment from the proceedings convinced them. Nor had they mentality high enough to read thoughts… That had been Jelfel's particular prerogative…

I watched intently whilst that brilliant brain transference took place—saw the neat, bloodless action of golden drills, the glitter of electric knives and saws, and smelt the sweetly-odorous ointment that welded the cuts into position with perfect, instantaneous smoothness. Then the restorative. The patients rose slowly from their tables.

"Sa-Sandy!" Elma breathed shakily, clutching my tentaculate hand. "I've—I've got my own body back for—"

"Hush! No names!" I said to her, sharply. "Thank God these fellows don't know the Earth language…" I stopped and turned abruptly on the surgeons. "These Jovians, to whom their rightful bodies have been restored—see that they are imprisoned. His Serenity's orders!"

"Imprisoned?" the leading surgeon repeated in surprise.

"You dare to question the word of the Master?" I demanded, and at that he looked away.

"So be it," he assented solemnly.

"Quickly, out of here," I breathed, "They'll be asking me next why I'm using two languages. Come—there's a lot to be done yet."

We left as rapidly as possible; evidently the Jovian surgeons believed me to be a type of intermediary between Earthly and Jovian peoples, understanding both languages. Whatever it was, they didn't attempt to follow us. The fact, that I assumed the role of a guard, was the main reason for us passing unmolested to my domicile. Once inside, I shut the door and turned to my restored comrades.

"We're on the up-grade!" I said tensely. "What I propose doing, Frot, is to use your original plan and shatter Zagribud with sound waves. We have sound-projectors on the ships that survived the battle in space, and they should still be on the magnet where we left them. Valma made a fine job of those machines—"

"Truly," Valma assented. "I have turned them into perfect weapons, with no trace of dangerous recoil. Frot's idea and my perfecting processes have produced a masterpiece."

"I propose that we put a projector at the top of that great Tower in the city's center and rain vibration death on these devils," I went on grimly. "Jelfel is locked safely in a cupboard until I see fit to release him. I shan't harm him yet in case I lose my own body. That clear?"

"Yes—but what of the Earthlings who have been transferred into Jovians?" Frot asked.

"Unfortunately, we can't do anything about that as yet. It would take much too long. This is a case where the innocent are bound to suffer with the guilty. We can't discriminate, time is too precious. We cannot undo what has been done, but we most certainly can—and will—stop this butchery going any further. At nightfall we'll find a good time-space machine left, out of the few survivors that got here from the fight in the void, remove it to a place of safety ready for immediate departure, and then set to work to destroy the city. That is our plan…"

CHAPTER 16

IMPENDING DOOM

At nightfall we set forth. I was rather puzzled by the continued silence of Jelfel since my attack upon him in the morning; I had come to learn that silence on his part was usually the forerunner of exceptional, and frequently deadly, action—but I took heart now in my obviously superior knowledge.

The five of us made our way through the usual Jovian crowds in our transit of Zagribud, until presently we came to the comparatively quiet opening to the spaces beyond. It had passed the "mist-hour," and in the reflected light from the city and the glow from the slowly receding Earth we could distinctly behold the towering walls of the distant magnet, upon the floor of which there should be lying eight space-time ships—seven of them flight-worthy, for the door had been blown away from ours—unless Jelfel had had them moved...

"The Earth certainly is rapidly receding," Frot said quietly, as we progressed. "Much more of the sky is visible now. This movement won't do the Earth much good, I'm afraid. Tidal waves and such-like—"

"But didn't Jelfel say his rays and beams had so saturated Earth's atmosphere that it would take no harm if by some chance it suddenly were returned to its normal position in space?" Elna asked.

"That's right—he did!" Ronnit exclaimed. "That means Earth is relatively safe, Lee."

"Yes; we hope so, anyway," I replied. "It looks as though the Earth-Ondon transit stunt has stopped for a while. See—the spaceship grounds are quiet."

"Only because the massacre is done for the day," said Valma gravely. "They don't work by night, you know. A few more hours, and we'll blow the entire fleet to atoms. That'll stop any more of it...! But here's the magnet."

We passed at that moment through the doorway in the wall and entered the floor of the magnet. In an instant we noticed the lack of attractive force as compared to our earlier experience. Beyond doubt the magnet had lost at least fifty percent of its effectiveness.

"This is luck!" I breathed. "The lack of power will enable us to get our space-time machine into the air without being dragged back." I looked about me. "Well, Jelfel doesn't seem to have thought it worth his while to destroy these ships; they're all here. We'll take the second one—ours is useless without an air-lock door. Come on."

"I cannot see why we don't hurl vibration at Zagribud from the ship instead of from the Tower," Frot remarked.

"For two reasons," I answered. "One because we want a steady ground and a clear outlook on all sides—such as only the Tower can give—and the other so that we can be sure of what we're hitting. If we tried it from this ship we might hit the wrong place, and accidently destroy Jelfel, and incidentally my own body. I don't want that."

"Right enough. Lead on."

We entered the space-time machine and found it in comparative order. Obviously Jelfel had had more important problems to tax his gradually failing mind. Closing the door and moving the controls was but the work of a moment, and to our delight we rose into the air immediately, the power-effectiveness of the magnet too slight to hold us when our engines raced at full power. Once out of the direct line of the magnetism we did, of course, revert to normal powers of propulsion and ascension.

Seven minutes later we were floating high and silently about the massive city, then gently we dipped down and landed, with hardly a jar, upon the flat summit of the mighty two thousand five hundred foot Tower.

"There!" I said, switching off the engines. "We have two things here. Perfect and steady outlook, and a fine hiding place for the time-space machine, when it's needed. The last place Jelfel would think of looking in."

"Well thought out," Valma murmured.

Presently, with as much silence as we could manage in that dense air, we descended to the platform, carrying between us the sound-vibration projector with its ample lengths of power-cable...

Then suddenly, amazingly, the platform was alive with Jovian guards! The first intimation I had of the fact was a scream from Elna, and swinging around, I beheld her in the clutch of a powerfully built Jovian, struggling with all her power. Even as I stared she swung dangerously near the low rail. Below was a sheer drop to certain death.

"Quickly—pile into them!" I shouted hoarsely. "It's a trap! Throw them overboard—no time for ceremony! This is Jelfel's doing, I suppose..."

And the battle commenced immediately...

Aided by my earthly knowledge of wrestling and gifted with the mighty strength and four sets of hands of a Jovian, I soon gave a dangerous account of myself… The guard, who was bending Elna backwards over the rail, I suddenly seized by the shoulder, swung him around, and simultaneously planted my fists in his face. He tripped backwards, struggling to regain his equilibrium, but I inexorably followed up my advantage, clutched him round what was presumably his waist, and heaved with all my power. He rose ponderously from the ground, reeled sideways, then with an unearthly yell went toppling over the rail into the light-spotted abyss two thousand feet below…

I swung around to meet the onward attack of another Jovian, then suddenly Frot let forth a terrific shout. *"Elna!* Lee! For God's sake—"

I caught in my breath in horror, dodged the onrushing guard, and hurled myself forward. Another guard had seized Elna and borne her to the floor. She, unable to save herself, tripped over the flexed cable of the sound projector and rolled to the edge of the platform. The Jovian, perforce, relaxed his grip, which only served to make matters worse. I had one last glimpse of Elna's face, utter despair in her eyes, then she screamed hoarsely and vanished over the platform edge! Immediately afterwards something thumped heavily against the platform rail, but I was too horror-stricken to notice it.

The same guard came for me the instant he beheld my motionless attitude, but quite abruptly I saw his advance. Consumed with utter fury and fear I dealt him a bone-splintering on the jaw. He seemed to shoot backwards with the frightful impact; my whole double-fore-armed arm stung with the blow. In another instant he had struck the rail, failed to balance with his short body, and toppled helplessly into the void.

Instantly I was at the rail peering into the darkness; then I started violently. For the voice of Elna floated up to me.

"Sandy! Sandy! Down here!"

I strained my eyes, and at last beheld what had happened. In her fall Elna had made a last desperate clutch at the cable of the sound-projector, and was now swinging by her hands forty feet below the Tower summit. The thud I had heard had been caused by the projector itself slamming against the rail with the sudden pull. By a concession of Providence it had wedged itself and saved her from instant destruction. Even so, the cable was not meant to stand the strain of a heavy young woman's full weight.

"You attend to these remaining guards," I threw out, to the fiercely fighting Frot, Ronnit and Valma. "I'm going to help Elna…" Instantly I swung myself over the side of the platform, gripping the girder-work for all I was worth with my four hands. I went down cautiously perforce, hoping against hope that both the cable and Elna would be able to hold out long enough. As I went the cable before my eyes moved to-and-fro against the light from the Earth-ridden sky. A sense of giddiness sought to seize me at the awful abyss that yawned below in the hazy darkness. Instant death!

Then I again took a grip on myself and went downwards, but to my horror I now beheld the cable unravelling thread by thread beneath the strain! Stark horror swept in upon me. I struggled down faster, shouting encouragement, and once nearly missed my hold, to hang in shuddering horror to the main girders for an instant.

At last I came level with Elna, swinging like a pendulum in the void.

"Throw no strain on that cable!" I implored desperately. "Take it easy! Now, try and swing this way!"

"What am I to do?" her voice shouted. "I can't hang on much longer. Cramp in my hands—"

"Swing—towards me!" I counselled, admiration coming to me at her calm courage in her predicament. "Steady—now…" I watched, sick with fear lest the cable should snap and fling her to destruction.

With a skill that would have done credit to an old-world acrobat she began to impel her body backwards and forwards towards the Tower—a feat which would have been useless without me to catch her finally, otherwise she would undoubtedly have done it before now. I waited to seize her.

Then at last she came within reaching distance, and simultaneously the cable broke with a sharp snap. If ever I blessed a Jovian body, I blessed it then. For, holding on with two hands to the girders I was able to lean out with my two remaining sets of hands and clutched her as she jolted down into my grip. Another moment and I had dragged her up with superhuman strength and dumped her in a sitting position on the girder by my side.

She wiped perspiration from her forehead with the back of a red-raw hand—the cable had cut bloodless wheals into her flesh.

"Phew! Sandy, I can think of better places than that to try out acrobatics!" she panted. "Look at my wrists—not a bit of skin left hardly… But thank God for that cable—and you!" She looked at me for a space, sat recovering her breath. Then she looked down into the abyss and shuddered. "Where do we go from here?"

I looked above and behind me. For the first time I noticed a small lighted building, with three walls only, in the centre of the girder work near the Tower top. From it, stairs led to the Tower platform.

"Better go that way," I counselled, and helped her to her feet.

Carefully we struggled on our way along the massive cross-beams and lateral supports until at length we came within the three-sided division. It was quite brightly lighted with roof-bulbs. Upon one of the three walls reposed a large glass-faced dial, and in the centre of the floor a type of chart, resembling the Ondonian sky itself.

For a space I was deeply puzzled, then very gradually, as I studied the receding Earth reflecting on the shining surface of this floor chart, and beheld various needles quivering on the glass-faced dial, it came to me what the apparatus was. Jelfel's Cosmic Detector, as he had called it—for charting the movements of celestial bodies and to warn him of the presence of unwanted occurrences in outer space.

Quietly I explained all this to Elna and she looked at me with a quizzical pair of gray eyes as I inspected the meters with deep interest, I comprehending most of them as I went, thanks to my Jovian mentality…

"Well, what do you make of it all, Sandy?" she asked at last.

I shrugged; then at a sudden commotion I was instantly on my guard. Three figures came clattering down the metal ladderway from above.

"Oh, it's you!" I exclaimed in relief, beholding Valma, Ronnit and Frot. "What has happened to the guards?"

"We laid them out between us; they're unconscious on the platform," Frot replied. "Hello! What's all this?" He looked about him, and briefly I explained.

"This is interesting here," I remarked, indicating the glass-faced dial. "See this needle—it indicates the presence of anything liable to upset the Ondonian system. H'm—that's odd!" I looked more closely at the meter. "This needle is pointing to the Jovian words for 'Extreme Danger.' Now what the deuce is causing that, I wonder?"

Frot peered outside at the sky through the girders. "We can't see much of the sky with the Earth taking up so much room," he remarked, then quickly. "That will be the explanation, Lee. Earth itself is causing the disturbance."

I shook my head. "Not as I see it, Frot. The Earth is receding, therefore, it's not dangerous. No—there's something[1] else. Some terrific emanations in the cosmic which are affecting this delicate recording system. I wonder if—"

"Good heavens—look!" cried Lan Bonnit abruptly, pointing. *"Look!"*

At that identical moment two massive crescents, gleaming silver, were appearing from the edges of the slowly receding Earth—mighty objects that formerly had been hidden by the nearer bulk of Earth itself. With each passing moment they came nearer into view from their Earth-eclipse—one on each side of the globe.

"What the devil…" Frot began, and paused indecisive; then like a light, infinite remembrance came to me. I clutched his arm so tightly that he winced.

"Frot, those two planets which we saw before from the top of the power-house—then far off. They've been coming gradually nearer all this time, and until now the Earth has hidden them from our view. These instruments don't lie—they show what's coming. Quickly, man—from these instruments, which record rate of speed, direction, and everything else, can you compute what's going to happen to Earth? It looks as though she'll be jammed between them! Hurry—hurry!"

Immediately he turned to the instruments, and with assistance from all of us, and Valma in particular, charted the figures that were necessary. Then he set to work with the mathematical computations, to look up at last with an astounded, half-frightened expression on his keen visage.

"Lee, the most astounding thing!" he exclaimed. "Earth will pass safely between those invading planets—and their pull will save Earth from being drawn into our sun! Will, in fact, return Earth almost without tremor to its natural position in space. But—here is the amazing part of it all! Ondon has been slightly deflected in its orbit, as we know, by the force of my sound-projector vibration flung from Paliso, and it has made it that Ondon's orbit will pass *dead between those two planets!* It means the utter destruction of this world!"

"Good heavens—annihilation!" I breathed tensely. "The end of Ondon!"

"Exactly," Frot assented. "In fact, the end of the entire Ondonian Solar System. The terrific upheaval will wreck the remaining three planets—probably hurl them off into outer space. And to think that that sound-projector of mine has caused, in an indirect way, the destruction of everything! It's astounding! Almost as though it had been planned… Yes, Ondon will be crushed to powder."

"How long before the end comes?" I demanded quickly.

"At the rate of progress it will only be safe to stay another three nights on this world. By tomorrow, indeed, I anticipate the first upheavals caused by the approach of these two worlds into this system." He stopped, a puzzled frown on his high forehead. "It all seems so strange—so predestined. As though an actual mind had arranged it—"

"A mind!" I echoed hoarsely. "Great heavens, Frot, you're right! The mind of the Planet Brain! You remember! One of those two planets is the Brain itself—and the other is the mate it told us it was seeking. The Planet Brain has planned this, you may be certain. What fools we've been not to think of it before!"

"The point is, what's next?" Lan Ronnit asked cryptically.

"We'll carry on with our original plan," I answered grimly. "As soon as Jelfel realises what's happening he'll be off into space like a shot. We've got to stop him doing that, at all costs. Our future home is on top of this Tower, guarding our space-time machine—our only link with Earth and safety. We're all right for food. The other thing to do is to explode all those spaceships and all Jelfel's machines with your sound-projector, Frot. Yes, we've got him at last! But somehow, before we go, I've got to have my body back!"

CHAPTER 17

THE PASSING OF ELNEK JELFEL

We turned about, climbed the staircase, and presently regained the platform. To repair the broken cabling of our sound-projector was but the work of a moment. I glanced at the guards securely fastened to the railings, then at Frot.

"Everything ready?" I asked quietly, my hand on the guiding-handle of the machine.

He nodded, and immediately I pressed the button, directing the faint beam occasioned by the magnetite crystals towards the distant spot where lay the fleet of dormant spaceships. Instantly the space became alive with the most unholy series of explosions. Blue-white light poured upwards to the skies accompanied by dense columns of thick, acrid smoke. Ruthlessly I kept the projector going until the entire area was a seething holocaust of smoke and flame.

"A marvellous weapon, Frot!" I panted, between intervals. "How are we faring? Ask Valma."

Valma, at the controls of our periscopic telescope aboard the ship finally reported that the entire fleet used for Earth-Ondon transit had been reduced to ashes. At that, I smiled grimly.

"Now comes a point," I said. "If I destroy the magnet, will the sudden stoppage of power result in Earth going to destruction, or—"

"You couldn't do a better thing," Frot interrupted. "It will enable it to reach its own natural position in space before anything can happen, and these two planets will keep it in position. Carry on!"

So again I pressed the button, and that deadly vibration focussed on the distant mass of the infernal magnet. The air itself seemed as though it would explode as the terrific force of one energy struck the magnetism of the other, resulting in instant disintegration. The monster-magnet, that had enslaved a planet, vanished in a blinding sheet of flame, and with it went the remaining space-time ships that had come from Earth. There was only ours left on Ondon! Unless Jelfel had others hidden away, which was not very probable.

"Now the power-house!" Frot breathed, tight-lipped and eager.

We all stood at the rail and watched that miracle of machinery disrupt itself with colossal violence. Debris soared skywards, smoke belched its way through the air and along the ground. The whole mass of Zagribud and the Tower trembled with the concussions...

"And that leaves only Jelfel!" I breathed at last. "Ronnit, you stay here and guard the ship whilst we go and look for Jelfel. He's going to have an operation performed under pressure. Come along, the rest of you."

We descended the first flight of steps, passed the Cosmic Detector room, and then came into the normal galleries—when quite suddenly we were firmly seized from behind. I beheld a small army of Jovians surrounding us.

"Right into the trap, Earthling!" sneered the nearest. "His Serenity is awaiting you! Come!"

The four of us put up a stiff resistance, but it was useless. Cursing and fuming at our ready acquiescence to take things for granted, we were piloted down corridors and staircases and *via* elevators, until at last we entered the familiar instrument rooms of Jelfel's own headquarters. He rose from a chair as we entered.

"Oh, it's you, Commandant!" he snapped out viciously. "Sit down— you and the others! You can go," he concluded in Jovian, and the guards departed.

"I escaped from the cupboard, Lee," he said laconically. "You see, the locks opened from inside as well as out, so the moment I recovered consciousness I released myself. A trifling point you missed, I imagine. My Thought-Imager revealed your thoughts to me— Yes, I confess I could not read them myself. My brain is indeed becoming badly clogged with useless earthly blood." He hesitated, than leaned forward. "Commandant, I realise that I have fought a battle rare between worlds— and—and have lost it!"

"It's about time!" I snapped. "Elna was nearly killed tonight by your damned guards up on the Tower platform!"

"I know all about that. I had those men placed there, following your thoughts, and of course I hoped to again capture you by surprise and destroy you for all time. You were too quick for the guards, however. You have blasted all my spaceships to powder, you have ruined my magnet. You have broken all links with escape to another world—save one." He smiled strangely.

"You may have a space-time machine, Commandant, but I still have the sixth dimensional Rotator. I can project myself and some of my most intellectual comrades to yet another world..." He paused and seemed to consider; his next words were surprising. "I shall not again try to seize the Earth. I have decided it is better to seek an easier planet, where the inhabitants are not so tenacious in their opposition. A pity, for Earth is indeed a fair world...

"I find that Ondon is doomed. I have just been busy with my refractor, connected up with my Cosmic Detector in the Tower, and I have seen that Ondon's fate is to be crushed to powder. Before that happens I shall escape. But you will not...!" He smiled devilishly. "My intelligence is no longer capable of conceiving an interesting fate, so I will resort to the purely melodramatic. The four of you here shall be chained to the ground—to await the moment of cosmic catastrophe—alone on a doomed world! As for the space-time machine on the Tower top, containing Lan Ronnit, I will blow that to atoms—*now!*"

He reached forth his hand before we had an opportunity to stop him, but at the same instant the great instrument room trembled mightily from end to end. The floor under our feet heaved like a miniature ocean roller. Instantly I was flung off my feet, to be tossed with my three companions and Jelfel into a corner. Delicate glass tubes and dials splintered to pieces with the sudden shock—but the most noticeable damage was the throwing out of alignment, in the next apartment, of the sixth dimensional Rotator.

"Gravitational upheaval! The encroaching planets!" Frot panted hastily. "The trouble is coming earlier than I calculated owing to you stopping that magnet, Lee. Earth's movement is upsetting the equilibrium."

The opportunity in my hands, I literally seized it. I hurled Jelfel to his feet, and against the four of us he stood no chance. He glared balefully as I whipped my ray gun from his belt. "Listen here, Jelfel!" I said grimly. "I've got you where I want you, now. I want my body, but I detest you enough to blow you, and incidentally my own body, to pieces, if you dare to make a false move... Go straight to the surgical laboratories, and give us a free passage as you go!"

"I'll—" he began furiously.

"You'd better!" I breathed dangerously. "Remember, you can't think enough this time to put yourself in another dimension, as you did once before when I tried to kill you. Get moving—or it's certain death!"

Again he hesitated, then the ray gun in the small of his back prompted him to take the line of least resistance, and he led the way from the instrument room. We followed him, I for my part keeping closely in touch with him.

Out in the main pedestrian ways there were distinct evidences of the havoc that had been occasioned by the shifting of the planet, slight though the shifting had been. Masonry was lying in our path at several points, and many of the towering edifices bore fissures from top to bottom.

I shot one glance at the sky. The Earth had receded remarkably with the removal of the retarding force, and the two glowing planets—intelligent entities—were in the sky now at either horizon, one lower than the other. Finally, I presumed, one would vanish altogether on the other side of Ondon, whilst the remaining one swept ever nearer through space, until... I found myself wondering if the Planet Brain had deliberately planned this disaster. I could only presume it must have done so, even though it would certainly mean the inevitable destruction of all three planets...

We reached the surgical laboratories at last, and, still under the menace of my ray gun, concealed however, from the surgeons, Jelfel gave brief instructions and lay down on one of the tables. Before I took my place beside him I handed the ray gun to Frot, and from then on he became tireless in his surveillance. The anaesthetic hissed gently—I revived to find Jelfel reeling Jovian curses and holding a heavily bandaged head.

"What's the trouble?" I asked of Frot.

"Retribution indeed," he answered grimly. "Another ground tremor a moment ago, during the final touches to Jelfel's brain, and the instrument slipped! It has damaged Jelfel's brain somehow. That means—"

"Madness?" I interrogated in a whisper.

"I can't say. No knowing what the effect will be."

Frot became silent and Jelfel rose slowly from the table and dropped to the floor, still holding his bandaged head. For a moment or two he looked at us with burning eyes, then to our surprise turned and walked from the super-surgery without a single comment—a strangely detached, many legged figure.

I shrugged and then turned to feel my limbs with gratification. "That feels good!" I said in satisfaction. "My own body and my own brain. The only difference lies in a new face, but so long as it's Earthly what matters it? I don't quite understand Jelfel's mood, though."

"Be hanged to him," Elna said abruptly. "Our work on Ondon is ended, Sandy. Let's get along and find Ronnit. I'm uneasy without our ship."

We turned about and left the surgery, but the instant we set foot in the open again, the great gravitational upheaval was fully upon us. A sudden noise like the mightiest thunder crashed through the air, and we were all four flung headlong down the six steps to the pedestrian ways outside.

Sore and bruised we gained our feet, and as we did so the heavens above were slashed across with blinding lightning. The ensuing thunder in the dense air was the most devastating din I ever encountered.

"Disturbances in the air!" bawled Frot. "Moisture—condensation. Hell to come!"

But I had my hands too full to concern myself with his remarks. Zagribud was a suddenly changed city. Overhead, where formerly the sky had been clear, there was now a thickly swirling mass of inky clouds, seeming to make the great bulk of the threatened super-city all the more sinister.

Clinging to each other's arms we forced our way through the Jovians, who were by now too panic-stricken to notice us. Our one aim was to reach the great Tower where lay our last link with home.... Then abruptly it started to rain. I never knew such rain in all my experience of space and time. A tremendous deluge burst forth from the lightning-riven heavens above, boiling cataracts that hissed and swamped down upon us, bore us flat to the ground. Water was in our eyes, our ears—choking and blinding...

With enormous effort we struggled slowly up—I imagine the rain was so heavy owing to the extra gravitational pull—and fought our way inch by inch along the metal way, holding tenaciously to each other's sodden clothing.

"The Tower! Look!" Elna shouted suddenly, lifting a rain-splashed face and pushing damp, dripping masses of hair from before her eyes. "Look—it's collapsing! Oh, great heaven, that means our spaceship—!"

Petrified with horror we watched ensuing events. A tremendous fork of lightning was followed by another violent earth tremor. (I call it such for convenience.) The lightning blazed in fiery plumes about the summit of that two thousand-foot mass, and we distinctly saw pieces of metalwork go spewing outwards into space—but the earth tremor finished the entire catastrophe. The Tower visibly moved to one side even as we watched through the stinging sheets of rain, rocked dangerously, and then went crashing over away from us with a ground-shattering reverberation, ploughing down mammoth edifices as it fell, as though they were packs of cards.

"Our ship—Ronnit—it's all gone!" Valma choked huskily.

"Looks like it," I groaned. "There's nothing for it but to try and reach the fallen Tower. The ship might have been thrown clear. Come on..."

My idea was easier in theory than in carrying it out in practice. We left the pedestrian ways and went into the lower traffic-channels, dodging the curious vehicles, hopelessly out of control, as well as we could manage. Once we all fell into a water-choked gully, to find water chest deep. A sucking undercurrent from some kind of drainage system strove to drag us downwards, and only by enormous muscular effort did we manage to flounder out again, panting and exhausted with the effort.

The shaking of the ground had now become a constant thing. We went in terror of our lives, hardly aware where we were, only aiming blindly through the smother towards the distant fallen Tower.

Then suddenly our progress was halted. Ahead of us, clearly visible in the flashes of lightning, another earth-ripple was approaching, moving and razing buildings as it advanced. It had, however, a sideways movement, and seemed to be moving away to the left as it approached.

"Quickly—in here!" Elna suggested gaspingly, pointing to an open doorway that somehow seemed vaguely familiar, and we incontinently adopted her invitation, blundering after her in the darkness within. Then, as I chanced to lean heavily against the wall, it suddenly collapsed inwards and bowled me into a familiar room. In a moment I recognized it as Jelfel's instrument room. To our ears came the sound of explosions and splintering glass—a sound akin to the destruction going on outside.

"What is it?" Elna demanded.

"We'll soon see," I responded.

Cautiously we advanced along the shaking floor and peered into the next apartment—to behold an amazing sight. Elnek Jelfel himself was deliberately destroying his own instruments with a ray vibrator. Assiduously pressing the button on his weapon, he watched his glorious machinery, his masterly conceptions, blow to powder beneath the force.

Then suddenly he swung round to behold us. It was too late to escape... He smiled peculiarly.

"Come in, Commandant!" he invited drily. "You will be interested in what I am doing. You see, it is no use retaining instruments and devices which you do not understand."

"What do you mean by that?" I asked, moving forward.

"Just this." He motioned us to the familiar bench, then eyed us, still smiling very slightly. "In replacing my brain into my body, the instrument slipped because of an earth-tremor," he said quietly. "That mistake cost me all my knowledge! Ordinarily, I would have slowly risen again in knowledge as my blood-stream supplied my brain; as it is my brain will always be defective. I shall be no cleverer—if as clever—as a very ordinary Earthling. I could, of course, have used a sound brain from a Jovian and it would have perhaps served my purpose—but there is not the time. These machines, which only I understood, are, therefore, useless. Zagribud itself is on the threshold of doom, and I, my friends, am prepared, too, to meet my fate. The power of Elnek Jelfel is ended...

Maybe I do not regret the end of genius!" He looked at us thoughtfully before he went on.

"Strange Fate it is indeed that urges a man to achieve one fixed thing, and when he achieves it, it recoils upon and destroys him! So it has been with me. My one wish, besides transferring Jovian brains to Earthly bodies to enable our race to grow on Earth, was to put my brain in your body, Commandant. I did it, and that very act destroyed it! So be it, Commandant. There is, however, one thing I have discovered—"

"What?" I enquired, as he paused.

"Just this. With normal reasoning—I call my present state normal reasoning—there comes a tempering of mercy, of humaneness, and a vaster knowledge of the difficulties of others. It is difficult to have compassion when one is given the knowledge of a great genius. I am not egotistical when I say I have been clever—perhaps the most brilliant scientific creature that ever existed—but, somehow, I am glad to be natural... Commandant Lee, Miss Folson, Valma, Anton Frot"—he looked at each of us in turn—"you are among the most courageous Earthlings I ever knew. And I thank the queer Fate I am obeying that I have been prevented from doing any of you irreparable harm. I seek now only the peace of the cosmos... Goodbye, my friends."

And with that he turned back to his activities of destruction. We stood watching him for a space as he destroyed his amazing inventions one by one—his Emanation Detector, the remains of his Rotator—his Light-Wave Trap—all his super-instruments one after the other. In some unaccountable way I felt sorry for him, though I had no reason to be. He seemed an oddly lonely figure, fighting a last battle with the calm resource and courage that had always made him so outstanding a character... That was the last we saw of him.

We tip-toed from the laboratory and out into the seething hell outside.

CHAPTER 18

ANNIHILATION

The rain had ceased but the earthquake seemed more universal now. As we progressed, great masses of masonry and metal tumbled through space, narrowly missing us in several eases. The main lights of the city had gone out. From base to pinnacle Zagribud was becoming a collapsing ruin…

We staggered at last over the boiling torrent near the base of the fallen Tower, and finding a little more freedom raced along the two thousand five hundred foot length as fast as we could go. Once we reached the broken mass that had been the summit, our hearts sank. In the rain and murk and heaving mud there was no trace of our beloved time-space machine!

"It's no use—it's gone!" Valma panted hoarsely. "We—"

"Look!" Elna screamed suddenly, her arm shaking with terror as she pointed. "See—that fire! What is it?"

I spun round and gulped hard in my throat. Against the distant horizon loomed an encroaching luminosity slowly lighting up all heaven through the storm-racked clouds above. In an instant I realized the truth. The encroaching planets were almost upon us—were even now hurtling with terrific speed out of infinity towards each other—chained by the unbreakable force of negative drawing positive.

Zagribud lay a patterned immensity of toppling silhouettes, against that flaming abyss of destruction and death.

"It is the end!" cried Frot huskily. "Quickly! Run! Anywhere!"

"No use in running," I returned tensely. "We're done for, and we might just as well stand where we are." I kept my feet with difficulty on the heaving ground as I spoke—then suddenly at a different sound—a dull thud, I turned around. My heart nearly forced its way through my chest with crazy joy.

Not ten yards away stood the time-space machine!

"Hurry! Hurry!" thundered Lan Ronnit, from the air-lock doorway.

We did not need those instructions. Clutching each other we floundered through the mud and staggered through the open doorway. The clamps shot into place, the Particle Disintegrators instantly operated, and in another instant we were in the void and leaving the stricken planet far below us...

"Not difficult," Lan Bonnit explained, as we questioned him. "When the Tower was in danger I simply flew off into the air and moved on a few hours in time. Then I came back into the right time—but some providential fate guided me right to you; at the exact instant. Really remarkable! We're away in space now—safe. But look out there!"

In dead silence we stood at the window gazing upon the doomed planet of Ondon as the two planet brains came towards each other. It was even as we stood there that there came through the silence of the void outside us a familiar, profoundly deep bass voice."A sacrifice, my friends—the sacrifice of the Planet Brain! I planned it, and it shall happen. I shall return your Earth safely to its rightful place; I have already restored the Earthlings who were operated upon by the Jovians. They know nothing of what has happened to them. Henceforth there shall be peace! It was I who guided Lan Ronnit to you in your moment of need... And now to end this everlasting increase of knowledge. Even a Brain grows tired; I seek peace—and in reaching that ultimate of peace I will destroy forever a menace. Even a Brain must die. So be it—"

We stood in dazed fascination as the words ceased and then we beheld the three planets as three bright balls directly in line.

"Our work is ended," Frot said, "The Planet Brain has completed all the details— Ah, look at that!"

We watched, rooted to the spot. Suddenly the entire Ondonian solar system vanished in a blinding coruscation of light. Terrific glare that was blinding in its intensity— A silent and complete destruction—the fusion and disintegration of three planets—and the flinging into the void of the other remaining worlds. Then quietness again. A solar system composed of countless fragments of glowing particles—a massive nebula, to form one day another solar system. The inevitable law of space and time.

"It is ended," Valma said quietly. "Three words alone can sum it up— Expectation, Realization—and"—he smiled grimly—"Annihilation!"

ABOUT THE AUTHOR

British writer **JOHN RUSSELL FEARN** was born near Manchester, England, in 1908. As a child he devoured the science fiction of Wells and Verne, and was a voracious reader of the Boys' Story Papers. He was also fascinated by the cinema, and first broke into print in 1931 with a series of articles in *Film Weekly*.

He then quickly sold his first novel, *The Intelligence Gigantic*, to the American magazine, *Amazing Stories*. Over the next fifteen years, writing under several pseudonyms, Fearn became one of the most prolific contributors to all of the leading US science fiction pulps, including such legendary publications as *Astounding Stories*, *Startling Stories*, *Thrilling Wonder Stories*, and *Weird Tales*.

During the late 1940s he diversified into writing novels for the UK market, and also created his famous superwoman character, The Golden Amazon, for the prestigious Canadian magazine, the Toronto *Star Weekly*. In the early 1950s in the UK, his fifty-two novels as "Vargo Statten" were bestsellers, most notably his novelization of the film, *Creature from the Black Lagoon*.

Apart from science fiction, he had equal success with westerns, romances, and detective fiction, writing an amazing total of 180 novels—most of them in a period of just ten years—before his early death in 1960. His work has been translated into ten languages and continues to be reprinted and read worldwide.

JOHN RUSSELL FEARN

THE ANJANI SERIES

The Gold of Akada: A Jungle Adventure Novel
Anjani the Mighty: A Lost Race Novel

THE BLACK MARIA SERIES

Black Maria, M.A.: A Classic Crime Novel
The Murdered Schoolgirl: A Classic Crime Novel
One Remained Seated: A Classic Crime Novel
Thy Arm Alone: A Classic Crime Novel
Death in Silhouette: A Classic Crime Novel

THE HERBERT THE DINOSAUR SERIES

A Thing of the Past
The Genial Dinosaur

THE ADAM QUIRKE SERIES

The Master Must Die: Impossible Crime Science Fiction Novel
The Lonely Astronomer: Impossible Crime Science Fiction Novel

OTHER BOOKS

1,000-Year Voyage: A Science Fiction Novel
Account Settled: A Science Fiction Mystery
Before Earth Came: Classic Science Fiction Stories
Bury the Hatchet: A Crime Tale
A Case for Brutus Lloyd: A Science Fiction Mystery
The Crimson Rambler: A Crime Novel
Don't Touch Me: A Crime Novel
Dynasty of the Small: Classic Science Fiction Stories
The Empty Coffins: A Mystery of Horror
The Fourth Door: A Mystery Novel
From Afar: A Science Fiction Mystery
Fugitive of Time: A Classic Science Fiction Novel

The G-Bomb: A Science Fiction Novel
Here and Now: A Science Fiction Novel
Into the Unknown: A Science Fiction Tale
Last Conflict: Classic Science Fiction Stories
Legacy from Sirius: A Classic Science Fiction Novel
The Man from Hell: Classic Science Fiction Stories
The Man Who Was Not: A Crime Novel
Manton's World: A Classic Science Fiction Novel
Moon Magic: A Novel of Romance (as Elizabeth Rutland)
One Way Out: A Crime Novel (with Philip Harbottle)
Pattern of Murder: A Classic Crime Novel
Reflected Glory: A Dr. Castle Classic Crime Novel
Robbery Without Violence: Two Science Fiction Crime Stories
Rule of the Brains: Classic Science Fiction Stories
Shattering Glass: A Crime Novel
The Silvered Cage: A Scientific Murder Mystery
Slaves of Ijax: A Science Fiction Novel
Something from Mercury: Classic Science Fiction Stories
The Space Warp: A Science Fiction Novel
The Time Trap: A Science Fiction Novel
Valley of Pretenders: Classic Science Fiction Stories
Vision Sinister: A Scientific Detective Thriller
Voice of the Conqueror: A Classic Science Fiction Novel
What Happened to Hammond? A Scientific Mystery
Within That Room!: A Classic Crime Novel
World Without Chance: Classic Science Fiction Stories

www.ingramcontent.com/pod-product-compliance
Lightning Source LLC
Chambersburg PA
CBHW020131180626
46810CB00004B/1508